Underneath It All

It All

ALEXIS JENSEN

MILTON & HUGO L.L.C.
4407 Park Ave., Suite 5
Union City, NJ 07087, USA

Website: *www. miltonandhugo.com*
Hotline: *1- 888-778-0033*
Email: *info@miltonandhugo.com*

Ordering Information:
Quantity sales. Special discounts are granted to corporations, associations, and other organizations. For more information on these discounts, please reach out to the publisher using the contact information provided above.

Library of Congress Control Number:		2024912339
ISBN-13:	979-8-89285-188-6	[Paperback Edition]
	979-8-89285-190-9	[Hardback Edition]
	979-8-89285-189-3	[Digital Edition]

Rev. date: 06/25/2024

To My Sister, Aurora,
that put up with years of terrible fanfiction for this.

Playlist:

1. Underneath it All- No Doubt
2. when the party's over- Billie Eilish
3. Getaway Car- Taylor Swift
4. The One That Got Away- Katy Perry
5. Matilda- Harry Styles
6. At Last- Etta James
7. How to Disappear- Lana Del Rey
8. Emotions- Brenda Lee
9. Favorite Crime- Olivia Rodrigo
10. Ocean Eyes- Billie Eilish
11. Delicate- Taylor Swift
12. Love On The Brain- Rihanna
13. Heaven- Julia Michaels
14. More Than A Woman- Bee Gees
15. Sex on Fire- Kings of Leon
16. Casual- Chappell Roan
17. All I Wanted- Paramore
18. Apologize- One Republic
19. From the Dining Table- Harry Styles
20. Silver Springs- Fleetwood Mac

One

TESSA

When I clocked into work that August morning, the last thing I wanted to see was him. The tall, slender yet muscular, raven with the same typical scowl on his face, was early. His only intent being his father's monthly allowance. "Goodmorning, Mr. Finch." I greeted him with my stereotypical hospitality before I entered his father's room, which was met with a roll of his eyes.

Maurice, however, was the kindest of men. He would specifically request me when I was working as he knew I was always down for a game of Mancala in my free time. He would spend his days terrorizing the nurses, but me? He treated me as his own.

"Well, if it isn't my favorite lady." Maurice's wrinkled face pulled into a tight smile. I rolled my eyes playfully as his son followed behind me. "I've brought a visitor." I smiled with a sing-song voice, coming over to check his vitals. His son sat on the recliner in the corner of the room, texting on his phone. How he continuously ignored his father was beyond me. From the two years I had taken care of Maurice, he appeared to be a loving father, one that only wanted the best for his son. Yet the visits seemed to be the biggest inconvenience.

"Hey," Reese muttered, never looking up from his phone. "The guys and I are going on a ski trip this weekend." Reese spoke in a tone that to me, concluded with him asking his father for extra on his allowance. I muffled a snort, Reese's eyes flicking up to meet mine before he sprung from the chair.

"Did I say something funny?"

1

"Sit down, Reese. Don't get your panties in a twist." Maurice gave me a quick wink, sitting up in his hospice bed. I proudly smiled in response, filling out his chart with what was recorded on his vitals.

"I just thought it was kind of silly to ski in August." I mumbled with a light giggle as Maurice nodded in agreement.

"People who aren't forced to clean bed pans all day get to do fun shit like that." Reese snarkily replied. I wet my lips and softly shut my eyes, refusing to turn back around and face him with a mouthful of angry words. "Got it." I sighed in annoyance. The sound of Reese's voice is almost worse than the things he says.

"Alright, Maurice. I'll stop by later to bring your lunch." My face is tight as I force a smile, my hands are balled into fists in my pockets. "Enjoy your visit with your son." I turn around to leave, catching a quick glimpse of Reese who is back to whatever is so entertaining on his phone.

My shift is slow, not that I can complain. I almost prefer slow when it comes to working in a nursing home. When there's chaos, there's normally messes to follow. Or old ladies angry with bingo outcomes. I like to sit in the nurses station, catching up on all the workplace drama. I'm never involved, but I do enjoy hearing about it. Who's sleeping with who, who's on management's radar. The drama *never* ends here. But I love my job. I love the residents and the pride that comes with doing this kind of work.

I came back around 11:15 with Maurice's lunch. Reese nowhere to be found.

"Knock, knock." I greet in a cheerful voice.

"Mancala already?" Maurice smiled as I shook my head. "I'm working a short shift today, no mancala for me." I smile, setting his tray down and grabbing him water out of the fridge. "How was your visit with Reese?"

"Same as always. Needin' money for god knows what." He sighed, taking a shaky bite of his sandwich as I snicker to myself. The chair Reese once sat in is still warm, telling me he only recently left. "I mean, who goes skiing in August, Mr. Finch?" I giggle.

"People with no sense of responsibility, that's who." Maurice laughed, pointing his index finger at me.

2

He wasn't wrong. It seemed, at least from my perspective, Reese was handed everything in life, never learning how to be a functioning member of society.

From what I read in the tabloids of this wealthy family, Reese was the partying, black sheep of a son. I couldn't be so lucky.

My parents were hard workers. My dad was a carpenter, giving fifty years to his company before retiring. My mom was a nurse, now a volunteer at the blood bank. I wanted to follow in her footsteps, only finances were not my family's strongest suit. I paid for CNA school myself, but fell short for nursing school. I'm okay with that. I'm happy with what I do; I do alright for myself. I'm nowhere near Reese's life but I don't go without what I need.

I watch Maurice enjoy his lunch while I flip through this month's Fingerhut catalog. I'm not sure why he gets this magazine sent here. His room is beyond cluttered with knickknacks and different pieces of furnishings from his life before moving into Brindlewood. His room is one of the most beautifully decorated. But there would be no room for anything from this magazine.

"Reese… I just don't know where I went wrong with him." Maurice sighed, pushing his tray back a little. His statement makes my brows raise. Maurice didn't talk about Reese ever. It made my heart sink to watch this man looking back on his years of parenting, unsure of where the mistake was made along the way. "You can't blame yourself for how a grown man behaves, Mr. Finch." I smiled politely.

I don't think my parents had to worry much about my younger sister and I. We worked hard for anything we wanted. And kept ourselves out of trouble by being in sports or anything after school to consume our time. My sister in cheer, myself in track. The most my parents had to worry about was Kelseigh's boy crazy behavior. She never went without a boyfriend or someone that sauntered over her. I was lucky to have one boyfriend throughout high school. And I wouldn't have changed a thing about it.

Maybe Maurice's catering to Reese was his demise or maybe it was always in his blood to be a spoiled brat.

Two

TESSA

Thursdays. Thursdays are my favorite days. Three days off, every week. Friday, Saturday, and Sunday. All dedicated to me and what I want to do. Whether that meant sitting in my pajamas for three days or weekend trips with my girlfriends. The opportunities were endless. Though they were mainly the latter.

I stopped on my way into work, getting a coffee from the gas station and a donut for Maurice. I'm not sure what it was about those stale sweets. Maybe it was the idea of someone thinking about him for something other than his money. The only visitor Maurice ever received was Reese. He never came with a gift, or even a kind thing to say. Only an outstretched hand. But Maurice *loved* those cinnamon sugar pastries. As long as he stayed on top of his medications, I made sure to bring him a donut every Thursday.

"Special delivery!" I called sweetly, opening Maurice's door. The room smelled of Ombre Leather by Tom Ford, meaning one thing in particular. I am met with Reese sitting on that familiar sofa, my feet cemented to the ground. He'd been here only a week ago. He wasn't due back for another month. I take a deep breath, preparing myself for any dumb comments Reese could make. After all, that was usually all he said. Though based on the energy of the room, there was a heated discussion that had just taken place. "How were the slopes?" I ask in a sarcastic tone, locking contact with Reese's sea glass eyes. They're cold and jaded with a twinge of red, as if he was on the verge of tears before my entrance. He shook his head in annoyance, turning back to scroll on his phone.

I can't help but stare for a second, my head slightly tilted in confusion. There was almost a spark of emotion from him, but I can't make it out.

"Ah, there's my girl. Cinnamon sugar?" Maurice asked, his voice changing my direction of attention as he lifted his hospice bed with the small gray remote. The mattress was tattered, a shocking sight because of the amount of money the Finch family held. The fact that Maurice was even put in this home was rather confusing. I guess I would have expected him to get a live-in nurse.

Maurice always told me he was a social butterfly. He held the biggest events for his company, everyone in New York City attending. Everyone except Reese.

While his father was entertaining the socialites, Reese was snorting up all of their crumbs.

I nod kindly, making my way to his bed. After I placed the donut on his tray, I took a step back. "You've also got your bath today. I let you skip it yesterday, so don't even try to sweet talk me." I tease, pointing a playfully stern finger at his chest. The sound of Reese scoffing under his breath causes me to sigh, but I ignore it.

"I'll get everything ready." I talk as I disappear into his bathroom, grabbing the various soaps and towels, along with the small basin for warm water. I sigh, attempting to distract myself from what's about to come with the sound of running water.

Maurice's younger brother, Arthur, kept him rather stocked with necessities. I'd never had the luxury of meeting him, but Maurice always had name brand soaps, snacks, a fridge stocked with drinks, and the softest towels and bed sheets. Most people dropped their family members off without a word, leaving their social security to supply the cheapest materials.

When I return, Maurice is already trying to assist me by unbuttoning his gown. My brows furrow without my permission as my heart is pulled apart watching him try to do this simple task.

"Alright, Mr. Finch. I'm gonna have to ask you to wait outside, please."

I use my most professional voice when speaking to Reese to avoid my fist colliding with his face as he briefly looks up from his phone then back down. I wet my lips as I stare at the ceiling in annoyance. Reese appeared to not be moving anywhere fast.

"I'll wait here, thanks." He retorted, the sound of a football game coming from his phone. An announcer spoke of the Giant's stats at the end of the second quarter as Reese zoned back into his phone.

"I understand that you'd like to sit in here, but for your father's privacy and the sake of my ability to do my job-"

"What, are you gonna do something you're not supposed to?" Reese's brows furrowed as he stood up, meeting me at his father's bedside. His carved jaw clenched as his eyes darkened. I looked up at him, standing my ground as I exhaled rapidly through my nose.

He stood at least a foot over me. I've measured at 5'4 since freshman year with no chance of growth. There's no doubt he stands at an intimidating 6'5 as my head cranes all the way back to meet his gaze.

"Reese, that's enough." Maurice spoke with his usual calm demeanor.

"No. *Clearly*, your nurse thinks she can take advantage of you while I'm not in the room."

My chest is burning with rage. It's tight as if I can't take a full breath. My fists are clenched around the wash cloth. I would love nothing more than to punch Reese right between the eyes, and at this rate, I think Maurice would get a kick out of it. I wet my angered, quivered lips as he still stood over me, trying to make me cower. The last thing I want is to shed a tear and let him think he's won. I've always been tougher than I looked.

"You wanna stay? Grab a towel."

I force a wet, soapy cloth into Reese's hand. He looks down in disgust as I run my tongue over my top teeth. Maurice can't help but snicker in the act as the two of us stand on either side of his hospice bed, glaring at one another. Reese looked down at the towel, then to his dad, and then to me.

We were in a standoff. For at least three minutes, I watched his jaw lock and unlock as his full lips curled in loathing.

"Fine."

Three

REESE

God, the way she looked at me. I'd love nothing more than to throw this rag right in her face, watch the water drain her hair of its curls. After all, it was *my* father that signed her checks every week. And here he was, letting her talk to me this way. She wanted me to back down. She wanted to put me in my place.

Fuck that.

I took the rag and dipped it in the basin of water, my eyes never leaving her amber orbs. I smeared the soapy cloth across my dad's chest, making more of a mess than I was helping. He just snickered with his weathered face, watching her get frustrated which truly only fueled my desire to do it more.

"Can you apply just a little bit of effort?" Tessa sighed through her nose, wetting her lips. Which appeared to be something she did a lot when I was around. Almost as much as I rolled my eyes in response.

"Then don't ask for my help." I rebutted as soon as she finished speaking.

"I didn't ask for your help." Her eyes were beginning to wet as her stress levels went up. God, I was really getting to her. Her chest was rising and falling quickly, my eyes only broke her gaze to admire the form of her breathing for a second.

I took the cloth, wringing the water on my dad's withering ribcage. The soapy mixture dripped off in a rapid stream onto the floor, something she'd surely have to clean up.

Tess slammed her rags into the bucket. "I'm sorry. I just need a minute." Her hands were shaky as she held them up in defeat before wiping a tear that ran down her cheek. I snickered, watching her turn around. I had won.

Before I knew it, she was gone. I'd half expected her to dramatically slam the door. Shockingly, she closed it gently as if not wanting to draw anymore attention to herself.

"You really are a gentleman aren't you, Reese?" My father scoffed as I handed him a towel. I ran a hand through my hair, sighing as Maurice didn't have the same appreciation for my actions as I thought. I walk back across the room to the chair. "It was just a joke."

"Go out there and make it right, Reese." He ordered, making my brows furrow. I was now twenty-nine years old. Who was he to tell me what to do? After all, I was the product of an affair. He was never a real father to me until he got sick and felt like making peace before death.

"I'm not going out there." I argued. "She's a grown woman. If she can't handle-"

For the first time in two years, my father sat up in that bed on his own. Using all the strength left in his body with both hands on the guardrails. "If you can't see it in your heart to make it right to that girl, you can count yourself right out of my will." He spoke with strain in his voice. I looked at him for a moment, sighing as I shook my head. Maurice had threatened me on that several times in the past. All it took was one phone call, he'd tell me.

And unfortunately, I fell for it every time.

Unlike Tessa, I slammed the apartment door shut behind me, hoping my father shuttered at the vibrations. I moseyed down the hallway of Brindlewood, trying to find her in those tight, black scrubs. The soft sound of a cry could be heard from a utility closet. I stopped, staring at the ceiling tiles with a sigh as my tongue rested in the corner of my mouth. I use my index knuckle to knock on the door.

"Tess?"

"One sec!" She spoke in a sweet voice, trying to hide the shaky vibrato and causing me to roll my eyes. Why did she care so much about how people saw her?

Tessa stepped out of the closet, her face red and blotchy from her tears. She folded her arms, staring up at me with her dainty frame. She kept a solid foot and a half between us.

"Just wanted to say I'm sorry." I sighed, avoiding her big, brown eyes.

"Okay." She mumbled, her vision anywhere but on me.

"Okay? That's it?"

Tessa nodded, causing a groan to escape my lips. "I don't forgive you. You made my job ten times harder in there." She explained as my chest tightened. Was this guilt?

"Right. I'll stay out of your way from now on." I pulled my keys out of my pocket and held them up, showing her that I was leaving.

She nodded again, brushing past me and moving back to Maurice's apartment without a second thought. I watched her walk away, my head tilted as I wet my lips in her usual fashion.

I walk into my apartment, the cool brick stabilizes me as I toe my shoes off. It's cold, and it's empty inside. All of my friends are with their significant others or at the clubs and I am here. In this apartment, eating Chinese takeout.

My eyes are drawn to my phone, almost begging me to look Tessa up online. Yet every time I pick it up, I can't get myself to type her name in. Instead, I open my contacts for an old reliable.

Brooklynn. How ironic, Brooklynn in New York. It doesn't get more cliche. I shake my head as I tell her to come over. She was a year younger than me, graduating with my buddy Christian. I'd seen her in the halls, but never gave her the time of day. Brooklynn was known for her long line of male suitors, me being one of them. I was formally introduced to her in June and I'd seen her more times than I'd like to admit.

Looking around my penthouse, I scratch my head. There's several things in disarray but I don't care enough to clean it. My maid will be here in the morning. I'll let her deal with the mess.

I opened the door for her, her full lips and smooth skin resulted in a comforting sigh. Brooklynn was the exact type of girl you'd find lurking around my penthouse. Hell, she'd probably even snatch a watch or a bottle of liquor while I'm asleep to pawn. She'd done it in the past, but I was weak. Things belonging to my family go for a lot of money these days with Maurice's health declining. At least that's what I've heard. I try to dissociate myself from the media and the internet. I hate the shit they say about me. *New York's Drunken Playboy* is the most often used headline.

I'm the son of Maurice Finch, or lack thereof. As I've said before, he was never a father to me. All I wanted was his approval, maybe that's why I acted the way I did growing up.

As for my mother? How would you expect the media to react to a mogul such as Maurice having an affair with his secretary? Let alone getting her pregnant.

August 23rd

I open my eyes, Brooklynn is still asleep, the black, silk sheets tangled around her olive skin. I sigh, hoping she would have left in the middle of the night.

My phone buzzes as I roll over to grab it.

9:12 A.M.
C-Paradise Club tnt?
B-Hell yeah.
J-I'm in. Finch, you in?

I sigh in thought, glancing back at Brooklynn for a quick moment.

R-Count me in.

I text my group chat back. Paradise Club isn't my favorite place to go, but I never turn down drinks. While my phone is unlocked, I open Instagram. I squint at the brightness while curiosity gets the best of me. I type in her name, Tessa Dawson. Miraculously, she's the first to appear.

Her pictures are much artsier than I'd imagine from her. Genuinely, artsy. From museums to coffee shops. On hikes with friends at the crack of dawn, to her on a lake at dusk. I can't stop scrolling. She's accomplished so much in her time.

I look around my apartment once more and at the blonde whose life goals I'm unaware of, closing the app.

I get up for the shower, cautiously to prevent Brooklynn from waking up. I reach into my wallet, pulling out roughly thirty dollars for a cab and set it on her cell phone. I can only pray she's gone when I get out. I rub my hand against my sore back as I walk to the bathroom and turn the water on. The cold droplets strike my body, waking me up immediately.

My mouth falls open, letting some of the stream hit my tongue as I push my hair back from my eyes. I'm cleansed of my sins once more.

I dry my hair, absorbing the clean linen scent of the towel. It's tied loosely against my hips as I crack my head from the bathroom. I let out a breath I didn't know I was holding. Brooklynn from New York was gone.

Four

REESE

"Vodka Soda!" I called to the bartender over the thumping bass. My ears burned with every vibration that echoed in my body. I felt like a sardine, lined up in an overflowing tin can. "Who's dumb idea was this again?" I asked Brice, my best friend since elementary school, who appeared to be eyeing the crowd of women. The crowd being Bodycon dresses and chunky heels mixed with cheap hairspray.

Brice was my only beacon of light in this world. He worked for a big tabloid in NYC, the Stripe. It was his mom's magazine, but he always gave me a heads up when I'd be printed about. I could never thank him enough. He didn't really date or even hook up; I wasn't sure why he still came to things like this.

"Patience, Finch. The night is young and the women are sexier." Christian interrupted with a smirk, causing an involuntary roll of my eyes as I took a sip of my drink. I sucked in a breath through my teeth, my drink being more vodka than soda.

"You're a freak, man." Jody, Christian's roommate, snickered at his response. Everything seemed to swirl, lights flickered off of smoke in the air. I couldn't tell where one person's body ended and where another began. I was drowning in a sea of movement and sweat.

I ran my tongue over my teeth as I propped myself against the bar, trying to stalk my prey for the night. By my third Vodka Soda, I felt invincible.

"Have you found your target?" Brice smirked, bumping me in the side with his elbow. I sighed through my nose, my brows furrowed as I scanned the mob of people.

"Something like that.." I mumble, slamming the last of my drink and making my way to the dance floor. I slithered my way behind a brunette, hooking my index fingers in her belt loops. My head buried in her neck, her hair smelling of cotton candy vape and cheap shampoo.

She leaned against me, running her left hand from my neck down my torso until she turned to face me. My hands slid up her hips, wanting to swallow her curves. When she opened her eyes, her expression changed. The kind that makes you feel you just admitted to murder.

"Reese? Reese Finch?" She asked. No, *yelled* over the music, retracting from me.

"Yeah?" I replied with more confusion than necessary.

"Jessica Wilson? We went on like three dates. We had sex in the back of your Lincoln… You promised you'd call me and yet… Here we are." She folded her arms angrily. Jessica Wilson? My brain runs through the Rolodex of names in my head. It doesn't even ring a bell, nor does her face. There's no way I've slept around *that* much.

"Right." I stumbled over my words, my cheeks burning hot as she shook her head looking up at me.

"You don't even remember do you? Jesus, how embarrassing." Jessica held her hands up in disgust, turning to walk away from me. I felt like I'd been sucker punched in the gut.

The wind was completely taken from my body. I was the exact playboy the magazines made me out to be. I looked up to my friends, all of them laughing and pointing at my demise.

I wave my hands toward myself as I walk back in defeat. "Yeah, yeah. Let me hear it. Fuck you guys." I snicker, trying to cover the hurt and sheer humiliation in my voice. "How does it feel to be the disappointment of the night?" Jody grinned, sipping his Jack & Coke.

"Leave him alone guys, the bigger disappointment will be his left hand later." Christian elbowed Jody and Brice who both snickered. I sighed, nodding along with the banter. This was a typical move of Christian. From his light brown, gelled hair to his khaki pants and salmon button up, he was the epitome of white male privilege.

And Jody, God, who was even inviting Jody to these things? He was an outsider to our friend group. Every time he opened his mouth it made my jaw clench. Especially when he spoke on my behalf. But Brice?

Brice was the ultimate package. He was there for everything. Every fight with my parents, I'd get on my bike and head right to Brice's. Even at a young age, he was so wise and patient. He never had a bad thing to say about anyone ever.

August 28th

I sat down at the small cafe under my apartment complex, drinking a coffee and enjoying a danish while scrolling through my socials. My group chat spirals again, dinging before I can even catch up.

10:20 A.M.
C–Thinking about Malibu next week?
J–Sun and babes? I'm down.
B–Can't. Got a work thing.
C–Finch, waiting on you.

I mull over my cheek for a minute, opening my bank app.

My account drained all but five hundred dollars. I feel my heart fall into my stomach as my brows furrow. "Five hundred…" I mumble as I check the transactions. All the money was transferred back to Maurice's account.

My jaw slacks, searching for the reason he would have done something like this. I rise to my feet quickly, tossing my cafe treats in the trash and head for my car. I don't even turn the radio on, the sound of my thoughts would drown out any of today's hits.

I barge through the doors of the nursing home, making my way down the hall to his apartment. It takes everything in me to not kick the plastic plants that I pass on my way down. When I reach his apartment, I stare at the nameplate on the door. Maurice is written in girly cursive with a smiley face beside it. Probably the work of Tess. I mull my cheek, my hands on my hips as my tongue toys with the corner of my mouth in preparation.

I open the door, slamming it behind me.

"If it isn't my darling descendent. I knew you'd be here in no time." Maurice sighed, sitting up in his hospital bed. I always hated when my father had that smugness to him. It was something I often saw when he would argue with my mother. She would ask him for just a fraction of his time, only to be met with that same damn look.

"This is just like you to pull some shit- Tess."

I was sinking, drowning in quicksand at the sight of Maurice's nurse. She looked up at me with the mention of her name, but if I hadn't said anything, she wouldn't have given me the time of day. Her dainty hands were writing against a clipboard, my mind stuck on the sound of the pen sliding against the paper.

"Hm?" She asked, turning back to the clipboard. It was evident she was still mad at me for last week. I pursed my lips in annoyance before turning to face my father.

"What did you do with my money?"

My tone was louder and angrier than necessary but I couldn't control it. "Reese, you need-"

"No, I don't know what the fuck your problem is. That is *my* money." I argued, cutting him off without an opportunity to let him explain.

"I should give you guys some privacy." Tess whispered, hanging his clipboard on the end of the bed. "Stay." Maurice and I spoke, both turning to each other in confusion.

"Son, I think it's very important that I teach you the value of a hard-earned dollar." My father spoke smugly, causing my lip to curl. I hated when he did that, referring to me as his son only in that condescending tone. I was never his son. "What is that supposed to mean?" I rebutted, folding my arms as I stood at the end of his bed. Tessa looked at me with a clueless expression. Her face told me that she'd like to be anywhere but here.

"It means that I'm cutting you off."

Five

TESSA

Cut off? I practically hold in a snort at the thought. Reese's carefree life is now being burned at the stake. So long to yacht parties and playboy fantasies. At least that's what I assume he does in his free time. There were always rumors about the Finch family. About Reese, his mother, and how he 'coped' with fame. If you can even call it that.

I still don't understand what this has to do with me. His once icy blue eyes were now dark and full of hatred as they told me to stay, for what? A witness perhaps? Was he going to kill Maurice in front of me?

"Cut off?" Reese asked for verification, his jaw tightened as he spoke through his teeth. The muscles flexed against his protruding cheekbones. His skin was flushed against its normal ivory complexion. Reese's hands met the back of his head in frustration and practically tugged at his own hair. I sit back and observe the family brawl, trying to focus my eyes on anything except Reese's veiny hands now running through his once perfectly styled raven hair.

"It's time for you to learn that I won't always be around to give you everything you need. At nearly thirty years old, you are still dependent on me and an allowance. It's no one's fault but my own.." Maurice's voice was tender as he shook his head with a sigh.

Okay, this time I do snort. I can't help it. Reese Finch? Dependent on his father? I'd have never guessed. His eyes pierce holes into my soul as I don't hold back.

The veins in his hands are prominent and taut. For a moment, I can see right through him. Down to a little boy who begged his father for attention and love. I wet my lips awkwardly and cleared my throat, drawing my attention anywhere else as I still stand with my hands at my sides.

"I'm sorry, I guess I just don't know where I fit into all of this." I mumble with discomfort in my voice. My hands are clammy and I don't like the tension in this divided room. My mom always hated when I got nervous. I spoke too softly, my hands would sweat. Eventually, my legs would go numb.

I was nervous all the time.

"You, Tessa, are the one that can change him." The skin by Maurice's eyes formed tight crinkles as he smiled, seeming unfazed by his son's anger. A reaction I wish I could hone. Just the mere sound of Reese's yelling makes the hair on my neck stand. I open my mouth to speak but he waves me off. "I would like him to train under you, to learn what it is really like to work for what you've got."

I shake my head repeatedly, the word 'no' slipping out faster than I can control. Maurice paid no mind to my reaction, letting my unwillingness fill the atmosphere. Reese appears on the same page as me as he emits a scoff, running his hands over his face. I can see his foundation crashing, his kingdom being sworn over by trolls and witches. And it is oddly satisfying.

"Absolutely not. He will make my life a living hell." I felt bad for speaking so negatively of Maurice's son but I had to stand my ground, something I didn't do very often. I was always taught to listen to my elders, what they say goes. My father would die if he heard me now. I've never protested anything, but here at this moment? I would go down with this ship.

Maurice sighed as if expecting my reluctance to the situation. He adjusted his fringed and frayed hospital blankets with a wince, showing just how weak his state was lately. He'd been here every bit of two years. When he moved in, Maurice was always seen doing activities, at parties with other residents. After six months, he couldn't even be in his wheelchair anymore, strictly bedridden. Even the state of his hands, the thing I kept my eyes on as they wet with frustration, were different. They were modeling and tinged with blue.

"In exchange," He spoke with heavy breaths in between, as if struggling to breathe. "I will cover the cost of your nursing school, so you can flourish the way you were meant to." He smiled softly, his eyes telling me that this was serious. From what I knew of the family, Maurice definitely could afford my nursing school tuition.

My vision darted between the two men. One seemed so bitter while the other remained patient.

Maurice was begging me to help his son, while Reese was almost begging me to decline the offer. The words were on the tip of his tongue. His weight shifted between both legs, hands still on the back of his head as he searched the room for anyone to object. Reese's bottom lip trembled, the words begging to slip. But his pride and my inability to disappoint were much stronger. I wet my lips anxiously, my heart racing as I make the least thought out decision of my life.

"Okay." I spoke under my breath. I have the upper hand in this situation yet I cannot find the courage to show it. I've always struggled that way, but now it was painted on my face.

"Fuck..." he mumbled in exchange.

I have disrupted my only peace for this man. Someone who wouldn't spit on me if I was on fire.

Six

TESSA

I rubbed my temples as I paced outside of Maurice's door. My monthly run-ins with Reese were now promoted to every Thursday. My favorite day of the week now consumed with his suffocating ego and pungent hostility. I shook my head, replaying the invisible string of events as I walked down the hall. A slam comes from behind, making my whole body cringe. I jerked my head to see Reese staring in my direction. He wets his lips, parting them slightly as if to say something to me. His hands forced their way into his jacket pockets before I am met with his backside.

I take the rest of my day easier, keeping my head down and to myself as I try not to inflict any more reasons to have a heart attack by age twenty-six. Everyone took notice of my recluse personality today. I was now the topic of discussion with no one to talk to about it.

My eyes are heavy by the end of my shift, the stress of the day being too much to bear on my body. I pull my keys from my purse as I walk to the car, my beat up little Ford Ranger. It was my first car, a gift from my father. It was a rust bucket now, tears in the seats, and a smashed up driver side mirror from when my dad taught me to drive.

I swore to him that I'd drive that damn thing to the ground, and I meant it.

When I was little, my car seat sat perched in the back middle. I'd swing my feet, trying to rest them on the center counsel. My dad would hand me french fries from this little burger joint in Hoboken as Garth Brooks rang clear through those now static filled speakers.

I would beg and beg for my father to play my favorite Tim McGraw CD. He'd flop down his visor, scanning through all of his country discs until pulling it out.

My favorite feeling in the world was when he'd roll down all four windows on Interstate 78. The way the air would leave my lungs from the strong gusts of wind, leaving me weightless in the back seat of that '97 Ford Ranger.

I press the key fob, signaling the flashing headlights as it is unlocked.

Reese's figure created a shadow as he pressed his back against one headlight. I stop in my tracks with my heart thumping, a look of confusion and annoyance spread across my face. He was going to kill me, I just knew it.

"How'd you know this was my car?" I asked, tucking my left hand into my purse to reach for my mace.

"Shittiest one in the parking lot." He replied dryly, causing my throat to tighten. It's too hard to swallow. "It's not shitty." I mumble, covering the hurt in my voice. Reese's smug expression is like a knife in my chest as he points to my passenger mirror being held up by duct tape. "Did you need something or do you just genuinely enjoy ruining my day?" My tongue runs over my top front teeth as I ball my fists around my mace.

"I didn't know what time to show up Thursday."

My grip loosens slightly around the small plastic bottle in my bag. "Seven is fine."

Reese's feet dug into the broken up concrete on the ground as he nodded. The way he carried himself was so different from any other time I'd seen him. The confidence and swagger in his voice was gone, leaving insecurity in its place. He took a deep breath before speaking.

"Can I get your number?"

"Not interested." I scoffed, pushing past him and opening the driver door with a loud creak. Just another thing I was sure he'd make fun of me for. "Yeah, neither am I. I figured it'd be the best way to get a hold of you throughout this shit." My cheeks burn bright red as I close my eyes. I wanted to slam my head into the seat of my car repeatedly. My back is turned to him, thank god, or he'd see just how embarrassed I was. I couldn't place my embarrassment. It was almost jealousy, that a man like him, a man that slept around with all of New York, wasn't interested in me.

I threw my purse in the passenger seat and turned around to face him with my hand out. Never had I been so grateful for the moonlight. "Right, sorry."

He placed his phone in my hand and I typed my number in, saving it under Tessa D. This made a soft laugh erupt from deep in his chest, a laugh I wasn't used to. It made my brows crinkle briefly as I took a mental step back. "Is there a problem?" I asked, folding my arms. I can't help but take offense to every movement he makes.

"Nope, no problem. You're just always so damn serious." Reese smirked as my eyes involuntarily rolled back. If I spend any more time with him, they would get stuck like that.

"It's called being responsible. I believe your father asked you to learn about it today."

The second the words left my mouth, I wished I could stuff them back in. The color left his face as he lowered his head, tucking his phone in his jacket. "Right." He muttered, his voice back to dry and practically calloused. I sigh, letting my head fall back to view the stars. I wished my grandma was here, she always knew what to say and how to fix my mistakes.

I could be such a bitch.

"Sorry." Is all I can force out. Because in truth, I'm not sorry he is experiencing this. I *am* sorry that he was raised this way. I'm sorry he was forced to start over and to learn a different life. It's almost like culture shock. He was in a dystopian universe written by Nicholas Sparks.

Reese only nodded, seemingly done with any form of a conversation with me.

I climb into the truck and roll my window down as he begins to walk off. "Hey, Reese?" I squeeze my eyes shut, feeling my cheeks burn again.

"It'll be alright." My voice was sincere, no more of my snarky attitude. I can't see his expression as he stood against the moon's light. What I do know is that he stood in that spot for nearly a minute. His head cocked faintly to the left while he contemplated what to say. His right hand ran over his mouth with exhaustion and a scoff as he turned around to walk away.

I sit back in my seat, softly hitting the back of my head against the headrest.

What an idiot.

Seven

TESSA

"At least he's kinda sexy, right?" Kayla, my best friend, shrugged as she slurped her smoothie.

I met her when I had my 12th birthday party at the roller skating rink. She was playing Skeeball. Only, she was climbing onto the ramp to put the balls in the 100 point slot. I distinctly remember her moving her long, straight, auburn hair from her eyes every time she climbed back up the ramp. "You can't do that."

"Watch me."

My eyes were like saucers as she climbed down out of breath with the jackpot ticket prize rolling out.

Through all of my love for Kayla, her taste in men was clearly not a reputable source as she mentioned Reese's looks.

"You're so dramatic." Kayla rolled her eyes, turning to walk into the *American Eagle* and disappearing in a rack of sweaters. I take a drink of my mango pineapple smoothie, trailing off on my own toward the wall of jeans.

The mall was rather busy for midday Friday. I hadn't expected there to be so many teenagers. Summer was over, school was back in session. Yet they polluted the stores like lemmings, lingering and never purchasing anything. I can't say that I blame them, I was their age once too.

Most of my best memories in high school included meeting my friends and making our way through the candy stores, loading up on sugar only to talk about boys and which classes we hated. Kayla's brother, Timothy, worked at the movie theater in the mall. Everyone called him Tim, but I called him by his full name. It started as a way to pick on him, but it became my favorite name.

The mall theater was quite small, only two show rooms. So they would only pick certain movies for certain days. We'd get in for free, Timothy giving us all the popcorn we wanted. That was until Kayla found him and I making out behind the concessions during a lull in *The Stepfather*. I've never been a fan of horror films, but they were Kayla's favorite. Her brother and I had been sneaking around for a few weeks at that point, it was only a matter of time.

That year, I ran for president as a freshman, and Timothy won prom king.

My first impression of Timothy was that he was annoying, rude and everything in between. He was the epitome of all big brothers. I wouldn't know personally, as I only had a younger sister. But I'd seen enough movies to figure it out.

Kayla and I would lay out by her pool, Timothy and his football buddies would splash the icy water over us in pursuit to make us scream. Every war ended with the same battle cry for their mother, who typically laid the gauntlet down no matter what.

"Sweetheart, I don't know why you stick around." Kayla's mother would sigh at me, returning to whatever it may be that she was doing.

It wasn't until a get together in the summer of '07 that I really noticed Timothy in that new light. My parents, along with several other families, were having a get together at the Lorne's for the end of summer. Kayla and I were starting high school, Timothy entering his junior year. My house was neither large nor equipped enough to host an event for all the neighborhood kids.

All of us were in the basement after a swim while the parents discussed the predicted housing crash to come the following year on the patio. It was funny. Timothy had no problem being one of the only four boys in a room full of 14 year old girls. Of course, every last one of them had a crush on him. Including me.

My body was covered in goosebumps, my lips blue as my teeth chattered.

"Jesus, Daws. Are you cold or what?" Tim snickered, using the nickname he'd given me over the two years of knowing the Lorne's. His top teeth were exposed in a lazy grin as he draped a quilt made by their grandmother over my goosebumped shoulders.

"You got your braces off." I smiled excitedly, moving to sit on my knees. I wrapped the blanket tighter around my shoulders, inhaling the comforting basement smell. "Show me." I am only a few inches from his face, my lips parted in focus as I look at his perfect smile. From this angle, I can see every freckle that constellates his face. I could now appreciate the strains of denim that ran through his light blue eyes. "Does it feel weird?" I asked with my face contorting in concentrated expressions. Tim let out a soft laugh and nodded.

"Slimy." He simply responded, running his tongue over his top teeth. I mimicked it the same, a trait I would pick up for the better half of my life. My teeth weren't perfect, but my mom said they were too good for braces. Though I was always jealous of Timothy for having them. "I got a job at the movie-"

"Ahem." Kayla cleared her throat, her green eyes glaring at the two of us. I sat back on my bottom, my hands in my lap, twiddling the rings my sister got me from *Claire's*. She told me that she read in *Seventeen* magazine that they would make me look older. I could see Kayla's knuckles turning white against the bowl of popcorn she was holding. I scooted over on the cheap carpeting, allowing her to sit in the middle of us.

The opening credits began of one of those movies where sharks get put in a pond and all the college students die one by one. They were so unrealistic, but it was Kayla and Timothy's house. The rest of us were merely guests. I still remember the floor was covered in pillows and miscellaneous tie blankets as we all laid in different sections. Classmates scattered around as Timothy, Kayla and myself lay with our heads on pillows in the dead center of the floor.

Timothy laid on the end, glancing at me every so often.

The second the basement was silent, apart from the disc's title screen and everyone's soft snores, Timothy was waking me up to go hang out in his room. We stayed up till four in the morning, laughing and diving deep into each other's secrets. And before we came back downstairs, we exchanged a soft kiss goodnight.

We were inseparable from that day on.

In 2009, Timothy graduated, and I was only going into my junior year. A full ride to Texas Tech for football really put a damper on dating the star running back that lived three blocks away.

And just like that, every good thing in my life had ended. Right on track.

Eight

TESSA

"You only think that because you don't know him."

"Yeah but do *you* know him?" Kayla folded her arms as she sighed. I ignore her comment as I focus on the jeans on the wall. I catch her staring at me from the corner of my eye, waiting on my response. "I know enough." I dramatically move my head as I speak, feeling my claw clip full of tangled curls bob along. I didn't sleep well last night, tossing and turning as I thought about my new position at work. I had no strength to get ready for that shopping trip, nor did I care how I looked. I zipped my gray jacket up a little more, betraying my carefree mindset as the teens in the store made me feel more insecure.

"No, you know what the media *wants* you to know." Kayla, pointed her smoothie cup at me with a smile. I sigh in annoyance. She just didn't see him the way I did. I saw the way he spoke to his father every month. Hell, I saw the way he spoke to *me*. My only response was a shake of my head as we left the store, walking down the marble tiles of the shopping center. "There's more to this story than TMZ, Kayla." I sigh.

Kayla stopped in front of me, folding her arms as people pushed past us.

"Then tell me. What do you *know* about this man? Like *really* know?"

I run my tongue over my top teeth, avoiding her gaze. I always hated people putting me on the spot. "I know he's a dick to his father." I matched her stance, trying to remain stoic. "Why?" She asked, her tone telling me that she already knew the answer.

"It doesn't matter."

"Yes, it does. He's a dick to his dad because his dad was a dick to him his *entire* life." Kayla was really trying to sell me on this guy, wanting me to give him a chance. It's so foreign to me, seeing her try to stick up for the guy who'd made my life a living hell, when she was always quick to pull a gun on anyone who merely looked at me funny. "Kayla, if you want him just fucking say that." I groaned, pushing past her. My angered tone only struck a pitiful laugh from her.

"Don't get mad at me because you're being a bitch without the facts."

I understood where she was coming from to an extent. Living the life Reese did, a child of an affair, was definitely grounds for daddy issues. But that didn't write him a pass to being an asshole to everyone around him.

Kayla quickly caught back up to me, a snicker plastered on her face. "I wasn't trying to piss you off. I just think you should make the most of this. I mean, his dad's literally gonna pay your tuition." She spoke this time with more sincerity, losing her forceful tone. I nodded along as she was right. His dad was doing me the biggest favor, all at the expense of teaching Reese how to be a functioning adult.

I sit at the table in the courtyard, opening the container of Indian food. The smell is comforting, reminding me of my high school years. I watch as Kayla waits in line for hers, mulling over the inside of my cheek in thought. I pull my phone from my pocket, opening Safari. I stare at the search bar for a while. I'm unsure of what I want to search for. So I start with the simplest thought.

Reese Finch NYC.

Several articles appear, along with a few images. Him golfing, him intoxicated in public. His mugshot from the same intoxicated night. His eyes appear bluer from the bloodshot twinge that surrounded them. His lips are together, his expression was hard with furrowed brows and lazy eyes. His cheeks are sunken in and I can tell his jaw is clenched. His sharply cut cheekbones and jaw looked as if it were molded from marble. A pure portrait of masculinity. The entire image makes my stomach tighten, like he's staring right at me.

The articles all read about the same things. 'Troubled youth socialite cracks under pressure' type of thing. I take a deepened breath, one that makes me feel like my lungs are maxed capacity, and hover my finger over the bold, blue writing.

"If I gotta hear about one more girl's homecoming ideas, I'll lose my mind." Kayla sighed, knocking me from my trance. I lock my phone, taking her arrival as a sign to not dive deeper into Reese. I nod with a soft chuckle, truly not listening to what she was saying. I found myself glancing at my phone on the table periodically, distracted by the thought of him.

August 28th

As I aimlessly scrolled through my socials, a voicemail from my mom plagues my entire focus.

"Hi, honey. It's mom. Haven't heard from you in a few days, give me a call and we can arrange a way for you to come visit. Don't work too hard. Love you, bye."

Her voice was soft, comforting in all ways but physical. The sound of her voice is like a warm sweater on a fall day. My eyes shut as I play it over again. The static is soothing, as if it's her heartbeat.

Since they moved to Florida on my twenty-third birthday, I saw them once a year. After dad's retirement, he decided he was done with the finicky New York weather.

I can't even force a phone call back without her catching on to something being wrong immediately. I sigh, shooting her a text in response.

T- hi, mom. love you more, talk soon.
M- Perfect.

I'm grateful this appeased her. If I don't call tomorrow, she'll be certain something is wrong. It'll end with my tears and her telling me to leave New York and come be with her, dad and Kelseigh. It was always her go to response. And though I loved my mother more than anything, I wished she would give me advice, versus a solution that I never asked for.

Kelseigh was so comfortable living with mom and dad at twenty-three. She was in college part time, mainly staying at home in Daytona. I was on my own by 19, living with girlfriends I'd met through my CNA program. Though from what Kelseigh had told me through the phone these days, mom and dad were rarely ever home. They spent most days in hotels around the country or on cruises. So I guess it would be like owning your own home for free. A luxury I don't think I'd ever come across being in my position.

I looked around my apartment, though small and quaint, it was a lot like that '97 Ranger parked out front. It needed so much work. I tried my best to make the chipped paint and peeling wallpaper look artsy and poetic. In truth, it was a shithole. But it was mine. I had a stove, a bed, and a bathroom. Things lots of people had to go without. I told myself every day how fortunate I was to have what I have. Even if I did climb the fire escape every time my key got stuck in the front door.

The sun melted to orange hues over the city horizon as I adjusted my clip. I needed to shower, but I couldn't get myself from this position on the couch.

The television was off, the only noise came from the traffic outside as I stared at my reflection in the dark screen.

I wanted nothing more than to call into work. I wanted to tell them I was sick, that I had a case of incurable diarrhea and I would never be able to return. But the motive of a free ride through nursing school was keeping me together.

I felt my eyes growing heavy, my body still cemented to the cheap material of the sofa.

August 29th

When I open my eyes, I see the sun is comfortably resting in the sky. I rub my eyes, squinting as I look out my living room window. It takes me a moment to recognize where I am. I grab my phone and spring from the couch when I notice it's dead.

"Shit.... Shit, shit, shit." I mumble, rushing to the kitchen for my charger. My hands tremble as they struggle to plug it in and I glance at the clock on the stove, 7:05 A.M. My jaw drops. I slip into the bathroom, quite *literally* slip as I still have my socks on from the night before, taking the fastest shower of my life. Before I can react, I'm out the door.

I crank the old door of my Ranger open and slam it shut so hard I'm afraid the whole thing will fall off.

"Is Mr. Finch here?" I ask my tending nurse for the day, grabbing my pager and tying my wet curls back into my signature clip. I check the time on my watch, it's 7:58. She nods, pointing to a conference room that we typically only used for potluck weekends. I groan, cramming some gloves in my pockets and walk that way.

Reese is sitting with his chair facing away from the door. I can tell he's wearing a ribbed knit polo, the collar appearing to be open as if a button or two was undone.

It wasn't until he spun his chair around that I could see it was tucked into a pair of black slacks accompanied with a Saint Laurent belt. I wet my lips and squeezed my eyes tight, nervous for what he had to say.

Nine

REESE

"Nice of you to show up." I toss my phone on the table and fold my arms. My eyes trail over Tessa's curves, so haphazardly tucked into her black, tight scrubs. The few curls that didn't make it into her clip, frame her face. They were a wet and tangled mess. I didn't know much about girl hair, but I knew she'd have one hell of a time brushing that out later. She had no makeup on, still her skin was so even and velvety. Even her eyes, they were so hazy and sleepy yet I couldn't get myself to look away. I kept my smirk at bay as she turned and scrambled through some cabinets.

"I'm sorry I'm late. I had kind of a tough night." I can tell it's a lie, a vague one at that. I'm a pro at making shit up, she'd better take a lesson if we were to be spending every Thursday together.

"Oh, yeah? What happened?"

She stops, her back turned to me as I let out a small chuckle. My tongue traced the corner of my mouth as I shook my head.

"You can just say you overslept. Not everything needs an explanation or an apology." I teased as she finally turned to face me. Based on her expression, I can tell she was trying to appear unbothered by me, but even I knew she was having a hard time hiding her true emotions.

"I only overslept because I was nervous."

"Do I make you nervous?" My face contorts to a snicker as I feel my ego growing tenfold. "No, that's not what I meant." Her rebuttal was quicker than I imagined she was capable of at this hour, assuming she did only just wake up. "Sounds like that's what you meant."

"Well, it's not." Tess's face is gravely serious, making my stomach drop. I hadn't seen her this way in all the times I'd riled her up. She's so much smaller than me, yet she was intimidating at this moment. "Got it." I put my hands up in defeat as I stood from the chair. She rubs her hands over her face with an exaggerated sigh, taking a moment before speaking.

"I'm sorry. I'm just a little thrown off of my routine."

I stared at her for a second, appreciating her apology as it seemed more sincere than the one earlier. "It's alright, really." My words seem to put her at ease. I could tell by her aura that she was a perfectionist. The mere idea of being late today, whether I was involved or not, was excruciating to her.

"Have you stopped in your dad's room yet?" She asked, applying some hand sanitizer before stepping into the hall. I close the door behind me and scoff. "Maurice? What for?" I replied. Tessa's expression softened as she looked up at me with those amber pools. "Because it's the kind and mature thing to do." The words made me want to lash out, but I knew she was saying what I needed to hear. Or maybe she just wanted her money. Which I couldn't blame her for even if I tried, because I wanted my money too.

I wave my hand for her to lead the way, ultimately deciding on the 'kind' and 'mature' thing to do as she so sweetly put it. Tessa nodded, walking in front of me. I watched the way her arms swished against her hips that swayed so effortlessly. My head tilts on its own chemical reaction to the tightness of the scrubs, I almost don't hear her voice.

"Reese?" The way she said my name snapped me back to the dreary nursing home. I looked around, making sure no one noticed me staring so long. "Hm?"

"Are you ready?"

I wet my lips and noticed her crinkle her brows as I did so. She definitely picked up on the fact that I've learned this habit from her. "Chapped lips." I point to my obviously well moisturized lips with cheeks now burning crimson. Am I a fucking idiot?

"Okay." Tess's expression was that of unease as she weakly chuckled to clear the awkward air. I held my breath as she opened my father's door. His wrinkled face shining brightly as he was met with her bubbly greeting. "Good morning, Maurice." Tessa spoke in a melodic voice that sounded like warm sunshine.

As I came around the corner, I saw the smile become replaced by a blank, sullen expression. The anger begins to bubble in me yet again. Tessa turns around to look at me, her eyes telling me to hold off.

"I see you've shown up for your first day." Maurice looked me up and down, shocked at what he was seeing. He looks like shit, worse than when I saw him last. I wish I felt something besides anger towards him. I'd probably be more torn up about his condition. "Yeah, I even beat your precious daughter here."

Maurice snickered at the thought. His biggest disappointment and failure being on time to a job was unbelievable. "Don't worry, Reese. She'll keep you on your toes today."

I watch Tessa snicker at his comment as she takes his blood pressure. "I didn't have time to get your donut this morning."

"That's quite alright. I know where to find you." He was so playful and witty with her. It made my stomach churn. I felt like an outsider in my own father's bedroom, like I was unwelcome.

The words were caught in my chest. I wanted to scream at him. I wanted to blame him for the way he'd treated me, the way he raised me. But I knew he wouldn't care either way.

My earliest memory of my father was held in a courtroom in upstate New York. The room smelled like a stale basement, reminding me of when we'd do laundry in our apartment complex.

My mother battled for child support after Maurice fired her for coming forward about the affair and me belonging to him. I sat in a pew, a five-year old boy, dressed in a suit my mom had bought for Easter that previous year. I can remember the way the pants hugged tightly against my ankles and how taut the sleeves were. My legs dangled off of the cold, wooden seat. My mother's tears combined with my suffocating suit prevented me from taking full breaths. Why was she crying? Why didn't he want me? I had so many questions and no voice to use.

Maurice sat at the other end of the courtroom, pinching the bridge of his nose as if I was already deemed a nuisance to him. "I'm not just gonna cut a check because Miss Taylor *claims* this kid is mine." He scoffed. I remember he talked with his hands a lot, deflecting most questions. The voices of adults floated past me like clouds, using words I didn't understand. I also remember my mom holding my hand as a man in a white coat approached me with a cotton swab. "Stick your tongue out, baby." My mother's voice was always so soothing, reassuring like Tessa's.

Maybe it's because she was so young in comparison to my father. My mom was twenty-four when she began working for Maurice as his assistant. He was fifty-four. By her twenty-fifth birthday, she was pregnant with me. My mother was practically a baby, raising a baby.

I stared at the back of Maurice's head as the man with the white coat swabbed the inside of my cheek, memorizing the exact moment when I knew I wasn't supposed to be.

Ten

REESE

"Can we get this over with?" I groaned, interrupting their banter and folding my arms as I leaned back on my heels. Tessa's eyes spring up from her clipboard as she nods, hanging it back on the edge of the hospice bed. "I'll bring your lunch around 11." Tessa smiled, spinning to follow me out of the apartment. I don't stick around to acknowledge what he says.

I hear Tess's small feet patter behind me as she catches up to me. She can sense the shift in my mood, I know she can. My frustration is a stench that is just wafting off of me. "Reese–"

"Just tell me what to do here, Tessa. I wanna go home, I have shit to do." The words are colder than I'd like them to be. She takes a step back from me, nodding as she pulls out an iPod from her scrub pocket. Perhaps that's what she dug in that cabinet for.

I can tell her wall is being built brick by brick, I'd almost prefer it that way. She placed the iPod in my hand and I raised a brow at her. "You're on activities." She spoke walking off, leaving me without another instruction. "What is that supposed to mean?" A question I was getting all too familiar with asking.

"It *means* Lena is on maternity leave and Salsa class starts in…" She checked her watch. "Ten minutes, so you'd better get in there." My eyes grow large as she speaks so nonchalantly, heading toward the activity room. All the kindness in her voice has melted into nothing.

"Get in there? I don't know the first damn thing about salsa." I argue as I stay on her heels, my body practically pressed against her as she walks. I watch her shoulders heave with a heavy breath. "Reese, it's

36

nine in the morning in a nursing home. Most of these people aren't even sure who the president is. Trust me, you know enough."

Tessa snatches the iPod from my hand and plugs it in, queuing up Ricky Martin's version of *La Bomba*. I thought I was going into cardiac arrest, that or I was going to explode from embarrassment.

"Tessa, please don't make me do this." I begged. I'd get on my knees if she asked me to. I wet my lips nervously, my eyes softening in desperation as she only smirked back at me. This was revenge. For what, I hadn't yet figured out.

"Good morning, everyone. As you know, Miss Lena is on maternity leave. Which means… Mr. Finch will be taking over activities on Thursdays." Tessa had such a magnetic personality when talking to these old people. They smiled and listened to every word, proving they were enamored with her presence. It was like they couldn't get enough of her, hanging on every word and hooked on that damn smile. All I could do was stand behind her like an absolute dork while she controlled the room, something I was typically known for. "Take it away, Mr. Finch."

Tessa sat in a chair in the front row. The mildewy room held maybe seven residents though my heart thumped like it was a full house. One lady knitted, a man read the newspaper, leaving only a few interested in the class.

"Take your shirt off!" A woman called out, others cheered as my eyes were saucers. Tessa buried her mouth in her hand as she muffled a chuckle. I roll my eyes at her reaction, taking a shaky breath. *Come on, Finch… You can do this…* I tuck my nerves away and relax my shoulders, pulling out my infamous charisma that had gotten me much farther in life. "I think the ways of Salsa are better *shown* than taught. Miss Dawson, could you please join me?" My lips curled to a lazy grin as her tongue ran across her top teeth.

"No, thank you." She was still clearly annoyed with me.

"Suit yourself." I winked in her direction before turning to a woman in the front. She stood at about Tessa's height as I pulled her up and into a dance, making lots of random foot movements. I don't think I'd ever seen anyone Salsa before, nor was I completely sure what it was. But I know I wasn't anywhere near *Dancing With the Stars*.

I spun the old woman, looking up to find people partnering up. The activity room appeared to be filling up. I felt a sense of pride, knowing I'd brought these people together. Even if it was just for a silly class.

Tessa sat in the chair, her left leg over her right and shaking her head with a smile as I shrugged. She was right, I was a natural to them.

The older woman rested her head on my chest while we danced in a circle, slowing down as the song *At Last* by Etta James began to hum over the cheap radio. The salsa playlist was finally over, and I knew I'd be thanking God for that later.

If there is one thing I *can* do, it's slow dance.

An old man with a fall risk band sways his way to Tessa with a cheerful smile and pulls her up from the chair. I've never seen her smile like this in person, not even with my father. It's reminiscent of the candid photos I scrolled through a while back. A smile that is truly lost in the moment and under no sense of pressure from the outside world. I can faintly hear her laugh over the music and I find myself grinning at the sound. She truly had every person wrapped around those little fingers of hers.

I dance my partner in her direction, smoothly spinning her out to the old gentleman and spinning in Tessa. "How'd I do?" I asked her with a lazy grin.

"The bar was pretty low." Tessa teased back to me as my right hand lay at the small of her back. My thumb caresses the smooth fabric of her scrubs. Her right hand is folded with my left. I try not to focus on the tingling sensation I get when she twirls the hair on the back of my neck. She probably doesn't even realize that she's doing it. Or that it's driving me absolutely insane.

"How low?" I'm lost in those caramelized honey eyes as I wet my lips, this time not out of nervousness. But out of attraction. I slide lower on her back, cupping her ass and my neck grows cold as she removes her hand to lift mine back up. "Not that low, we're working." Tessa's tone was sharp, but like the absolute idiot that I am, I rolled my eyes. "Well, what time do you go to lunch?" I asked. No, I *flirted*. I was genuinely trying to get this girl in an empty apartment for ten minutes or hell, a janitorial closet.

In a matter of one day, I'd thrown all hatred for her out the window. I just wish I could say the same for her.

A frown forms on her face as she lets go of me completely and stands back to get a good look at me. I was proving myself to be the same sex driven moron that she knew me to be.

"We're done for the day. You can go." She spoke in a meek voice under the crooning music. "Tess, wait." I called after her but she was quick on those damn legs, already off helping a resident down the hall. I ran my hand through my hair and sighed.

Eleven

TESSA

R- I'm sorry I'm a dick.
R- Nothing to say?
R- Seriously? Not even an 'I know?'
R- I'll see you next week I guess.

I groan, tucking my phone into my pocket. His apology was dull and insincere. Empty words without a hint of remorse or regret. The heat of his hand swindling its way to my ass can still be felt as I bump open Maurice's apartment door with my hip.

"Oh, Lucy! I'm home. And I brought lunch." I giggle, using my best Ricky Ricardo impression. Maurice let out a laugh, followed by a barky cough, the kind that sounded like an old engine running out of gas. "Gee, Ricky. For me?" He smiled.

He raised his hospice bed to a sitting position, wiping the corners of his mouth from his cough. "How're you feeling?" I asked with pulled down brows, my right hand rested on my hip. He'd really seen better days. If I knew any better, I'd say he had one foot in the grave.

I open his lunch container and the plastic silverware, setting him up. "Never better." He smiled through his pain as I grabbed the newest issue of Better Homes & Gardens.

"How was Reese?"

I cringed at the question, though I knew it'd be coming. "Fine." My reply was short but to the point. He wasn't amazing, but he wasn't terrible.

"Hey, how long am I doing this for?" I asked, closing the magazine and folding my right leg over my left. My fingers crease the corner of the magazine, looking at Maurice as he chews his food. His gaze is on his muted tv, an episode of Gunsmoke told in subtitles. I try to catch his eye, but he doesn't respond for a moment.

"You'll know."

I'll know? God, did I hate word problems. I needed an answer, a date. A damn timeline.

"Right." I let out a soft, frustrated sigh, going back to the magazine. I try to read but I can't focus. I flip the pages to this year's top color pallets. I would have killed for a renovation or even a new dresser set.

From the watermarks to the crooked drawers, my dresser told a story. My dad's first bachelor pad, the place he brought my mom to after their second date. The first piece of furniture he lugged into his apartment, somehow trudged its way to me, thirty years later.

I could have taken out a credit card, or got a payment plan, but I've always been a sucker for the sentimental value of things.

"Up for a game?" As Maurice finishes his lunch, I'm jolted back to reality. I rise back to my feet with a shake of my head. "No, not today. I think I'm just gonna head home for the night." I smile politely. It isn't enough to convince him. He wanted to ask me what my problem was, where my big personality was. But he seemed to respect my decision.

"Enjoy your long weekend." His wrinkles crease as he smiled, leaning his bed back. I nodded, exiting the room.

I closed the door to my truck, both hands rested at ten and two. My forehead is pulled to the steering wheel like a magnet. I shut my eyes, listening to the seatbelt ding. A sound that is so rhythmically relaxing. A vibration comes from my phone and I pull it from my pocket with a sigh, expecting it to be Reese. I'm met with a picture of my mom and I on my prom night. My brown curls in a taut updo, my skin glowing against the black sequin dress. And in the background, a scene practically painted of Timothy and my father laughing as they talked.

"Hi, mom."

"You said you'd call." Her voice is like a warm blanket wrapped around me and I try not to cry. I'm not sure why my trigger reaction is to cry. Maybe I miss her more than I give myself credit for. My tears are threatening to escape. "I know." I whisper into the phone, leaning back against the seat.

"Honey, talk to me."

She can see right through it, she knows I'm not okay. It's like I'm a window, transparent and visible, exposed for everyone to see. "I'm just so damn stressed at work right now." I croak out, it's the vaguest I can be.

"Tessa, baby, you can always come home for a while. Clear your mind."

Home. She says it like we grew up in Florida. Like we didn't spend our summers in Coney Island, with Kelseigh begging me to ride the Cyclone again. Or Timothy kissing me at the top of the Wonder Wheel as the humid summer air blew through our hair.

I wasn't from Florida. None of us were. We were from New York.

When we hang up, I feel worse. I wipe the one tear that dared to escape and start the engine. There was no sense in crying. It wasn't going to make me feel any better and it sure as shit wasn't going to fix anything.

September 2nd

The windows in my apartment are open, and I'm enjoying the golden air that blows through. During the fall, it smells less of pollution and more of burning leaves and apple cinnamon. Maybe it was just my candle I was burning. But all around, the quality of life was better. It was Monday; I worked in the afternoon. The morning was for me to do whatever I'd like. Shop, journal, bake, clean. But mostly, I scrolled through videos and laid around. That crisp September air was different though. I *needed* to be up and moving.

I took a colder shower, basking in the icicles against my skin. I apply my makeup in natural nudes, actually participating in my curly hair routine. I've got on my black scrubs, the ones that hug my body in the right place. Or maybe they were just my most expensive pair. I had to justify the amount somehow.

I knew when I arrived, I'd get to play a quick game of Mancala with Maurice before tending my rounds. I owed him that much as I had robbed him of his Thursday donut and his games all last week.

The nurses all looked at me with confusion as my cheery personality had returned. I greeted them all with jovial hellos and waves. Deep down, I think I truly bothered them. I was one of the few people in that nursing home that didn't take my work home with me. My Reese drama did not count.

I would walk away from that place at 2:30 every afternoon and turn my mind off. I didn't worry about anyone or anything in that building the second I clocked out.

I knock twice on Maurice's door, holding the mancala board under my arm. "Mr. Finch?" I smiled, walking in. I felt the wooden board slide from my grip and land on the floor, marbles echoing as they hit the ground.

Reese's eyes meet mine.

I didn't know what he was doing here. It wasn't Thursday, and he didn't care to visit his father ever. "Joyous, darling." Maurice smiled, leaning over his bed slightly to watch the marbles ricochet and disburse. Reese stands to his feet to walk to me but I'm quick to my knees to scoop the marbles before he can speak.

"You never texted me back." He mumbles in an attempt to keep Maurice out of our business as he meets me on the ground. His larger, veiny hands scoop more marbles faster than I can. "I don't need your help." I refused to look at him. I wasn't going to let him destroy my good mood. My eyes are watering, forcing me to blink faster.

"I didn't ask if you did. Would you just fucking look at me?" His tone was low and deep. I wet my lips, slamming the marbles into the board as I look at him as requested. "I told you I was sorry." He whispered.

"I know." I replied, standing back to my feet. I place the wooden board on Maurice's overbed table.

"I'll come back later." I smile through the lump in my throat. Reese was practically stepping on the backs of my shoes as he followed behind me. He gripped my upper arm, pulling me into his father's bathroom and shutting the door behind us. "Get your fucking hand off of me." I scowled, ready to claw his eyes out. Reese's lips are parted as he breathes from his mouth. He's out of breath from the fight I put up. His body is practically pressed against mine as he looks down at me, one strand of his raven hair falling forward in his vision. My heart is beating from my chest with adrenaline, he has to hear it. The silence is deafening as he wets his lips to speak to me.

"Look, I know you hate me. Trust me, I'm not too fucking fond of you either. But I'm *really* trying to make the best out of this." His voice was low but whiny as he finished his sentence, my stomach tightened as I clenched my jaw.

"Now, I said I was sorry. I didn't mean to take advantage of you." I can't help but notice the way he struggled to keep his eyes on mine, his trailing from my lips to the notch of my neck.

My chest rises and falls rapidly as I chew the inside of my cheek to keep myself from screaming. "Say something." He demanded, his crystal blue eyes dark and stormy. There was a hint of danger and intrigue in his gaze. His lips were still parted as he hovered over me. I took in a shaky breath, feeling my body buzzing at the sensation of him so close to me.

"I'll see you Thursday." I swallowed hard, watching his lips curl into a devilish grin. His eyes kept me guessing, creating a menacing yet captivating expression.

Reese opened the door for me, waving me to walk through first. I flattened out my scrub top with two hands as I cleared my throat, leaving the room without another word.

Twelve

REESE

"You up?" I knock on the door lightly. Maurice peers his head around the corner as he sits up, a sigh escaping his lips. "You're a few days early." He scoffed, muting his television. His face was gaunt, his eyes sunken and dull from the ravages of age. I feel my lip twitch with emotion as I stare at him in the bed before responding. I'm not sure if I'm upset about how he looks, or about the way he greeted me.

"I came to talk to you."

Maurice gave a hoarse laugh, tainted with bitterness as he cleared his throat. "Right, I told you I'm not writing any more checks."

My jaw twinges at his comment as I'd *kill* to blow up. "I'm not here to ask you for money." In truth, I wasn't sure what I was there for. I take a deep breath, wetting my lips. "How are you feeling?" I practically speak through my teeth. Deep down, I didn't give a fuck how he felt. But I was on the path to maturity and responsibility. And the responsible thing to do was ask my father how he was feeling.

"Reese, please don't act as though my health is of concern to you." Maurice sighed, pinching the bridge of his nose. Suddenly I was a little boy again. In that stale courtroom, swinging my feet in that pew.

My breath is caught in my chest, trapped in my lungs, pinched tight. I feel my face burning with hatred as I grip the foot rails of the bed with white knuckles.

"Mr. Finch?" The voice is like a harp in an '90s rom-com. My head darts to the right and I lock eyes with her. So hard, that she drops the things in her grasp and a pleasant melody of marbles bounced off of the floor.

I shut my eyes slightly, watching her leave the room. My body heat is through the roof, my chest panting with uncontrollable desire for this fucking girl. Both hands are on my hips, my thumbs rubbing against the leather of my belt as I regulate my breathing. I can feel my dick still twitching at the thought of how close our bodies were when I was in her face. My lashes flutter as I force my eyes closed. I tried to think of anything besides her bratty lips as she had that look on her face. I wanted to wipe it off myself.

When I head home, my apartment is quiet in comparison to the outside world. It's dark and cold. I flick the light on to my kitchen, pulling out leftover wings. Normally, I'd be at Marc Forgione. Engaging in a four course meal and drinking with my friends. I take one bite of the wing and toss it back into the greasy, saturated styrofoam.

I throw myself into the sofa, my legs spread slightly as I slouch into the leather material. I see the same posts from the same friends on *Instagram*. Christian updates the world on his Malibu trip he took and I groan, double tapping the post in support.

Her name is still in my recent searches.

I mull over the idea, deciding to go back to her profile to see one new post.

@tdaws93: missing FL extra today #dontbeabeach

I crinkle my brows with a snort from my nose, only Tess would say something corny like that. I zoom in on the image of her in the white sands and a bright pink bikini. If you could call it that. It was more like cheap strings tied around her curves. It would make any man's mind wander to the pits of Hell. The sun is reflecting off of her golden skin, she'd been in that Florida sun for at least a week. My breath was fragile and shallow. Her curls were loose from the salty water. She looked so relaxed, a version of her I had yet to see. I zoom in more on Tessa, shifting slightly in my seat.

My jeans tighten as I run my trembling hand over my dick to calm the growing feeling, my mouth sweating. I continue to look at her picture and grit my teeth, cursing under my breath. I unzipped my denim prison, wondering if I was really this hard up for sex. It had only been a few days since my last Brooklynn call. Sliding my hand into my briefs, my length is swollen and throbbing as I groan from deep in my chest. A wince escapes me as I relieve my twitching urge. I can feel small beads of sweat appearing across my forehead as I play the scene in my mind. Tessa is standing in front of me, her hands running up and down my thighs.

"Tessa, fuck…" I whimper, my tongue tracing the corner of my mouth as my thumb reaches the tip of my dick. I imagine it to be her tongue, as she sits on her knees in front of me in that stringy, pink bikini like the good girl I know she can be. I just have to break her of that bratty fucking attitude.

A ding startles me enough to drop my phone between my legs on the floor. "Shit." I mumble, feeling like a teenage boy being caught in my room by my mother. I pick the phone up, a text glows across the screen.

11:49P.M.
T- hope you like ice cream. see you at 10 on thursday.

The blood had been drained from my face. A doctor would be gravely concerned about an EKG of my heart. Tessa knew. She *definitely* knew. I look out of my 28th story window down at the New York skyline. Could she see in my apartment?

No, this was stupid. She didn't know I was jacking off to her. Maybe she did, maybe she was a witch. I decide to play it safe, my heart practically escaping my chest.

12:02A.M.
R- Thinking about me? At this hour?
T- no.

I can't help but smirk at her quick reply, feeling the blood return to every appendage. I run a clammy hand over my face, still shaking from my denied release. I purse my lips as I think of a reply.

47

12:20A.M.
R- Then what are you doing up so late, Tessa?
T- typing…

I snicker, watching the typing appear and then disappear. She doesn't respond. Not now, not in an hour. Not even the next day.

September 5th

I walk into Brindlewood Assisted Living, a black coffee for me and a danish for Tessa. She's standing at the nurse's counter, her hourglass being squeezed into electric pink scrubs. I trace my eyes from her shoulders to her hips. The way her body appeared so smooth yet snug into that matching set, I wanted to tear it off of her. My breath is sharp, reflecting on my private rendezvous last night. My legs go numb, I shift my weight to one side, trying to not focus on the way my khakis graze my briefs. "Christ.." I mumble, wetting my lips.

A nurse points at me standing by the door, causing Tessa to turn and look. Her curls are down today, cascading just over her middle back. For a second, I caught a smile. Not an overly ecstatic smile, but one that she seemed to have put on just for me. "Hi." She greets, walking over to me with her hands in the pockets of her top.

I noticed she changed her name tag to one with tiny red and orange leaves. The entire nursing home was decorated for fall, something I would have remembered the last time I was here. There is a faint smell of cinnamon, like the Christmas pinecones my mom would put out to cover the smells of the leaky pipes in our apartment.

I push the memories from my mind as she stands in front of me. Tess looked up, a sparkle in her eye by default. It had nothing to do with me, and everything to do with her seeing the best in people always. I can't even use my fucking words as I hold the bag with the danish out in front of me. Tessa raised a playful brow.

"Figured you haven't been sleeping the best lately, so I brought breakfast." I teased about the other night, finally finding my voice.

She rolled her eyes, reluctantly taking the bag from my hand. I'd hoped her hands would touch mine so I could feel her skin on me just once.

Jesus Christ, I really was desperate for sex.

Without a second thought, she was already on the move down the hall. "I've got you set up in the activity room whenever you're ready." Tessa takes a bite of the pastry, licking the glaze from her lips and I feel my mouth sweat. "Please tell me there isn't any dancing involved." I beg as the music gets louder the more we walk down the hall. We pass several residents, all smiling and throwing their one-liners to Tessa. Most of them just greet her, others ask her questions. She's amazing with them. The way she carried herself was enigmatic.

"No dancing."

She finishes the danish, licking her index finger. I nod, avoiding her in every way possible. She turns her back as we enter the room. There is already a crowd, some dancing to *Emotions* by Brenda Lee, other's playing cards and doing crosswords.

"But I am gonna have to ask you to wear this." She turns back, holding a hairnet and I feel my brows lower and my eyes grow with concern. "What the hell for?" I ask, masking the panic in my voice. This is social suicide. Her voice erupts a giggle as she stands on her tiptoes, making me realize how much smaller she is once again.

I crouch, giving her better access to put this hairnet on me. "You didn't think I was asking you to an ice cream date the other night, did you?" She snickered as I was still in her eye line, I felt my breath shift as I grinned.

"I guess not." I spoke in a low tone, admiring her lips before rising back to my original height. She waves me to follow her to an ice cream cart, just like you'd see on a street corner in 1960. "Your toppings are all right here. Fudge, caramel, nuts, and maraschinos." Tessa used the tongs, plucking a cherry from the small plastic container. She held the stem by two dainty, manicured fingers, putting the cherry between her teeth and popping its stem.

"Good luck." She winked.

And I watched, like a dog on the hottest day of summer.

Thirteen

TESSA

My eyes linger into the activity room every time I pass it. I catch myself grinning at the way Reese conducts himself. His nerves were all over the place. Condiments fell to the floor and residents grew annoyed with him. But by the second hour, he was a natural.

I checked my watch, deciding now was a good enough time to go to lunch. My legs have a mind of their own as I try to prevent myself from entering the ice cream social. I take a deep breath, walking up to his cart.

"What can I-" Reese wipes the sweat from his forehead with his forearm. His tongue meets the corner of his mouth as a smirk finds its way to his face. "I'm not even gonna ask. Close your eyes." I fold my arms playfully, an exhale escaping my nose.

After a few minutes, Reese lets out a snicker. "Open your mouth for me, Tessa." The sentence made my stomach tighten as I did as told. My body buzzed feeling his heat radiate off of mine as he stood closer, waiting for the ice cream to hit my tongue.

The cold cream is covered in nuts and caramel. I lick the sauce from my lips, my tongue lingering a moment too long.

Reese is staring at my mouth, still holding the cup of ice cream in his hands as he imagined the taste of my lips. He's mesmerized by the sight of me, practically melting the ice cream in his hands by the heat of his body. The lustful look in his eyes tells me he's enjoying himself. Maybe a little *too much*.

My eyes grow wide as I pretend to be worried. "Reese, were there nuts in that?" I asked, putting my seventh-grade drama class to work.

"I- Yeah. I-Is that a problem?" Reese's face is white, worried at what I might say. His eyes dart between mine as I take a labored inhale.

I struggle to breathe, faking a wheezy cough as I fight to get any air in. "I'm allergic." I mutter, trying to make it sound authentic. Reese's eyes were full of panic as he looked around frantically, trying to find some indication that I wasn't really in danger. "Holy shit... Okay. Um, okay." He looks in fear, taking my hand to pull me from the activity room before I could even get a word in edgewise.

"I need an EpiPen!" He called for help, his voice laced with panic, drawing the attention of other residents and nurses in the hall. I quickly placed my hand over his mouth, trying to prevent him from yelling anymore. We turned down a secluded hallway, his back to the cold cement wall as he towered over me.

"I'm not allergic." I whispered playfully with a naughty smile, so no one could hear us, except for him. Reese rolled his eyes and sighed against my hand.

"You're a fucking menace." Reese smirked as I removed my hand. I lick the sticky remnant of caramel from my lips, stifling a laugh. "I thought you were gonna die back there, Tessa." He ran a shaky hand over his face as he chuckled. "I almost had a heart attack."

"I tend to have that effect on people." A snort erupts from my nose. He leans his head back against the wall letting out his final sigh. "I'm on my lunch. Hungry?" I hate that I'm offering to spend any more time than legally required with him. Reese nodded, groaning as he went to his full standing position.

"What's for lunch?"

He sat at a table across from me in the courtyard. "Good old fashion PB&J." I wink, breaking it in half. I extend one to him and he shakes his head in disgust. "Really?" I can practically see his face turning green. "Reese, it's a damn sandwich not gravel from the driveway." I groaned.

"Let me take you to lunch, show you a good meal." He folded his hands at the table, leaning forward with that dumb, smoldering grin. I wet my lips, this time in frustration as I stand up from the picnic table and move around to sit on top beside his half. I extend the sandwich down in his direction again.

"Part of being *responsible* is understanding that you don't always get to eat a five star meal when you're hungry." I sighed with a devious smirk. I wasn't going down with a fight. After all, I was to be teaching him responsibility. He reluctantly takes the sandwich and takes a bite, tearing the bread between his teeth like a savage in an attempt to prove a point. "Think about it, you go to some fancy ass restaurant, spend $100 on lunch, including drinks... You could make a peanut butter and jelly sandwich for about $3 in your kitchen. Put that $97 toward something useful. Gas, bills, investments." I shrug taking another bite.

"Not if you don't have bread at home... Or jelly... Or peanut butter." Reese spoke under his breath, causing me to nearly choke on my sandwich. "We're grocery shopping for you this week." I laughed. He was someone who probably didn't even know how to cook for himself.

Reese runs his index finger over the crust as he holds the remainder of his sandwich. "We used to live off of sandwiches like this my entire childhood." He scoffed, setting the crust back in my tupperware. "Right, Reese Finch of *Finch & Co.* I'm sure you had gourmet peanut butter and organic jelly, right?" I laughed, his eyes meeting mine without the same reaction. My brow involuntarily raised, waiting for an explanation.

"I didn't always live with my dad."

"Oh?" My head leans to the right as he nods. I take a bite of my crust, watching as he toys with his fingers, folded against the table. "I know you love Maurice and he's great to you. But I don't even recognize that man in there, the way he is with you." Reese's voice was low and almost sullen. I can't bring myself to say anything. What the hell am I supposed to say to that?

"He was a fucking asshole. Always will be."

I nod, wanting to place a hand on his tightened back muscles but deciding against it. "You know, we had my tenth birthday at the park. Just a shitty little playground and a gazebo not far from our place in the Bronx." His brows furrow, focusing on a hangnail on his thumb. "It was my mom and some of her friends from work before Sal's opened. Maurice showed up. I'm sure my mom gave him some big speech about being a father. I can still hear his car door slam, the way his suit jacket flapped with the strides he took across the grass." Reese's head falls back as he shut his eyes

"The motherfucker threw a blank card on the table, right in my cake. Not 'to my son'. Hell, I would have taken 'Reese'. It was just a blank fucking envelope."

My heart plummets, I'm sinking in a world of dread *for* him. "Inside, no signature. No fucking note. Just a check for $25. I handed it right to my mom because she deserved it more than I did."

My brows are furrowed. I can't imagine this to be the same Maurice that I laugh with and receive advice from. The same man offered to pay for my nursing school. "I'm so sorry." I whispered, chewing the inside of my cheek as my body was pained with awkwardness.

"Well, don't fucking apologize. Because the last thing I want is your sympathy." Reese piped back at me, causing me to shift in my seat. "Sorry." He mumbled, pinching the bridge of his nose for a quick second before breaking himself from the scene.

I can't focus on anything around the courtyard. This is an unlocked piece of information that I hadn't read from *TMZ* or *The Stripe*. "That's why you don't like to see him?"

My tone was full of sincerity. I wasn't asking for information to run and tell everyone I knew. "There's more than that." He groaned standing from the picnic table and I looked up at him.

"Are we done for the day?" His voice was defeated, his eyes dull and his gaze focused on nothing and full of emptiness as he tried to look at me. I nod softly, standing beside him. "I'll see you next week?" My hands are in the tight cotton pockets of my top as I try to wipe the sweat from them.

He nods, a weak smile on his lips. It's more than forced.

"See you Thursday, Tess."

Fourteen

TESSA

"He's been alright otherwise?" Kayla asks, poking at her Thai noodles as we walk from the food truck. I bite into my spring roll and nod, choosing to avoid sharing the information he told me about his childhood. "Have you guys fucked yet?" She teased, elbowing my side. I nearly choke on my food.

"Gross. Absolutely not." I shake my head, setting my spring roll back in my little paper bowl. Kayla smirked, rolling her eyes. "Don't play dumb with me. Reese Finch fucks anything that can walk. Count your days, girl." She giggles.

That is something I've begun to forget these days. He had seemed so different this morning on the picnic table. It was a side of him I don't think anyone had ever seen before. Though Maurice and him never saw eye to eye, I was quickly learning that his mother meant the world to him.

"One second," I stop walking, pulling my buzzing phone from my pocket.

9:31P.M.
R- Sorry for unloading on you.
T- no worries.

"Unloading? Unloading what?" Kayla pressed for information. "Nothing, drop it." I shook my head, shoving my phone back in my pocket. "Well, it sounds filthy."

I roll my eyes and continue walking. "You're an idiot." I finish my food, tossing the flatware into a trash bin. I couldn't help but relish in the

54

thought that he was still thinking about me after leaving Brindlewood at noon. Nearly nine hours later, I'm circulating his mind.

After parting with Kayla, I walk upstairs to my apartment. My tongue runs across my teeth, mischievously as I decide to use his own lines against him.

10:10P.M.
T- thinking about me at this hour?
R- typing...

I set the phone on the counter, grabbing a jar of peanut butter and a spoon. I hike my body on the fake granite and sit with my legs crossed, scooping the topping from the jar and eating it.

10:12P.M.
R- Yes.

My stomach drops, yet I pull in my bottom lip instinctively. "Nope. Not today." My hands are up in the air in defeat, as I decide not to reply. There is enough chaos in my life right now, the last thing I need is to mix Reese into it. I toss the spoon in the sink and decide to take my dumbass to bed.

September 6th

I groan as my phone rings, I stretch in bed and try to reach my phone.

"Yeah?" I ask with my eyes shut, mouth hanging open as I attempt to stay asleep.

"Tess?"

My body jolts to a sitting position, I wipe the corners of my mouth and slick my hair from my face. "Reese? Is everything alright?" I clear my throat, wetting my lips. I can practically hear him rubbing his jaw as he lets out a husky laugh.

"Did I wake you?" His voice was deep like the ocean pulling me under the tide. It filled empty spaces in my imagination on what it was like to wake up with him.

"No, no. I've been up for a while." I lied, my heart skipping a beat as he sighed softly. "Well, I *believe* you said you'd take me grocery shopping."

"I did?"

"I think those were almost your exact words." He mimicked my laugh, possibly smiling into the phone. I sigh, happily.

"That doesn't sound like me." I groan teasingly as I fiddle with the frays on my bed sheets. His breathing echoes through the phone. "Look, I'm outside. Just get your ass down here."

My eyes go large and I spring to my bedroom window. When I crack the curtain, I see him standing in front of his Lincoln with his black Ray-Bans on. He waves with his free hand, the other still against his ear. "How'd you find my address?" I whispered into the line, eyes still locked with him.

"Google." Reese's lips pull into a snicker, hanging the phone up. I rush to the bathroom, swishing my mouth with Listerine and tucking my curls into a clip. I look in the mirror, I'm in black sweatpants and a white top from last night. It'll have to do.

I close the door behind me and walk to his car. "My address is on Google?" I asked with confusion as he snickered, opening the door. "Just get in, Tess." I wished I could see his crystal pools behind those glasses. I'm feeling deprived. I buckle up, observing all the different buttons and settings on his dash. The Ranger could never sport this many gadgets. I was grateful to at least have working heat in the winter months.

"Where to?" He begins scrolling on his dash maps through the different high end grocery stores in the upper east side. "I'll just give you directions." I smirk, getting comfortable in my seat. A soft groan escapes his lips as he puts the Lincoln in drive.

My directions lead us directly to a run down market owned by the nicest old couple in the entire city. "I'm not getting out, someone's gonna steal my tires."

Reese shook his head, refusing to turn the car off. I place a hand on his upper arm. "I promise, no one cares about your damn car." I smirk, opening my door and stepping out. He growled, following behind me. The sidewalk is busted up, causing me to walk with caution yet his steps are still quick on my tail as if something bad would happen. A bell jingles above the door and I grab a small basket.

"Grocery shopping is all about essentials. Bread, eggs, milk. Things like that." I smiled softly as his chest practically pressed against my back. "You can make just about-"

"Tessa Ann, is that you?" The frail old man stepped out from behind the counter, cane in hand. "I've got a fresh shipment of blueberries. You want 'em?"

I nodded as Reese still hovered so protectively. I could hear his breathing through his nose on the back of my neck. "Reese, I'm fine." I whispered, his brows furrowed and eyes dark. "I know." He mumbled.

"Then back up, please." I smiled. He put his hands up in defeat, following me throughout the store. We throw all the necessities in the basket and make our way to the snack aisle. "What's your vice, Finch?" I smirk, looking at the different chips, nuts and candy. I grab a bag of gummy sharks for myself. I could live on those alone. "I don't really like snacks." He answered, looking through the different choices with his hands tightly in his pockets. I turned to face him, standing just a few inches away as I glared up at him. "Why?"

"I just don't." He snickered, the smile lines creasing darker as he stared down at me. "Then, I guess I'll have to pick some out for you." I groan.

"Okay, you carry this." I giggle with exhaustion in my voice as I hand the basket to him. Reese sighs, bringing it to the check-out.

"I'll wait in the car." I smile, holding my hand out for the keys. "Don't go stealing the car, baby driver." I give an unimpressed look as the metal clinks in my hand.

I close the door behind me, looking over the settings in the car once more. I don't even know where to begin. Seat warmers, google maps, Onstar. Hell, maybe he could get *Netflix* on here... He can do anything with this dash computer.

A text appears across the screen, interrupting my scrolling. I take a soft breath, a girl named 'Brooklynn'. I run my tongue over my teeth as I look to see him talking to the owner inside still. My heart races as I click the red bubble.

9:56A.M.
B- was thinking of you the other night... LMK
the next time you wanna hang. 💋
B- photo.jpg

Fifteen

REESE

I open the trunk, tossing the bags of groceries in. "Seventy bucks. Can you believe that?" I chuckled under my breath in disbelief of just how many things I got. I looked at Tessa, her honey skin looking ghostly. "You alright?" I grinned, buckling up. "Hm? Yeah, yeah. I'm not feeling well. You got a text."

My jaw slacks slightly, taking my phone from my pocket to see a text from Brooklynn. My phone was connected to the car. I glance out the corner of my eye, she's looking straight ahead. I hope to God she didn't open it. Or the picture of Brooklynn naked in bed. Which was nothing to write home about, I might add.

"My uncle." I sigh and hold up the phone, knowing the lie was fucking stupid. She stared at me for a second, opening her mouth to speak. "You don't have to lie to me, Reese." Tessa scoffed, her tone was cold and no longer affectionate. "Unless if you're ashamed of the women you fuck in the city."

My brows crinkle at just how vulgar she worded it.

"I like to call it soulmate searching." I smirked, playing up her bratty attitude. "Right." She folded her arms as I drove. My right hand gripped the gear shifter hard as a low groan escaped my lips. I hated when she had her tantrums. "Tessa, you can say you're jealous of the women I sleep with." I sighed with a devilish grin. Steam was practically rolling out of her ears as she continued to face forward. She was horrible at the silent treatment. I know she wanted to cave.

"You don't want me fucking them, admit it." Hesitantly, my hand moved from the shifter to her thigh. The material of her sweats glided across my fingertips as my middle finger drew circles.

"You'd rather I'd be fucking you, right?"

I hear her breath hitch, my fingers tracing their way to where her thighs met. "If you want me to fuck you, I will. You just have to ask." Her head meets the headrest, a sigh escaping her lips as my ring and middle finger slide against the waistband of her pants. Tessa refused to open her eyes, I struggled to keep mine on the road. I pull the strings to loosen her pants, my hand sliding in against her lace panties. She's already so wet for me. I lick my lips, my dick throbbing against my leg. "Jesus, Tessa. You *do* want me to fuck you." I smirked. My driving was falling more erratically. I was drifting over the lines, my speed picking up and slowing down in the middle of intersections. I had to be fucking calm. I had to give her what she wanted from me and save mine for later.

My ring and index lift the lace seam to feel the *real* her, immediately dripping in her honey. I can feel her clit pulsing. All for me, just like I knew she would be. "You're so bad at hating me." My lips curl into a grin as I toy with her entrance. Her chest is heaving, her left hand cradles my right and guides me the way she needs. My fingers slip deep inside her, moving and curling slowly. She's so fucking tight, I can barely fit two fingers. She softly bucked her hips against me, all I can think about is how she would react to my dick in her. Her thighs are twitching as sweet, sticky sweat pools in the notch of her neck. I can tell she's working closer to her orgasm. I won't let her finish. Not until I know she's fucking broken down for me.

I retract my hand, a whimper escaping her lips as she practically claws at me. "Reese, please." She groaned, her body shaking.

"Hello?" Tessa groaned as I blinked rapidly. "Shit, what did you say?" I ask, wiping my hand over my face. I realized I'm practically panting over a fantasy. "I *said*, why the hell would I be jealous of them?"

I'm not even in this car right now, my brain was left at the fucking store. My hands are trembling, I can't remember anything we were talking about before I blacked out. I keep swallowing hard, my mouth chalky as I steady my heartbeat. "What?" My voice was full of annoyed confusion as she waved her hands in defeat.

"Never mind." Tessa groaned, turning her attention forward. I nod softly, still unsure of what the hell was going on. I turn down her street, stopping in front of her complex. "I'll see you Thursday?" I asked her, knowing our obligation is most important. She grabbed her purse, slinging it over her shoulder and nodding before getting out of the car.

10:39A.M.
R- You make it inside okay?
T- typing...

What the hell do I even care for? Tessa typed for a few minutes, never sending a reply. My eyes darted around, looking for an excuse to stay in my car. A groan erupts from my chest as I put my hazards on and slam my car door. I count the windows going up to her curtains that she looked at me from this morning. Sixth floor. I marched into the building, looking around. No God damn elevator.

I tighten my laces and get to jogging up the stairs, at least this way I can skip my gym routine today. This place is a shit hole, it's blasphemous that someone like Tessa could live here. Her bright and enigmatic personality secluded to an apartment just like the one I grew up in.

My search was over as I reached the sixth floor. I rest my hands on my hips, mildly out of breath as I look at all the doors. It takes only a second to figure out which is hers. A flowery doormat with the most stereotypical nursing shoes outside. She's nowhere in sight, so I pounded on the chipping wood as if she was being hauled away.

Her scowl as she opens the door mid bang catches both of us off guard.

"Do you not know how to answer your fucking phone?" I asked, trying not to take in the soft scent of vanilla and apple coming from her apartment. It's warm and welcoming, like I could lick it right off of her. I rapidly blink as the fragrance is just seeping from her. I wet my lips, her gaze softening for only a second. She wanted to let me in. Both to her apartment and her heart. If only my words hadn't come out so harshly.

"Why the fuck do you care?" She scoffed, folding her arms, seemingly as confused as my brain I left behind. I stepped back mentally, why did I care? She wasn't my girlfriend, we hated each other most days. My jaw twitched, practically grinding my teeth down to the nerves. I opened my mouth to speak but fell short of anything but a pitiful laugh. "I don't. Have a good night, Tessa." I put my hands in my pockets, shaking my head as I turn to leave. She was such a bitch. Here I was thinking I was a gentleman, making sure she made it into this dump, and she'd painted me into a dick yet again.

I walked down the hall, fists clenched as I had yet to hear her apartment door shut. I'm fighting every urge in my body to not collide my fist in the wall. It's like crack to me. I want that pain. I want the blood gushing from my knuckles. But it's only fuel to her fire. When I turn the corner to the stairs, she closes her door softly. Just like in Maurice's apartment, she does things without drawing attention to herself. Where I would have slammed it so hard the hinges would have fallen off.

I take a minute in the car before driving off, occasionally glancing at her window. She doesn't appear to have given me a second thought. Not that I can blame her. I pull my phone out and look at the picture from Brooklynn. Her thin figure bundled up in black lingerie, I can't help but sigh. I'm weak. I can get whatever I want from whoever I want. My tongue runs over my teeth as I look back up to that sixth-floor window. Fuck it.

11:01A.M.
R- Tonight?
B- Can't wait. (;

Sixteen

REESE

September 8th

I crack my eyes to the sun peeking through my hanging blinds. What fucking day is it? I sit up in bed, my body is stiff and aching like I'm in my sixties. My brows are buried in confusion as Brooklynn's leg hangs over mine. She's passed out, God knows for how long. There is a buzzing coming from my phone, a text from Tess. The buzzing turns into thumping as my heartbeat skyrockets. I can't bring myself to check it. My eyes are burning, my mouth is parched. I looked around at all the empty liquor bottles. Fuck, I'd done it again.

It was time to retrace my steps, starting with what I remember last.

Friday.

Brooklynn practically breaks my front door down as she knocks. I open the door, this time sporting the same expression Tessa gave me only hours earlier. "Hey." She smirked, her lips were sticky red. God, I hated lip gloss. It was tacky and her long, blonde hair was always clinging to it when she spoke.

"What's up?" I give her the same look of arrogance that always reeled her in. It didn't take much, she was always all over me.

I never gave her the chance in high school, it made her crazy for me now.

I made the most of my time with her, bringing her immediately to my leather sofa out looking at the skyline. "Can I get you something to drink?" I offered, standing at my bar cart in the hall.

I pour a cup of tequila and stare into the clear liquid, deciding against the cup and swig from the bottle. "No, I'm okay... How've you been?" Brooklynn asked, slinging her arm over the couch to look behind at me.

"Actually," I scoffed. "Not great." The liquor burns my throat as I take another gulp. I sauntered over and leaned down, inches from her face as I can't hide my disgusted expression.

"Why are women *so* fucking mean?"

She looked away from me, avoiding my gaze as she rolled her eyes. A scoff erupts from me as I sit on the armchair across from her.

My legs spread as I slouched comfortably. Brooklynn looked at me with annoyance and confusion. She stood from the sofa, the leather creaking underneath her as I groaned. I knew where she was headed, I knew her intent.

"I'm not mean." She had this sultry look in her eye as I took another drink. My head cocked to the side, as I shifted in my seat. I truly felt bad for her, her upbringing was shitty like mine. She'd do anything for male attention and I was so weak for a piece of ass. All it took was a woman looking at me and I had a fucking boner. "You're right about that." My hand goes up her thigh and under her mini-skirt. I search for the material of her panties and come up short of nothing. Tessa would never be caught that way. She was so uptight, I don't think she ever *could* be caught that way. Brooklynn straddled my lap, taking the bottle from my grasp to give herself a drink. My pants grew tighter, a sigh escaping my lips. Brooklynn reached into her bra, pulling out a small vial of white powder. Now this was my idea of a good time.

I'd dabbled with coke more often than not, but it wasn't my drug of choice. Truthfully, I preferred just smoking a bowl with my friends and hanging out.

Cocaine made me too... Reckless, blinding me to the consequences of my own actions. I was impulsive. Hence, my mugshot from a few years back, public intoxication and drug use. The one thing Maurice did for me was clearing that from court records.

When I looked back at her, the substance was gone. Brooklynn poured out another line on the back of her hand, offering it to me. I wet my lips, looking at my phone on the counter across the room. My hands go up her thighs as I sigh. As if instinctively, I leaned forward, closing one nostril with my index finger. It was cold and sharp, my heart immediately jolting. My pupils dilate. I'm trembling as my laughter is uncontrollable. The mere idea of Tessa was floating away as my lips met Brooklynn's neck. I'm ravenous for her. Okay, maybe not for *her*. But she would have to do.

And that is where I fade to black.

1:57P.M.
T- hello?
T- i just want my wallet back, Reese.

Her wallet? I look around confused. My stomach drops when I remember the time I saw her. The way I paraded up to her apartment, the last words we exchanged. She was without a wallet because I was too busy with my head in my ass.

Two days. I was unconscious for two fucking days. I ran my hands over my face. My hands are shaking, both from my nerves and the cocaine still exiting my system. My stomach is churning, I feel like I'm trapped in a spin cycle at the laundromat. Brooklynn is still unconscious, I hope she's fucking alive. I stand up, my legs vibrating with every step.

The entire apartment is destroyed, top to bottom. The curtains are torn, my dining table flipped on its side, which means I got paranoid. My maid will have a fit. As usual. I hate cocaine.

My head hangs over the toilet, my hands gripping either side of the cool porcelain. The nausea began to seep forward, the bile ready to fill my throat. Throwing up after a cocaine binge was the worst feeling. My stomach tightened as I hurled myself into that toilet. Between loud, forceful retches, my front door could be heard being pounded on. I sat up, wiping the puke from the corner of my mouth.

"Just a fucking second!" I yelled over the flushing. My feet scuff against the floor as they drag me to the front door. Before I open it, I say a silent prayer, hoping it isn't the police. It was a thought that hadn't yet crossed my mind. I clear my throat of the burning liquid and calmly open the door.

With her fist in the air, getting ready to barrel again, Tessa looks up at me. Her cheeks burned red, mine reciprocating. "Tess." I mumbled, unsure of what else to say. I was just trying to keep what was left in my system down.

"I dropped my wallet in your car." She whispered, peering over my shoulder the best she could through my height. "Did you get robbed?" Her eyes wander across my body, I realize I'm in only my underwear.

"Oh this? No, redecorating. Uh, while you're here I wanted to talk to you about something." Maybe it was my newfound sobriety, but I was feeling ballsy. Tessa was looking breathtaking. Her curls were styled perfectly, her makeup was dark but not too cakey. Her hips were screaming in those skinny jeans. She was clearly going somewhere. She had plans that didn't involve me. "Look, I have to be uptown in thirty-"

"I'll drive you." I didn't even let her finish the thought, even though I was in no goddamn condition to drive. I could only hope she'd decline the offer. Something about her made me want to bend over backwards.

"Reese!" A sleepy groan came from the back of my apartment. Tessa's eyes lock with mine. I try to clarify who that was, but what was I to say?

Oh, yeah. That's my coke whore that I blacked out with just to get you off of my mind.

Tessa's eyes are huge, and almost sporting a sense of hurt. I don't know how to respond to this emotion.

"Reese, come back to bed!" Brooklynn groaned, making my body burn with anger. Could she not shut the fuck up? "It seems like you're busy. I'll just have my friend cover my drinks tonight." Tessa sighed, taking a step back. I feel her retracting from me, both physically and emotionally. "Tess, wait. I can explain this."

"No need, she sounds very... Sweet." Tessa put her hands in her jacket pockets with a soft smile and turned around. "Tessa, please." My voice was weak, begging for her.

"I'll see you Thursday, Reese." She sighed, stepping into the elevator. I groaned, resting my forehead against the front door while Brooklynn let out a tired whine down the hall.

"What did we do last night?" She gave that same lazy smirk, her blonde hair disheveled and matted against the back of her head. "It's fucking Sunday." I replied, walking past her without a second glance and slamming my bathroom door. I could be so dramatic sometimes, but I just wanted her to get the hint to fucking leave.

Seventeen

TESSA

I walked into the restaurant, late as usual. I hate not being on time, but it was somehow my nature when it came to things like this. Doctor's appointments, volunteering, work, I was always ten minutes early. But doing anything for myself? Consider me late or not going.

"I didn't get my wallet back, can you spot me tonight? I'll pay you back." I whispered to Kayla who nodded in reply. Everyone appeared so attuned with Quinn, a girl we went to high school with, story. To everyone else, her energy was just captivating. But I just saw her as an influencer who got paid to post certain opinions.

She had only just gotten back from L.A. where she had a 'new outlook on life'. It sounded like a bunch of bullshit to me. Life was the same there as it was here, only more heatwaves. I loved the rainy NYC weather, I loved everything about this city. Why did people always go searching for better?

"Gimme your card, I'm gonna go order a drink."

Kayla doesn't even look at me as she pulls her wallet from her pocket. I roll my eyes, standing up and making my way to the bar.

"Malibu and pineapple." I smiled at the bartender, playing with the zipper on the old designer wallet.

"Still drinking the same drinks I made you a hundred years ago?" A voice comes from behind me. The room begins to melt and I can smell the Lorne's basement and chlorinated water. I take a deep breath, my eyes closing softly.

"Timothy." My heart flutters at the sight of him. His sandy hair is perfectly quaffed, a full scruff covering his jaw and cheeks. He was wearing a navy blue button up, an aviator style jacket and some nice jeans. His style was always so simple but he made it look so elegant. "I usually just go by Tim these days." He smiled. A genuine, free spirited smile. It wasn't fueled by lust, or something dumb I've said.

He was just happy to see me.

"By who?" I furrowed my brows playfully, making light of his newfound maturity. "Coworkers mostly." Timothy snickered as the bartender handed me my drink. The pineapple juice was sticky on my lips as it went down. Its taste was just as memorable as when I was in high school, like I'm standing in Kayla and Tim's basement during a party. The sound of the restaurant feeds my delusion of our parents upstairs as we poured more liquor than mixers. I felt at home again.

I giggle in response to his answer, my cheeks burning a little. So many years had passed yet his expressions and humor were still the same.

"So you turned down the big leagues, huh?" I smirked, catching Tim's chuckle.

"Something like that. Dad got sick, remember?" He sighed, resting his elbow on the bar. I nodded, remembering how distraught Kayla was six years ago.

The funeral was hard on everyone, Jake was just as much a father to me and Kelseigh. He was very active in town, a good father and often helped out with our school functions. If he had decided to quit drinking when the doctors told him to, there was a chance he'd still be here today. The Lorne's were just stubborn that way. Hell, Kayla was 26 and still refused to listen to anyone that wasn't a beauty guru online.

Still, Jake's passing was unexpected and devastating to the entire community. Timothy finished college online to help his mom take care of things here before moving away at twenty-three.

Rose couldn't keep their heads above water without Jake's salary. And Tim was the type of son who wouldn't let them suffer. It was the only time I'd seen him cry, nor did I see him much at all after that funeral.

I'd often kept up with Timothy through stalking his social media, never would I let him know this of course. He traveled a lot in his adulthood. He loved to hike, seek out different shops, and of course help people in need. It was like his personal mission to be the good guy in every book.

"Are you still at that retirement home on 11ᵗʰ?" He asked, flashing me a half grin. My tongue instinctively runs over my teeth just like when he got his braces off. I nod, cramming my straw in my mouth with blushing cheeks. God, I was an idiot.

"They gotta be about to rent you a room, huh?" Tim snickered, bumping me with his elbow. "I'm there enough, hopefully they'll give me a deal." I giggled, feeling my stomach go light and my head go dizzy. "Where are you working now?" I asked softly, my eyes focused on him but my ears listening to all the bustle. All I can do is pray that I'm not interrupted by Kayla. Does she even know he's in town?

"I'm in Seattle, actually. I run my own firm, just here on some business." Timothy held up his hands in a jazzy way as he rolled his eyes. "You have your own business? That's amazing, Timothy." I smiled at something he seemed so nonchalant about. His cheeks flushed as his full name slipped out again.

"Tim, I mean. Sorry."

"It's fine. I can't say I didn't miss that." He chuckled, looking down at the bar with a soft laugh under his breath. "Truly, Tim. That's really great. I'm so proud of you."

Sure it wasn't the national football league, but being a lawyer was a steady, promising career. "I'm sure people are always looking for a reason to sue someone." I laughed as he nodded.

"You're not wrong, Daws." He smirked, putting down a ten for my drink and grabbing his keys. The way my nickname fell from his lips, I felt like I was that meek high school girl, in love with her best friend's brother again.

"It was really great to see you, Timothy. Kayla's here too, did you want to go see her?" I point my thumb behind me, a kind smile still on my face. "No, God no. I don't need her knowing I'm in town." He teased with a wink.

"Got it." I exchanged the same expression before he walked off. I looked down at the drink with a smile. Never did I think my day would end here.

I make my way back to our table, Quinn's story must've ended as there is no conversation anymore. "Guess who I ran into." I whispered to Kayla, opening my menu. "Don't say Reese."

"Timothy."

Kayla whipped her head around, searching for her brother in the crowd. "My brother was here, and you didn't think to come tell me?" She scoffed playfully. "I was told *not* to inform you."

She shook her head, turning her attention back to the menu. "Sounds like him. Did you guys bang behind the bar? You're pretty good at things like that." I swat her arm, causing a snort to erupt from Kayla.

September 9ᵗʰ

My morning began just as they always did. Those three days off were so refreshing in just about every way. I remember when I first started working here years ago, at the bottom of the totem pole, I worked just about every day. My first week I think I cried twice a shift.

Then one day it just… Clicked. I knew my residents, their routines, their likes, dislikes. Just about every day was the same, and I was always prepared for it.

"Good morning, Lynn." I smiled at the nurses that were exchanging shifts. The third shift staff were true heroes. I couldn't imagine being here those hours. I stopped into each of my residents' rooms, doing all of my daily tasks. Mr. Gonzalez needed his insulin, Mrs. Claywell always liked a protein shake drink with her pills, and Mrs. Freeman liked her television on her 'programs' by the time breakfast came in. And I was happy to do it. I loved all of them as if they were my own grandparents.

By nine, I headed down the hall of Maurice Finch. A sigh escaped me when I opened the door to see Reese sitting against the arm of the couch. "Just tell me what you did with the money and I'll write you a check, Reese." Maurice pinched the bridge of his nose, something I noticed he did a lot when Reese was around. "Tessa,"

He sprung to his feet, but I chose to ignore him. It wasn't a Thursday, our friendship was strictly professional now. "Good morning, Maurice. You've been keeping up with your meds, yes?" I asked, checking his blood pressure. "Always, doll." Maurice took a labored breath. "Tessa, would you talk to me for a second?" Reese spoke under his breath, his hand on my back. Maurice caught this interaction, but stayed silent. I could tell something was up with him.

I lifted the blanket on his feet. They were still modeling with no sign of improvement. Almost his entire lower half had stiffened. "Has hospice stopped by today?" I asked, pushing Reese's voice from my mind and focusing on my job.

"No, not yet. I'm sure they'll be in to give me that whole 'death' spiel again." Maurice groaned playfully, his chest rattling with every breath. I rolled my eyes, swatting his hand softly as I went back to vitals.

"Please." Reese whispered once more.

"You know they just want what's best for you and want you to have the best care possible." I reassured his father, playing up my kind and sweet demeanor. "I'll be back around 11 for Mancala before lunch, okay?" Maurice shook his head no, something that made both Reese and I stop in our tracks. Maurice had *never* once denied a game.

"I'm very tired today." He sighed as I nodded, trying to save face in front of his only son. "Alright then, maybe tomorrow." I smiled, closing the door behind me.

Unfortunately, the sound of heavy, quick footsteps could be heard behind me. "I want to talk to you." I could practically feel Reese's breathing on my neck. "About what, Mr. Finch?"

"Please don't call me that. Don't act like we're not-"

"Not what?" I cut him off, my words like a dagger as I turned to stare at him. We were nothing. We weren't even really *friends*. Reese appeared to dodge my rebuttal, his fists clenched at his side as his jaw pulsed. "I just want to explain what you saw in my apartment." He exhaled shakily as I watched him calm. This was different compared to his normal angered reactions. "Reese, please come back Thursday when I'm court ordered to speak to you." I sarcastically spoke as I turned to leave.

"Can you just stop for one second?" He scoffed, still hot on my trail.

"Oh, Ms. Dawson! There you are. You had a delivery at the front desk." Nurse Lynn smiled as she pushed her med cart past us. We saw enough crazy things in the nursing home that she hadn't even looked twice at the large, deranged man chasing me down.

I nod and take a quick left to the front of the building. "Delivery?" He asked, trying any tactic in the world to speak to me. I shrug, still feeling him on my tail.

At the front desk, is a small vase of pink roses. I raise a brow as the receptionist, Francine, gives me a wiggled brow smile. I wipe a hand over my face in exhaustion. Maybe they were from my mom. She tended to do things like that when she knew I was having a rough go at life.

"You don't even like roses." He scoffed as I rolled my eyes at his presence. Francine hands me the small white envelope as Reese's body leans over me, his right hand braced on the reception desk as his heart beat rings from behind me.

You just couldn't keep my arrival to town a secret could ya?
–Timothy

I feel my jaw slack as I wet my lips. A smile creeps on my face. Kayla must have called him. "Who is that? Who's Timothy?" Reese asked quickly.

"A friend." I sighed, tucking the card in my shirt pocket. I'll leave the flowers at the counter until the end of my shift. "Friends don't buy friends roses. Those are sex roses." Reese argued, following me down the hall. "You're an idiot." I scoff, unable to hold my smile back. He was truly rattled. I open the utility closet door, stepping in and grabbing a box of gloves. Reese stands in the threshold, a hand on the doorknob. "I'm a guy, Tess. I know what sex roses look like."

"Would you stop saying that?" I speak with my back turned as I stand on my tiptoes to reach the top shelf for a new pager. "Here," Reese sighs, walking over to me. "Let me help you."

"No, no. You have to hold the door or–"

I'm cut off by the latching weighted door. I softly shut my eyes. "It locks behind you."

Eighteen

TESSA

I let out a sigh as I hang my head back. Here we go. Reese's hands are on his hips as he wears the same expression of annoyance. I see his tongue flick against the corner of his mouth. "I didn't know that was gonna happen." He mumbled in embarrassment.

"I know." I sighed, trying to keep my temperature gauge on cool. He turned to look at the door and then back to me. "I'm sorry." He moved to sit in a creaking chair we used to have in the activity room. Its fabric cushion was dated and just all around broken-down. "I know."

I needed a break anyway. I sat on the floor, my legs stretched out in front of me and parted slightly. A quick smile met his face as if I was forgiving of his behavior. "Not just about the door." He sighed, resting his elbows on his thighs as he stared across the closet at me. "Also about the way you saw me on Sunday."

"What? With Brooklynn?" I catted back. His face scrunched for a moment as he realized I never forgot her name. I couldn't figure out to myself why I remembered it. "Yeah, Brooklynn."

He looked around the room, irked with my attitude. "She's not my girlfriend, y'know?" His voice was soft, his blue eyes coming back to meet my gaze. "I never said she was."

"Right."

We weren't getting anywhere with this. I didn't have anything to say to him that wasn't about teaching him the responsibility of having a job. And based on the conversation I walked in on with Maurice, he wasn't learning a damn thing.

"Why were you asking your dad for more money?" I took a leap on the topic.

"I don't want to talk about that." Reese sat back in the chair, shifting his legs a bit as he folded his arms. "Why not? Did Brooklynn steal your black card?"

Reese scoffed, looking at the ground. "No, she did not steal from me."

"Hmph." I nodded, staring straight ahead at the old mop buckets against the wall. The closet reeked of cheap floor cleaner and nitrile gloves. I was going stir crazy, and it had only been fifteen minutes. "Can you just call the front desk and tell them to let us out?" He asked with a dry tone, he was done trying to get my attention. A part of me longed for that feeling again. The feeling of him begging for me to just look at him. "No, I leave my phone in my locker. You call."

Reese groaned, running both hands over his face. "My phone's in Maurice's room." He stood from the chair, walking to the closet door to bang on it.

"We're at the end of a hallway in a place where people cannot find their hearing aids half of the time, no one is gonna hear us for a while." I sigh, pinching the bridge of my nose. He turns to look at me, as if to say something snarky. "I fucking hate when you do that."

My brows furrow, my lip turning up. "Do what?"

"That thing with your nose. He does the same shit." He shook his head in reference to Maurice as he went back to pounding. I rolled my eyes and stood up. "Well, I hate when you do that." I point my index finger right at him.

"What?" He doesn't even turn around to notice me pointing. "Ignore my advice and just do the same stupid shit you wanna do."

"You just think you know everything. It's obnoxious. No one ever told you to shut the fuck up when you were little and it shows." Reese's tone hits me deep in my chest. My lips part and I feel my eyes wet with anger. "I'm obnoxious? You literally walk around like some angry man child with daddy issues and think society is supposed to cater to you. It's the real world, Reese. Figure it out." I was shaking with rage. I didn't know 'everything.' I just had common sense. I was raised in a way to figure it out and that's exactly what I did.

"Fuck you, Tessa." His tone isn't as angry anymore as it is hurt. He stands a foot away from me. "Fuck me? I'm sure you'd like that. Considering you can't keep your dick out of anything with a pulse."

Reese scoffs, shaking his head. "You couldn't pay me enough to fuck you. I'd be doing you a favor." He looks down at me, his eyes dark as I chew the inside of my cheek. My hands are sweating, I rub my fingers against the palms, trying to calm myself. I could smell him, I wanted to bathe in it.

"Don't tell me I'm making you nervous, Tess. How fucking pitiful." A vindictive smirk is on his face as he steps toe to toe with me. I take in a deep breath, my brows still furrowed in anger as my eyes flicker up to his. "You're an asshole." I breathed, feeling myself believe it less and less, my body vibrating. His brow raised with a douchy grin as a teasing exhale left his nose. "I can hear you throbbing from here, Tessa."

I stare up at him, my underwear practically flooding without my permission. I'm doing the best I can, staying strong against his charm. My chest is heaving as my eyes leave his gaze only to glance at his wet, full lips. I swallow hard, the moisture leaving my mouth. "I'm not gonna fuck you, Tessa." He snickered, causing me to feel more lightheaded. Every time he spoke my name, my vision got blurry, and he knew it.

"That would be *so* easy. And you're not easy, right?" His thumb met my chin, grazing it side to side before it moved to my bottom lip. My head reaches the back of the shelf as I switch to breathing from my mouth. I'm panting like a damn dog.

"Or *are* you easy?" He whispered, his thumb entering my mouth brushing against my tongue. I can't pull myself from him, I can't get a word out.

"Yes or no, Tessa?" He whispered, his thumb pushing further down my throat. My body naturally responds, letting it slide further back without a gag. Kayla told me it would get me farther in life than nursing school.

"I thought so." He smirked, retracting his thumb. He gave a soft laugh, taking a step back from me. "Look at you, so weak for me. I wish I could say I'm surprised or even disappointed." His smile was devilish as he wet his lips again. Reese turned away from me, looking back at the closet door. I wanted to grab him and turn him back to my attention again. I wanted him to be all about me; I hated the girls that occupied his time. I hated that they saw his bedroom, laid in his sheets, felt his lips.

I needed him in the most desperate way.

It was a craving. I was overwhelmed and couldn't get enough. The feeling was an insatiable urge, flooding my mind and body. "I hate you." I purred. I knew it'd make him turn back to me. And right as rain, his crystal pools met me with a look of intent. He groaned, rolling his eyes as he came back to me.

"Tell me again." He growled, fueled by my degradation. "I hate you." I whispered, his hands moving to grip the shelf on either side of me. "Again." He spoke against my neck, his tongue licking and teeth nibbling against my skin. My hands reach to his back as he pushes me against the shelf harder. Small boxes fall beside us as a weak moan escapes my lips. "I hate you... So much." I pant, my right hand sneaking into his hair. His styling products leave my fingers feeling like I had a piece of him, something that only *his* hands had been on. I savored the scent as his head pressed against my collarbone.

"Tell me you want me. That you fucking need me."

I'd do anything this man asked of me right now. I didn't care if it meant chewing my arm off. I'd do it just to keep feeling him against me. "I need you, Reese." I gasped, feeling his right hand slide into my scrubs, his left lifting my thigh to hold me open. I could feel the muscles in his arms flexing as he showed me just how much he really did work out.

"I've been thinking about this moment for weeks, Jesus Christ." He panted, his finger wasting no time to slide inside me. I moaned loudly, grateful to be at the end of the hall.

My hand tugged at his hair as my leg wrapped around his waist. "You are so tight, baby." He whispered in my ear, kissing the space below it as he slid his ring finger in to partner his middle. "Oh my god," I whispered. I haven't had sex in almost two years. I'd gotten so caught up with work and my social life, that I'd forgotten how amazing this was. His fingers curled inside, brushing against my inner walls as I lost sight of my sanity.

"God damn, Tess. Can you feel me stretching you out with *just* my fingers? I can't wait to fill you with my cock."

I felt his lips pull into a smirk against my neck. I don't think my eyes can roll back any farther. I'm ready, I need to experience what he'd given to every other girl.

"Please."

Nineteen

REESE

"Please."

Tessa lifted my head from the crook of her neck, my mouth was glistening with saliva from peppering her with kisses. Was she really begging? Begging *me* to fuck *her*? That was not where I saw this going. I thought for sure she'd need more convincing. Maybe I was better at my craft than I thought. She was like a kid asking for dessert before dinner. I put her leg back down, retracting my fingers. I kneel at her feet, untying her scrub pants. Her hands meet the bottom of her top, lifting it up over her head. I gripped the pants on either side and tugged vigorously down her curves. I wet my lips, staring in awe at her beauty until my gaze met hers. "You are so pretty, Tessa." I kissed both of her thighs, practically wheezing with excitement.

As I stood back up, I undid my belt, my head cocked slightly as I appreciated the lace design of her bra and matching thong. I can feel my dick twitch as I drop my slacks to my knees, Tessa looks at me like she has something to say.

"What is it?" I asked, making sure she still wanted to go through with this.

"How did you know I hate roses?" She asked, her fingers teasing at the hem of my briefs. I sucked in a breath between my teeth, my hands lifting to my shirt. "Because I listen when you talk. You may not think so, but I do, Tessa."

Another brick down in the kingdom of Tessa's heart. She wasn't expecting that answer. My hands go over hers that are still on my underwear. I help her pull them down slowly, taking our time so I know she's comfortable.

"Your favorite flowers are daisies." My length springs out of the material and I see her take a deep breath. It was always an ego boost, but something about the look in Tessa's eyes tells me she was ready for it. "But not the shitty ones from the gas station." I want to turn her around and bend her over this fucking shelf. But I must be gentle. I *need* to see her reaction when I enter her for the first time. It'll kill me to lose that image forever. I lift her leg again, leaning her back against the cold metal.

"You like the ones from the florist down in Greenwich." I used my free hand to grab my length, working my hand up and down to ready myself for her. I stretch the material of the thong to the side, smirking at the sound the torn fabric made. Tessa can only work out nods as she felt my length toy with her entrance, sliding up and down but never fully pressing inside.

Her face scrunched as I pushed in slowly, a whimper coming from her throat. My lips part as I exhale. It's like the world's warmest vice grip. My eyes are shut, I'm breathing from my mouth loudly.

"I'll go slow, I promise." I stutter out.

She nodded quickly, the feeling of her nails digging into my back burned vigorously. It was the fuel I needed to keep from burying my dick inside her immediately. Her walls were so tight, I knew there was no way to do it without hurting her. My head falls back as I'm about half-way inside. I pulled out delicately, moving back in a little further as she moaned. Her sounds are like a symphony.

"Reese," She panted, her legs quivering. I moved my head back to look at her face, a cold sweat pooling in the notch of her neck. I wanted to lap it up. "You want me to stop?" I was ready, I'd do anything for her. Even denying myself what I wanted most in this world.

Tess quickly shook her head no. I took it as my sign to push myself in about three quarters. The feeling of her back arching against the shelf and her chest thriving up and down was better than any drug-induced high. It was better than the alcohol. This was my drug now. And I'm already fucking addicted.

"Give me all of it, please." She begged.

"I don't wanna hurt you." I shook my head, my body vibrating as she found her voice. "I can take it, Reese." Her brown eyes sparkled at me; I knew she was serious. I nodded, wetting my lips and scooping my other hand up under her thigh. She was going to get what she asked for.

I forced my length the rest of the way inside with a loud guttural moan. "S-Shit, Tessa. Holy shit..."

My head is empty. Completely fucking empty. The only thing I can hear is *'don't cum, don't cum, don't cum.'* I've never felt anything like this. My breath quickened, my entire body heating up as I got my way with her. I was going to explode just at the idea of being inside her. I was trembling to the touch, our warm breaths filling the room and covering the smell of the dusty, chemical closet. The shelf banged louder against the wall the harder I thrust myself into her, my length sliding in and out vigorously.

Tessa's hips bounced against me in the most intoxicating way, as if she was already a professional. I leaned back, watching her bounce on my dick and letting her take control for a minute. She wasn't as innocent as she'd let on. My body was growing weak, I wasn't going to be able to hold on to this feeling much longer. I moved my hand down to her pulsing clit, using my thumb to draw slow circles. I want her to have everything in this world. "Look at me, or I'll stop." I watched her breathing shift, she tried so hard to open her eyes. Tessa's body trembled; she was closer than I thought. "See how nice I can be when you're not being a brat?" I spoke through my teeth, trying to keep my focus on her satisfaction as she nodded. "Don't stop." She whined.

Tessa's lips parted, her body twitching as she reached the peak of the coaster.

"You're doing so good, baby. Finish for me." Her nails dug into the back of my neck as a moan escaped her lips, her walls tightening around my length. Fuck, it feels so good, I can't stop myself. "I gotta pull out," I stuttered, my mouth open wide.

"No, I'm on the pill." Tessa squeaked out, hooking her arms under my own and pulling me all the way in her as I came. I muffle my groan against her shoulder, filling her while my body struggles to stay up. There was no feeling like it. No feeling like her.

"Jesus." Tessa whispered, her head hitting the shelf in exhaustion. My length is still inside her with my arm's looped under her legs. I rest my head on her shoulder a little longer, my body still trembling.

"I didn't hurt you, did I?" I asked, using my free hand to steady my dick on its way out. Tess rubs her thighs as she meets the ground again, I can tell she'll be sore tomorrow. I pull my briefs back up, my slacks still around my knees.

She shook her head, her hands now covering her torso as she slowly knelt for her top. There was no fucking way she was feeling embarrassed. "Hey," I reach it first, looking up at her with a sloppy grin. I wet my lips, taking in her thick thighs with the now stretched out thong draped over them. I'll have to get her a new one for next time. My mouth hangs open just enough to let a sigh out, admiring the sticky sweat dripping from her body.

"I meant what I said earlier. You are *so* fucking pretty." My hand moved to her thigh, caressing with my thumb. "Yeah?" She whispered, her voice hoarse from the thickness in the air. I nodded, with a smirk. "Let me help you." I bunched the top up and put it over her head. Her smile as she pulls her arms through is captivating. I want to bathe in her radiance. She reminds me of a sunset, the way her skin glows like golden embers. She *is* the sunset, fleeting and precious.

Tess grabbed her pants, clearing her throat as I pulled mine back up. I watch her squeeze her full thighs into those tight scrubs, practically drooling. They were too small, suffocating everything in just the right way. The silence is deafening as my phone falls from my pocket. I immediately squeezed my eyes shut. I was busted.

Her eyes darted to the screen; she's pissed.

"You had your phone the whole time?" She spoke in a hushed tone as I still squeezed my eyes shut. "I had to get you to talk to me." I don't bother to sugar coat anything.

I did what I had to.

"I can't fucking believe you." She shook her head, tying the strings to her sweatpants quickly to end her time with me. "Tess, listen to me." I weakly laughed, there was no way she was *actually* mad.

She grabbed my phone from the floor, pressing it to my bare chest. "Call the office." She ordered. I'd fucked up yet again. "No, not until you listen to me."

"You lied. And I don't like liars." Tessa folded her arms, back to her bratty attitude. I hung my head back with a loud groan. "I hate when you talk to me like that." Lie. That was a fucking lie. If I hadn't just emptied myself inside her, I'd be twitching at the tone of her voice. "Would you rather me call you a selfish asshole?"

God, yes. Please say it again.

"Fine, I'll call the office."

Pussy.

Twenty

TESSA

"Same time Thursday?" Reese called from behind me as I walked down the hall. My whole body cringes as I squeeze my eyes shut. "Go home, Reese!"

I can hear his laugh echoing as he leaves, and I am already imagining the next time I'm alone with him.

I had experience, sure. At least I felt like I did before him. But I was born again. He knew the exact places to touch me, to kiss me, hell, to breathe on me. I grazed my fingers against my thigh as I walked, feeling the indents of his fingerprints lingering behind. If only he wasn't such an asshole, lying about having his phone. I would have left with him.

I made my way to the lockers, grabbing my stuff at the end of my shift. "Don't forget your flowers." Francine smiled, scooping the last of her yogurt from the tiny, plastic container. *Right, my flowers.* I sighed, remembering Timothy, as I grab the small vase on my way out.

They weren't daisies. They were roses, exactly what any other girl would have wanted. I took a long look at them in the passenger seat. My mind drifts back to when we were younger. His senior prom. I was the only sophomore and the talk of the event. Timothy was a true gentleman, making me feel comfortable in the sea of older girls that all would have killed me for a taste of him.

I remember looking down at my corsage, red and black roses to match my dress, thinking how much I hated it. But Tim had it custom ordered, so I appreciated the gesture.

I decided to pull out my phone, scrolling through my contacts. I hadn't texted him since Jake's funeral, I could only hope he sported the same number. I mean, people didn't change their numbers *that* often.

5:14 P.M.
T- what are the odds that this is still your number?
T- typing…

My fingers trail to my lips, tugging at the chapped skin anxiously. Please, don't let me make a fool of myself.

5:19 P.M.
T- Depends. Were the flowers too much? Lol.
T- not at all (:

Still the same old Timothy. He was like a worn out copy of a movie I'd seen a hundred times. Never changing, just repeating the same lines over and over. I knew what to expect, and something about that was comforting. He was exactly the way I expected him to be, the same old Timothy.

September 12th

The smell of coffee fills my senses as I walk into the Java Bean, a locally owned coffee shop that Timothy demanded he show me while he's in town.

"What are you getting?" I asked, my hands crammed into my scrub pockets. I convinced a girl to switch me shifts, giving me the morning off. Since there were no activities planned for today, I'd string something together for Reese later.

I wasn't worried about it or him. I was focused on the man in front of me. The man with goals and a vision on how his life was going to be.

"Chai, of course." Timothy scoffed with a sly grin as he stood with his legs spread a tad. I roll my eyes, mimicking the same grin. "God, you and Kayla really are the same person."

"Hey, I still take offense to that. Even at this age." Tim elbows me, approaching the line. My phone buzzes in my pocket. I follow Tim in line with my feet. My eyes, however, are glued to the text I'd received. "I'll do a large, iced chai." Timothy's voice is a soft hum in the soundtrack of my life.

10:56 A.M.
R- Don't wear any panties to work today.

I don't even know how to respond. I feel my mouth parch like a California drought. My breath hitches as I remember the way he tore my thong only days ago. "Tess?" Timothy pulls me from my heated trance. And a part of me is angry about it.

"Hm?" I look up, face white as a ghost as I take a deep breath.

He motions to the barista that's waiting for my order. "Oh! Yeah, I'll do the same. Sorry." I smile politely as Timothy's brows furrow for a second. I can tell he's trying to figure me out.

"I've gotta take this really quick. Work." I roll my eyes, holding my phone up. Tim nods with a chuckle, paying for our drinks.

11:08 A.M.
T- gross. don't say panties to me.
R- Don't be a brat.
T- don't act like you don't like it.
R- Just do what you're told please.

I pull in my bottom lip, feeling myself pulse with desire as I read his texts over and over. I shift my weight to one side, my body trembling as I'm glued to my phone.

"The Lorne Special." Tim smiles as I lock my phone, cramming it in my pocket.

"Thanks." I smiled, wishing I would have put my hair up today. There is an overwhelming sense of self-consciousness about me. I can't shake the feeling. "You alright?" Tim asks, pulling out a chair for me. "Hm? Yeah, yeah. I've just been stressed with work." I swirl my finger around the plastic lid on my drink, admiring the cinnamon dusting inside. My nerves were eating me alive. "You wanna talk about it?" Tim leaned forward, folding his large hands on the table. I shook my head, following a reassuring smile. "I'd much rather hear about what business you have in New York." I rest my cheek against my hand, a curl falling in front of my face.

"Jesus, kid." Timothy snickered, pushing the curl from my face. I hated when he called me 'kid.' It was a lifelong nickname that I just couldn't shake. His fingers are calloused, like they were the summer he picked up the guitar. "I feel like I've been doing this for the last fifteen years."

"God, don't make us sound so old." I giggle, my cheeks hot. "You'll be forever young in my eyes." Timothy teased with a wink as he took a drink, I felt my stomach tighten. "You'll be twenty-nine in three months, I'm not sure I can say the same for you." My tone is playful as he laughs, and it makes me smile. Timothy checks the time on his phone with a sigh.

"Can I take you to work, Tess? I've got a meeting to get to soon."

I ponder the offer, sucking in a breath through my teeth. I could just take the bus to avoid suspicion. Maybe I even had enough time to walk.

"Fine. Let me use the bathroom quick and we'll go." I smile and ignore my better judgment, grabbing my cup and standing alongside him.

We walked out to his car and before I can reach, the door is already open for me. I look at the buttons on the dash as I buckle up. There is no screen or anything that looks remotely space age. It's comforting in the same way as Tim.

"Toyota?" I snicker.

"Rental." He chuckled under his breath, putting the car in reverse and gripping my seat with his right hand. I watch his muscular arm tighten as he backs from the parking spot. I cleared my throat, realizing I was staring with my mouth open. I turn the radio on with a sigh, trying to fill the humbling silence.

A tune of *Beautiful Girls* by Sean Kingston makes us both erupt in laughter. "Tim, it's your song!" I tease with excitement.

The summer of 2007, Timothy wore clothes two sizes too big for him to look 'cooler'. As if he needed it. His jeans were so baggy he needed to wear Kayla's belt. His shirts hung to his mid thighs with long sleeves underneath. For the decade, it was epitome of cool.

Along with this new sense of style, he played this song on his iPod *every* damn day. "Turn it off." He rolled his eyes with a smirk.

I swat his hand away from the radio as his cheeks flushed. I sing along with the words, more than likely out of key. He doesn't seem to mind as we continue to drive, approaching the nursing home.

"Someone looks lost." Tim points to a figure out front, causing me to stop singing and I feel my stomach drop.

Twenty-One

REESE

I check my watch; Tessa would be pulling in the parking lot in that shitty ass Ford any minute. I realize I'm early. I could go in and see my dad, but truthfully, I'd rather stick needles in my eyes. It's bad enough that I'm forced to see him every week. I don't want to do it any earlier.

I lift my sunglasses as I spot Tess in the passenger seat of another man's car. My lips part slightly as I withhold my smirk. I can only expect it to be Timothy. She's laughing and dancing, her curls bouncing around as the man laughs with her. That is, until she locks eyes with me. She really wasn't as innocent as I thought.

I open the car door for her as he pulls to the drop off lane. "Ms. Dawson." I hold my hand out for her to take, but she rolls her eyes and declines it. I snicker to myself as the man steps out beside her. "Who's this?" I point a lazy finger to the man who appeared around the car to begin walking her inside. I leaned back slightly, my arms folded as they walk right past me. *Am I fucking invisible?*

"Tim." He nods at me as he opens the door for her. His demeanor is arrogant, like I'm a threat. Which is *exactly* how I should be viewed. My mouth falls open. I can tell Tessa finds this hilarious just by the speed she's walking.

I want to tell him about how *I* fucked her in the closet, how she moaned *my* name, how *my* cum is probably lingering inside her. God knows it's all I've thought about. I know Tess would absolutely murder me for it. I've already fucked up enough.

I watch the two of them talk from the reception desk; he stands too close for my liking. He could lean down and kiss her at any second and I would rip him in half. My jaw tightened, flexing as Tim crammed his hands in his pockets and took another step closer. I swallow hard, my breathing picking up. Tess stands with her back to the wall, looking up at him. She was so pretty, her small frame pinned against the wall. If only it was me standing in front of her.

She was laughing at his jokes, her breasts rising and falling with every slow breath.

I look to my left; the receptionist watching with her mouth open, as if invested in the same drama unfolding. Tess doesn't even remember I'm here and my body is burning because of it.

Tim leans in, whispering something only inches from her face.

"I need you to page her to a room. Now."

"I- I can't." The receptionist shifts back to her desk quickly, looking at all the buttons on her phone. "If you don't wanna lose your job, then I suggest you stop them." I ordered, leaning over the desk and looking at her phone. My heart was pounding, I needed to prevent them from kissing. The receptionist scrambled from her desk and ran around the corner.

"Ms. Dawson!" She called frantically as I stayed hidden. "Mr. Reed paged, he's on the floor again."

"Can someone else get it?" Her voice was annoyed, almost unrecognizable. My Tessa would never push off work to someone else. The receptionist looks at me out of the corner of her eye. I shake my head, telling her to stick to her guns.

"Um... No. He requested you."

Tessa doesn't respond, I look through a magazine as I spy at the desk. "You want me to pick you up after work?" Tim asks, grabbing her hand. No, God no. The last thing they need is to be alone together.

"No, that's okay. I'll just take the bus." I watch her smile between my spying fingers and a sigh escapes my lips. "Tess, please. I'm only in town for a little while. I'm not letting you take the bus as long as I'm here." Tim pleaded.

"Fine."

I was going to put a hit out on this man.

They say their goodbyes, Tessa making her way back to the reception desk where I'm still hiding behind my magazine. "Mr. Reed isn't on the floor is he?" She smirked at the receptionist. The lady shakes her head 'no' and points a finger at me.

"Thank you for being discreet." I sarcastically spoke, pushing off the desk and closing the magazine.

"What was that all about?" I ask, following Tessa as she walks to the locker room. "What?"

Though I'm behind her, I can feel the smirk on her face. "I know what you're doing."

"And what is that?" She giggles, stopping in front of her locker.

"You're trying to make me jealous."

Tessa's laugh makes my blood boil, like the mere *thought* was astronomical. "Baby, my world doesn't revolve around you." I want to soak in the way she calls me baby, though I know it to be sarcasm.

"I beg to differ based on your behavior in the closet." I crack back, her cheeks burning. I wet my lips, stepping closer to her as she smirks up at me. "Are you jealous, Mr. Finch?" Tess raised a brow, her fingers hooking into my belt loop.

"Of that guy?" I scoff, I look to the window where he is still sitting in his car, probably texting Tessa already. "Never. That tool could never fuck you the way I did." She takes a sharp breath, my bluntness catching her off guard. I toy with the strings of her scrub pants, my eyes flicker to hers.

"Did you do what I told you?" I ask, untying the knot. Tessa looks to the door that lacks a lock and nods.

"I ditched them in the bathroom of the coffee shop." She purred, pulling in her bottom lip with excitement. "That's my girl. I didn't take you for being such a good listener." I slide my hand into her untied scrubs, feeling the soft skin with a deep breath.

"I bought something for you." Thank God for dad's allowance. I retract my hand; she lets out a soft whine. I'd like to put all the sounds she makes on a CD. She's so angelic in everything she does.

I reach into my pocket, pulling out a black Givenchy thong. "I believe I owe you this." I stretch the material between my fingers.

"How much did this cost?" She folds her arms, a teasing pout on her face. I just know she's going to hit me with some bullshit about responsibility. Fuck the responsibility, I wanna give her everything.

"Don't worry about it. I had a little extra lying around."

Tessa takes the thong from me and rubs the material with her small thumbs. "Hm..." She whispered, a sinister look on her face. "You'd better hold on to this." She balls the material into one hand, pinching my cheeks with her other to open my mouth. "I mean, you don't expect me to put it on myself, do you?" She puts the thong in my mouth, and I roll my eyes back with a guttural groan. My dick throbs against my now tight jeans. She was so sexy, the urge to throw her over my shoulder lived on in my mind as I watched her walk out of the room.

I rush to cram it in my pocket, catching up with her.

"So, what's on our agenda today?" I ask, staying as close to her as I can. I can smell her coconut shampoo as she walks. "Nothing." She answered, blankly.

My brows raise in concern as I chuckle. "Nothing?"

"I forgot to plan any activities this week." Tessa stifled her laugh. "Tessa Dawson falling off of her high horse?" I tease, catching the blush in her cheeks. This was so uncharacteristic. Tessa was on the books about everything. I didn't recognize her. "I've been busy." Tessa pulled out her pager, looking over her calls. "I can see that. Are you boning Timmy too?" I poked in a playful tone, though I am completely serious. I hate him so much for even getting her to smile.

"His name is Tim." Tess smiled as I refrained from pinching the bridge of my nose like my father would.

I take her hand, pulling her down the hall. My back is against the cold, chipped paint. She stands so close to me; I can feel her breasts touch my torso as I look down at her. "You didn't answer my question." I watch her big amber eyes roll back as my fingers intertwine with hers. "What question?" She looked up at me with the most innocent pout and I'm back on immediately, strapped for whatever coaster we're going to be on today.

"Are you fucking Timmy too?" I asked in a low voice, watching that pout melt into a grin.

"Not yet." Her eyes graze over me like I'm lunch and I feel my stomach go light. "You know... My birthday is October 1st–"

I immediately cut her off. There's no need for her to finish her sentence because I can top whatever it is she's going to ask. "Done."

"You don't even know what I was gonna say." She smirked, fully pressed against me. *Don't let her feel your boner, Reese.* "You were going to say," I cleared my throat, raising my voice two octaves.

"Gee, Reese. I would love for you to take me somewhere warm and secluded for my birthday." Her eyes sparkle in a way I've never seen before when I suggest taking her away. I could already see her reeling and living out fantasies in her mind.

"I would never say that." She smirked, taking a playful step back. I looked toward the end of the hall, making sure we were still alone. "Not yet." I winked. My brain is turning to mush as I think about her in the pink bikini from her Instagram. I'm swallowing so much saliva as I stare at her, trying to keep myself from collapsing.

"A vacation would be fun. But I know what your finances are like."

"All I gotta do is mention your name to Maurice." I smirked because it was true. Shit, if she asked him for a new car he'd give it to her. He wouldn't do a damn thing for me, but for Tessa? She was more his child than I was. And I would play that to my advantage.

"Hm. Should you mention a private jet?" She teased against my exact thought. It was like she could read my mind.

"That could be arranged." I bring my right hand to her cheek, caressing her velvet skin. I want to tell her how beautiful she is. How I've never seen anyone as daunting and as breathtaking as she is. Or that she literally makes me feel like a crazy person. But I can't. I can't use any words.

I lean in, our noses grazing each other as she cuts me off. "Oh! I know what we can do today." Tess smiles as I sigh. "Does it involve our tongues?" I ask, my eyes still closed and an inch from her lips. When I open them, she's giggling and shaking her head. A groan escapes me, and I motion for her to lead the way.

"The Turners always want me to spend extra time on some care for them. Nails, lotion, shaving, but I don't have the time." I stop walking, my hands up in defeat. "I'm not shaving no man's balls, Tessa. I really like what we have going on here, but I draw the line at balls." Tessa rolls her eyes. "Beard, you dumbass."

I nod, my feet moving quickly to catch up. Tessa stops outside of the door, pulling out her skeleton key. "Are you *sure* there's not another closet around here?" I asked.

"Reese, I have work to do. And *you* have responsibility to learn."

Twenty-Two

TESSA

I file Mrs. Turner's nails as Reese stands beside us, shaving her husband's face. I admire the way Reese's tongue peeks out the corner of his mouth in focus. I smile softly, turning my attention back to my resident. I dig in the bucket of different nail polishes and pull out a peachy tone.

"How's this?" I asked, my head cocked to the side. "Beautiful, just like you, sweetheart." Mrs. Turner winked. "You are a lucky man, Mr. Finch." She teased as Reese scoffed playfully.

"I suppose so." He shoots me a quick glance before turning back to Mr. Turner. It's evident to me that Reese is being diligent with his work. He wants to prove to himself that he's changing, or maybe he doesn't even realize it.

I sigh with a weak smile. I appreciate the compliment from the elderly woman, but being linked with Reese was something that I still wasn't sure how to handle.

"Alright, let's go look in the mirror, eh?" Reese grinned ear to ear at his work, tossing the hand towel onto the table I was working at. I feel my heart swell when I hear the two of them chatting away about keeping a woman happy in the muffled room.

Reese's phone begins to vibrate beside the towel, my eyes flicker to catch the text before going dark.

2:12 P.M.
B- We need to talk about this.

I directed my eyes back to the manicure I was finishing. I needed to mind my business. Yet, I couldn't help but be intrigued. Brooklynn was beginning to play a bigger role in Reese's life. I chew the inside of my cheek, cleaning up my mess and walk into the bathroom.

"Well, I'll be damned. That's a nice shave, son." Mr. Turner gave a wrinkled smile as Reese stood proudly. He looked younger now without all that scruff. I listened as Mrs. Turner's walker crept up beside me as her eyes lit up at her husband's appearance. I'd half expect them to start dancing at how good they felt about themselves.

"I'm all done out here." My voice was soft, trying to hide any form of hurt. I wasn't exactly sure *why* but my stomach was in knots, my brain foggy. Reese nodded, holding Mr. Turner under his arm and guiding him back to his recliner. He grabbed his things, glancing at his phone and taking a hard swallow.

Reese checks his phone as we say our goodbyes, I watch him wet his lips from the corner of my eye.

For the first time, Reese looked horrified.

"Everything okay?" I asked in a tender voice, listening to the vigorous keyboard clicks behind me. "Why wouldn't it be?"

His guard is up, and it makes me roll my eyes. I can tell his body is tense when I glance back at him. His brows are furrowed, his eyes are dark and full of hatred. If Maurice had a phone, I'd almost expect him to be talking to his father. When he acted this way, it made me want to slap him across the face, get him to snap out of it.

"Sounds like a lot of typing back there, that's all." I tuck my hands in my pockets, my body beginning to sweat. I was psyching myself into being sick from this unknowing doom. I took a deep breath, exhaling slowly as Reese finally tucked his phone away.

"You alright?" He asked, coming to stand at my side. His eyes softened, no longer dark and gloomy. I nod, pulling my claw clip out of my pocket and scooping my hair. "Here," Reese took the clip from my hands. "I wanna do it." His voice was low as a smirk met my lips. He tucked the clip in his teeth and ran both hands through my curls, my eyes softly rolling back as he tugs my hair in his grip. I've suddenly forgotten all about Brooklynn's text. My head tilts back and I can practically feel his grin.

"Just put my hair up, you freak." I tease, feeling the teeth finally meet my scalp. Reese moves his hands from my head down my waist in a lingering way. "You're the definition of no fun." He groaned, moving to stand at my side. "I'm also at work." I snicker, turning down Maurice's hallway.

I notice Reese's footsteps slow and I'm dreading the way his mood will shift in this room. "Can't we just leave?" He sighed as I pulled out my key. "Reese, I have a job to do." My eyes are sympathetic to his expression. He's uneasy.

"What's going on?" I asked, pulling my key from the door. I knew he hated Maurice, but he didn't struggle this much when visiting him.

Reese shakes his head and runs a hand over his face with a dramatic groan. He wets his lips and finally lands his icy eyes back on me. My heart flutters at the way his eyes are lazily open as he smirks. "What if I can get us out of here?"

I'm a little annoyed that he ignored my question, but if I've learned anything in my month with Reese, it's that I can't pry. "How?" I folded my arms, amused at his eagerness to leave. His smirk grows and I can already feel myself getting written up about this. "Go wait in the bathroom."

He turns me around and gives me a slight push as I laugh under my breath. I pace the stall for a little while, counting the tiles on the floor as I step over them. I avoid the cracks like I was a kid again.

Kelseigh was horrible at that game. It didn't help that I'd trip her or scare her. I often think back to when I was younger and our relationship. I wasn't mean, but I wasn't the nicest big sister. And Kelseigh was no saint. It's amazing that in our adulthood we've grown as close as we have. She comes to visit once a month, this time for my birthday.

Finally, the bathroom door opens. Reese pushes himself past me to the sink, turning it on and wetting his hands. He places them on my forehead, and I flinch at the hot water. "Jesus, Tessa. You're burning up." He smirked, standing with his body pressed against mine.

"This is not how a fever works, Reese." I snickered at his lack of medical knowledge. "Look at you. You don't even need to go to nursing school; you're already a genius." He winked; his wet hand still pressed against my forehead as his other hooked the curve of my neck to hold me in place. I watched as his eyes lingered down to a droplet of water, dripping to the tip of my nose.

He has something in his mind, something he wants to do. God, I want him to kiss me. I would sell my soul for him to kiss me. But I was never the girl to make the first move.

A heavy exhale escaped his lips as he removed his hands. I was good enough to sleep with but not enough to kiss? "Now, I need you to pretend you've just violently thrown up." Reese talks with his hands as I groan. "Are you serious?" I rub my face strenuously as he chuckles.

"Matter of fact, you just let me do the talking." He gives a smug wink, draping his arm over my shoulder.

"This isn't gonna work..." I whisper as he glares at me. I take the hint and shut up, giving him full control of whatever it is he thinks he's doing. My heart is pounding.

I wasn't a great liar, I never lied about anything. I never so much as cheated on a test in high school. My pulse is pumping through my fingertips as my mouth goes dry with the reception desk insight.

"Tessa, you look awful! Get some reset, okay?" Francine gives a pouty lip, looking up from her desk. She's buying it. Whatever Reese told her is more believable than I thought. He keeps his face full of concern as he looks down at me, checking me over as if I'm really sick. I feel my heart pumping faster, like I could keel over any second. "Thank you, Francine. I'm gonna go get her in the car and I'll be back in for her things."

She jolted up from her chair, the wheels sliding back against the linoleum floor. "Let me go get them for you. No need for you to walk all the way down the hall again."

"You're a saint, Miss." Reese exhaled from his nose, his lips pulled into a closed, tight smile. I stay silent, giving a soft wave because I know if I open my mouth, I'll mess this up.

Reese opens the passenger door to a different vehicle. It's a BMW. He places his hands on my back and under my thighs, scooping me up to put me in the truck. "I can get in by myself." I whisper confused.

"Shut up, you're sick. It's the least I can do." He smiles, pulling my seatbelt over me. I take a deep breath as he opens his mouth only a little while stretching over my body to click it. He closes the door, turning to be greeted by Francine who is even smaller than I am. He looks down at her with a smile as I rest my head in my hand. If she talks to me again, I'll fold.

"Thank you again. Please apologize to Nurse Lynn for us. I cleaned up all the puke in the ladies' room." Reese's tone is fake and schmoozy, one that I assume he uses with Brooklynn.

Before I know it, he's back in the SUV. "How many cars do you have?" I asked, only half annoyed. "Just the one. This is my friends, mine is getting detailed."

I've never in my life had my truck detailed. I wondered what it was like to just have the need. "I'm sure your truck could use it. Hell, after all this is over, the first thing I'm doing is buying you a car." He snickered.

"Who says you're gonna look at me twice when all of this is over?" I asked with a sassy brow. I had to admit, it was something that had been weighing on my mind over the last month. He'd be back to his old ways.

Hitting the slopes in the middle of summer, surfing throughout winter.

His brows furrowed for a second, his lips wet as he thought about his answer. "Do you think I'm just gonna go back to my life without you?"

"I dunno." I spoke distractedly, scrolling through my phone. "Hm." Reese rested his elbow on the window sill, rubbing his chin.

"So where are we going?" I asked, changing the subject. I can tell he didn't want to stay on that topic either. His eyes are lit up, ready to say whatever stupid comment is eating him away inside.

"Well, you're sick. I have to take care of you." He sighed, turning his attention back to the road. He drives with his right hand atop the steering wheel and I take in the hills and valleys created in his veins under his skin. I could stare for hours.

"But I'm not sick."

"Yes, you are."

I sigh, realizing there's no way for me to win this battle. I was going to be 'taken care of' no matter what. "So, you're taking me home?"

"I didn't say that." He smirked, making a foreign left from how I would normally drive home. "I'm not going home with you, Reese." I sighed, tucking my phone away. Reese gasps dramatically, pressing the break in the middle of the road. "Tessa, I only want to help you feel better."

"We're in the middle of the road." I look over the seat to the cars in my back window now using their horns. "I know."

"Drive, Reese." I ordered, but he only put the SUV in park and folded his arms. I watched as people began to fly around us. I was worried we would get hit. My eyes jolted from the window to Reese as my jaw dropped.

"I'm not driving until you agree to let me take care of you." He softly shut his eyes and sighed.

"Fine, just drive!" I yelled with a giggle. He could be so annoying sometimes and yet here I was with a smile plastered across my face.

The apartment complex is bigger than I'd expected. I sighed, looking up at its height. "You coming?" he asked, shutting off the car.

I followed him up the stairs, to the elevator. God, an elevator? My eyes grow wide as he hits the 28th floor button. The ride is silent but comfortable. My hands are in my pockets, I'm unsure of what to do with them. I catch him staring at me from the corner of his eye yet neither of us speak.

"After you," He motions for me to step off the elevator. As I do, I follow him to the front door. There are only two apartments on this floor, and my heart is racing with nerves and excitement. My stomach is filled with butterflies and each beat of my heart is heavy with anticipation. I can feel the heat rising up the back of my neck. I'm filled with a sense of trepidation about what may come next.

Twenty-Three

TESSA

"Can I get you anything? Cough syrup? A cold compress?" Reese teased opening his fridge. "Very funny. Water is fine." I smiled, standing at the skyline. "The city looks so complicated from up here."

"The city *is* complicated, Tess." Reese startles me as he places a cold bottle of water against my bare arm. "How so?" My guard was up, I wanted to have an open-minded conversation, but I couldn't. My life was full of people tearing this place apart. I just wanted one person to see it the way I did.

"People come and go all the time, in the rush of making a quick buck but never stopping to enjoy the moment or see the beauty and joy here." Reese takes a drink of his own water and shrugs. "They are constantly competing, trying to outdo one another, racing towards this imagined idea of success that New York can offer."

Reese's words struck a chord with me, making me feel a strange mix of sorrow and bitterness. I couldn't help but feel like he was right, and it pained me to say that. I was one of those people quite often. I wanted to be a New York success story. But I was nowhere near it.

He accepted my silence as a response as he stood closer. "If it makes you feel any better, New York is my home, always will be. I'd die without this view. And the stench obviously." He snickered.

"Me too." I grinned ear to ear. The polluted air smell was one that took so many tourists by surprise. Something they complained about so heavily was something we became accustomed to.

I turn around, looking at the living room and what I can see of the kitchen. His space is so empty in comparison to the way it was when

I came for my wallet. I take it upon myself to walk toward the hall. "Where are you going?"

"Just looking around." I trace my hand along his sofa as I look over my shoulder. "Allow me to lead the way." Reese practically leaves a cartoon dust cloud behind him as he catches up to me.

The walls are white and barren. It's a place devoid of personal touches and decorations, just like a hotel room. I couldn't believe that someone could live here, in this bland space, without signs of self-expression or character.

"Here's the bathroom, but no one cares about that." He opens and closes the door quickly, pushing me toward his bedroom as I hold back my laughter. "Wait, I wanted to see that!" I tried to dig my heels, but Reese was so much stronger than me.

"And this is where I plan on keeping you tonight."

"You wish." My voice was dripping with sarcasm. As I walked over to his dresser, taking in my reflection in the mirror. My curls were a mess, falling from my clip. "I can be *really* convincing." Reese smirked, coming up behind me. His hands snake around to the front of my body as he unties my scrub bottoms.

I roll my eyes with a coy smile. "I still have that thong in my pocket, you know. Should we try it on?"

"So, you can tear that one too?" I raise my brow, turning to face him. His expression is blank, and I hear him dry swallow. "Only if you're giving me permission." His eyes darkened with lust and desire, the intensity of his stare making my body shiver with anticipation. I wet my lips anxiously. There's a newfound pressure here, I thought to myself.

This was no closet liaison; we were in his bedroom. Things were about to intensify, and I couldn't help but feel a twinge of nervousness along with my familiar excitement.

I wasn't sure how to feel about going so far so quickly, but there was an undeniable thrill in the rush of this experience.

"Do you trust me?" He asked, closing the gap between us. I craned my neck to look up at him. His breath was hot and shaky. I had every reason in the book not to trust him, yet I couldn't get it out.

"Of course." My eyes flicker between both of his. The blue was so bright in comparison to its usual hue. They were like the afternoon sky in the countryside in contrast to his dark lashes.

"Good." Reese's voice was deep and raspy, the moisture having yet to return to his mouth.

Reese walked backward toward his bed, pulling me with him by my shirt. He sits on the edge of the mattress as I raise my arms for him to lift the fabric off my body. I'm wearing my worn-out black *Victoria's Secret* bra. If I had any idea that I was going to be in Reese Finch's bedroom, I would have sprung for a new lace set.

He takes in a labored breath, running his hands up from my navel to my breasts. I'm looking down at him which gives me this overwhelming sense of power against him, like I was in control for once. He squeezes gently and I watch his dick pulse against his jeans. I swallow my pooling saliva as his fingers cautiously move to my back as if to undo my bra.

I quickly took his hands, moving them back to my stomach. I'm in charge, at least for now. And I need him to remove my pants. I pull his hands to the front of my scrubs, and he catches the hint immediately. His experience with every girl in NYC was only going to help him in a situation with someone like me. I had no idea how to give hints; I had no idea how to be dominant or even say what I wanted from a man.

Reese hooked his hands in the snug material and tugged them down. He ran back up from my thighs to my ass, squeezing with more intent and my eyes rolled back.

I slide my hands into my hair, removing my clip and letting my curls fall, something he seems to appreciate. Reese stands to his feet and turns my back to the bed.

"I want you to lay down for me, okay?"

I nodded, confused but in no position to question him. His voice is full of longing and eagerness in comparison to the way he is looking at me. I feel like he could rip me apart if he wanted and I'm both terrified and turned on. My legs are trembling as I comply with his request, laying on the silk sheets that have touched so many other women. I push the thoughts from my mind as he pulls his pants off, leaving his shirt and briefs on for the time being.

Reese climbs on the bed, stopping where I have my legs propped up. His breath is heavy, and I can tell this is different for him too. His fingers graze my thighs, making them twitch. "Open your legs, Tess." He spoke softly as they automatically widened to his request. He removed his shirt, wiping the sweat from his forehead before throwing it on the floor. I'd never seen this look in his eyes with the heat radiating from my inner thighs as he lowered his head to my most intimate spot.

He kisses my legs and I feel myself pulsing. His fingertips trail up and down mindlessly as I catch him glancing at my reaction. My body shutters to him, but I don't want him to stop.

"Reese, what–" My voice is cut off by his nose, finding the soft, silky place between my lips. My legs spread farther. One hand holds the bed sheets so tight I'm afraid they'll tear right through the fabric. The other instinctively locks in Reese's hair. I feel my back lift from the bed in an exorcism as his tongue flicks across my clit before pulling and sucking on it, treating my body like a fresh Georgia peach.

My body jolts up, my grip on his hair tightens as he slips his fingers inside. His left arm hooks my thigh, keeping me from inching away and holding my gaze. I'm going to scream. My body trembles as he slows down.

He swallows me, his chin dripping and I'm afraid he might drown soon. He seems more than willing to go out this way, moaning against my vagina as he devours what feels like his last meal. When he lifts his head and retracts his fingers, he looks me in my eyes. His chin glistened with all of me as he licked his fingers clean. I'm almost jealous. I wanted to know what he tasted and why he was so hungry for it.

Reese rested both arms on either side of my body, leaning down to kiss my breasts that are still covered by my bra. He pulled the material back, covering my chest with goosebumps. His tongue danced around the sensitive part, nipping and sucking as my arms linked around his neck. His breath was shaky, his nerves spilling over. "I need you, Reese." I begged for his length, my thighs practically quivering around his waist. I'd never wanted to feel something so bad again. He nodded; his lips parted as he sat back on his calves again.

His hand stroked his length. I watch as he tilts his head down, a slew of saliva hangs from his mouth as he spits on himself for lubrication. As if he'd need it, I was a puddle of my own honey and his saliva. I lay on my back, like a plastic doll at his whim, ready to be used and abused in any way he desired.

"G-go slow." I stuttered as he leaned back over my body, one hand in the down pillow and the other guiding himself inside. I watch as his head falls back, his mouth quivering as his face grows red. "Fuck," He growled, pushing himself inside gingerly. My back lifted from the sheets, his free hand sneaking between me and the mattress. I feel his length push further inside and my mouth falls open. Maybe I didn't want to be slow. The veins in his arms are bulging with adrenaline. "Are you okay?" He struggled out; I wanted him to stop talking. I wanted all of him right now, in the roughest way possible.

I nod, using my hands on his lower back to pull him closer to me. A moan escapes his throat as he buries his head in the crook of my neck. "Baby, please. We gotta go slow or I'm gonna fucking cum already." He was nearly whimpering against me, his entire body trembling. *Did I have that much of an effect on him?*

"I can't." My words come out in broken moans. I'm so weak for him, I don't even recognize myself.

"You want me to stretch you out. Don't you, Tessa?" He groaned, pushing himself all the way in. I can feel his length hitting my cervix. I can't explain the feeling, but it sends my body into a full twitch. I struggled to speak, feeling like I was going to convulse.

My phone rings on the nightstand, but he pays no mind. Reese forces himself back in as deep as he can go to distract me. My right arm scrambles against the table in a search. "Don't answer it." He growled, biting my neck more ravenously. "What if it's an emergency?"

He hits my cervix again and I whimper.

"I said *no*, Tessa." He grabs it before I can reach. "It's your boyfriend. Should I answer it?" He leans back, retracting his length from me and I am left out of breath and in tears, like a kid who's lost TV privileges for a week. My hands claw at him, hurrying to pull him back down. Reese places the phone on my sternum and grabs my arms with one hand, pinning them above my head.

He answers the call with his free grip and selects the speaker option. His expression is devious, and my heart is nearing cardiac arrest.

"Tess? Are you there?" Tim's voice is sincere, filled with genuine worry. I shake my head at Reese, the static on the line filling the void. Talking to Tim right now feels like talking to a priest in a confessional. Reese only nods his head, forcing me to talk.

"H-hey, Tim."

"Hey, I've been waiting outside for like ten minutes. You still needed a ride, didn't you?" He asks, his hazard signals filling the background noise. My eyes grew wide, I had completely forgotten about him picking me up. I was the worst person on this planet.

"I'm so sorry. I went home early. I couldn't stop throwing up." I squint my eyes shut, trying to wriggle from Reese's grasp to take the phone call more seriously. "Oh, I see." He doesn't buy it. I'm busted and I'm going to hell.

Reese drives his length back inside with no warning, a loud guttural most escapes my lips. "Tess? Are you alright?" The panic picks up in Tim's voice and I feel like an asshole, I hear him put the car in drive. "Yeah. H-horrible stomach cramp." My eyes roll back in my head as Reese pumps himself inside me faster, I can tell this entire phone call is getting him off. He's sick in the head and I'm completely fine with that.

"Jesus, kid. You want me to bring you anything?" Tim asked with a soft chuckle. I can practically see his smile when I close my eyes. Which is easy to do when Reese is fucking me so hard I can't open them. "No. I-I'm just gonna get some sleep. T-talk later, okay?" I'm forcing back my moan as I speak in broken words.

"Sure, call me when you wake up, Tess."

Reese hangs up the phone and tosses it on the pile of our clothes, letting go of my hands. "You are such a dick." I moaned, pulling him as close to me as I possibly could. "You fucking love it." He scoops under my right thigh, lifting it to rest on his shoulder. "I want you to feel me in your stomach, baby." He moaned, pushing against my cervix again. The wet, black tendrils are bouncing against his forehead with each movement.

"Reese, I'm so close." I panted, Reese gripping the sheets with his head hung back. His thrusts are losing their rhythm, and I can tell he's trying to hold on as long as possible. His lips are parted as he takes short breaths. "Let me feel it. I want you to finish on my dick, Tess."

My legs quiver, my body squirms. My head is dizzy and light as the mattress swallows me whole in my orgasm. "Fuck, Tessa." He moans my name and my high is stretched.

At this moment, I am the best and only thing on his mind. Everything about his attention and focus screams obsession, which is what I need.

I want to be his sole obsession. I am his drug, and he is mine. I never want to be out of his system.

Twenty-Four

REESE

September 11ᵗʰ

"Come on, dude. You seriously haven't fucked her?" Christian asks me. I roll my eyes, sipping my tequila and lime. My throat burned on the way down as I exhaled fire. I feel my phone vibrate in my pocket, a missed call from Brooklynn.

"No, man." I lied through my teeth. Something about what Tessa and I did in that closet made me want to relish alone. I didn't want anyone to know what I could do for her. "I'm not buying it. Reese can't keep his dick in his pants around any woman." Brice teased, elbowing me on our half of the table.

"I swear. She's persistent in hating me." I laughed with my hands in the air in defeat. "I checked out her Instagram," Jody sighed, setting his fork down. "I'll get her to fuck me if you don't." My body temperature rises, I want to rip his throat out and shit down his neck. I've already explained my dislike for this man but at this moment, I despised him. "If she won't sleep with me, she is certainly not gonna settle for you." I spoke with my jaw clenched, I could practically hear my teeth cracking at the pressure.

"He's got a point, J." Christian snickered. "No wonder you're still fucking around with Brooklynn, at least she's easy." He then shrugged, lightening the mood. His being a year younger than us put him in the same graduating class as her. I wasn't the only man to take a swing at that ball, Christian definitely had his share.

"Yeah well, she fucks like she's easy." I scoffed with a smirk. I sounded like a real piece of shit. But I had to get them to stop sniffing around Tessa. "And yet you still call her, Casanova." Christian winked, pointing his steak knife at me.

It was true, I'd had my share of run-ins with Brooklynn over the few months that I'd rather not divulge in. But after that day in the closet, my sights are set on one woman. It's a strange thought, I've never been one to be tied down.

I'm not sure that's even what I want, but I know I need to be inside her again. My mouth is salivating at the table thinking about how tight Tessa gripped my dick, how wet and sticky she was as she moaned in my ear.

I needed to know what she tasted like.

"Yeah, well. What can I say?" I bow out in defeat, they're off the topic of Tess and I can feel my ears cooling down. I'm not gonna snap. "So, where's everyone hanging out tonight?" I asked the table, ready to hit the town for the first time since working with Tessa. Everyone was quiet, speaking telepathically as they eyed each other. They knew something I didn't.

"Spit it out." I demanded sitting back in my chair, my arms folded. My brows are down and I'm ready to pummel each one of these assholes. "Well, we've all got a flight to catch." Brice blushes, pushing the wilted lettuce around his plate.

"It's a Wednesday." My voice is dumbfounded. Do they not have jobs? Am *I* the only responsible one here? "We're going to Miami. We would have texted you, but you never come around anymore." Christian sighed, mimicking my stance in his chair. It's been a month, not a year. I've already been written off. "I see. Did you guys make a separate group chat without me?" I already know the answer.

"You fucking blew off the Giant's game at my place on Sunday." Christian was standing his ground to me, something I could always count on. He was beyond hot headed, blowing my tantrums out of the water.

Sunday. Sunday, I was reeling from a coke binge. I remember reading the text from the guys. I had every intention of replying until I saw my account was empty. Assumably to buy more drugs.

"Don't be a pussy because I didn't come to your little party, Chris." I scoffed, treating him like the baby he was. "Don't take your bad mood out on me because you can't get Tessa to drop her fucking panties for you."

I want to tell him so bad; I want him to eat his words.

"I don't need this shit right now." I pulled out my wallet, throwing two twenties down for my food and drinks. Tessa was right, I should just eat at home from now on. "Fuck all three of you. Enjoy Miami." I stood from my chair and left. No one followed me, no one texted me with an apology.

We'll be fine in a week. Big personalities clashed like this at least once a month. It was like our lives were so boring having everything we desired; we had to create the drama ourselves.

When I step out of the restaurant, I'm greeted by a reporter. I roll my eyes, annoyed with their presence, but I hear Tess's voice in my mind. "Everyone has a job, Reese. They're just doing theirs." I shake my head, a coy smile reaching my lips.

"Mr. Finch! Is it true Maurice is rewriting his will?" The man asked, tugging his baseball cap tighter on his bald head. "How the fuck would I know?" I tuck my hands in my pockets, walking to my car. "It's rumored you're being written out of the will for your drunk driving scandal last year." He continued.

My hands are clenched into fists in my pockets. I'd love to knock his teeth out of his mouth but would only be another thing stacked against my odds with Tessa. "Could be." I fueled the man who began taking more notes. He was eating this up. I could say anything, and he would believe it. Though being written out of my father's will was the least surprising thing he could have said.

"Get a real fucking job." I sighed, opening the car door and driving home. Normally, I'd call for someone to meet me at my place. I needed to clear my head and sex was the only way to do it. This time, I opted for a more civil approach. Clearing my mind with the way God intended; forgiveness.

I opened my phone, texting Tessa. I knew she was annoyed at the fact I lied about having my phone on me. The way she was when I left, told me she wouldn't be mad forever.

6:22 P.M.
R- I'm sorry I lied about having my phone in the closet.
T- i know.
R- Are you pissed?
T- i wish.

I smirk to myself, reading the texts over and over as I step off the elevator. She was so quick to fold to me. I could hit her with my car, and she'd probably get up and apologize for being in the way. When I lift my gaze, I'm met with a blonde, leaning against my door. I can't help the groan that falls out.

"Where've you been?" She asked politely, tucking her hands in her pockets. She looks different. She's in sweatpants and a hoodie. Her stringy hair is in a high pony and her skin is gray with a lack of makeup. My face is full of disgust as I focus on the bags under her eyes and her all around shaky presence.

"Dinner. What do you want?" My tone is coarse. I don't want to ruin the slim chance I have of seeing Tessa naked again. "I tried to call." She replied with her head down, focusing on her sandals that dug into the mat outside my door. I raised a brow, annoyed with how vague she'd been.

"And I *just* told you I was out to dinner."

She nods, sniffling as I stare at her. "Can I come inside?"

"For what?"

"Because we need to talk." I can tell she's serious, her vision focusing all around to make sure no one else is near. "Don't take your shoes off, you're not staying long."

Brooklynn nods, stepping back as I unlock the door. I softly shut it behind us, something I'd picked up from Tess. Not everything had to be dramatic and about me, she reminded me often.

"Well?" I asked, leaning against the kitchen counter with my arms crossed. I was growing impatient as she twiddled her fingers. "I need money."

I couldn't help the laugh that escaped my lips. "Yeah, so do I." I replied with a low voice, my head falling back. My account was slim after our weekend together. "Reese, I *really* need it."

109

"For what?"

Brooklynn sighs, looking at the ceiling.

"I'm pregnant."

The saliva disappears from my mouth, the two words no man ever wants to hear from someone he's casually sleeping with. "It's not mine." I argue. There are no other words I can process right now. It's the first thing I can spit out. Surprisingly, it's the longest conversation I've ever had with her with our clothes on.

"It is. I haven't been with anyone else since the summer."

"Bullshit." She was a coke whore, plain and simple. Okay, that's harsh, but she did get around. Christian spoke from experience.

I ran my hands over my face that felt a million degrees. "I swear." Her voice was meek and broken. I turned, putting my hands on the counter.

"I don't want the baby, so you don't have to worry about that." Brooklynn sniffled between words as I ran my tongue over my top teeth. I threw my head back, groaning as my life ended.

"I don't know what you want me to say." I couldn't stop my tone from being so harsh. I wanted her to disappear. She was going to ruin this for me. I could already feel Tess slipping from my grasp like sand in an hourglass. "I just need your help."

"I need proof." I stared at the ceiling, my voice softer as I prayed to God, if he was even listening. "Proof?" she asked softly. "Get in the car." I grabbed my keys from the counter again with a sigh. This fucking day couldn't get any worse.

Twenty-Five

REESE

"Which one?" Brooklynn asked, pointing at the various brands of tests. "Does it matter?" I replied with a sigh. I looked around, making sure no one had been around or following us. Brooklynn nodded, grabbing the most expensive. Of course, it's only my money.

We walked up to the counter, without a word to one another. The old woman scans the tests, her eyes flickering between both of us, but no real words are spoken. She knows the situation. I can only imagine how many times she's seen it. At least we aren't teenagers.

She hands us the receipt, sliding the box of tests our direction. "Can you put it in a bag, please?" I asked before Brooklynn could pick it up. The woman sighs with a nod. I want to confront her, ask her just what exactly she thinks of me. Do I look as terrible as I feel on the inside?

Brooklynn pushes the door open, the plastic bag catching on the handle. "Shit, watch out." I take her arm to stop her from walking. She turns around, almost startled at my voice. It's the first innocent thing I've said to her in about ten minutes. "Hm?" She looks down at the bag and nods as I pull it off. "There's a hole, so be careful." I sigh, walking closely behind her.

"Do you want me to run in for a new one?" Brooklynn raised a brow, ready to turn back around as we walked down the sidewalk. I shook my head. "No, it's not a big deal." I waved her on to keep walking to my car down the block.

The dumbest decision I've ever fucking made.

I open the door for her, letting her step inside. I looked around again, no one following us, no signs of Tessa.

"Can I ask a favor?" I start the car, the dash lights up, and illuminating the car as the sky turns orange. She nods, looking at me.

"Keep this between us. I've got some real shit going for me right now." I sighed, feeling like a dick. She didn't deserve me treating her like this, but she wasn't someone who you ended up with. Tessa was the girl you brought back to meet your parents. Brooklynn was the girl you took back to rehab.

Brooklynn nodded, looking forward. I watch out of the corner of my eye as her fingers play with the hole in the plastic bag. There were so many things on her mind and unfortunately, I didn't care to listen. I knew it was wrong, I should have been there for her. But I was so selfish.

I stepped out of the car, quickly walking to her side to let her out. I offer my hand to her, and I'm surprised she accepts. "Shoot," The box slips from the plastic bag, both of us bending down to grab it.

From a distance, I've convinced myself that I see a flicker of light. Brooklynn doesn't seem to pay any notice to it. Maybe I've just officially lost my mind. I look around and see nothing more. My arm links around Brooklynn's side, pulling her up the steps to my apartment faster. Her feet stumble over one another and I don't care to slow down. I'm fucking paranoid.

September 13th,

Tessa lays facing away from me. The sun has yet to rise, and I can't get myself to go back to sleep. Her body is bare in my bed, a place I'd never expected it to be.

I can smell the coconut on her skin, and I want to drown in it. I want to run my hand down her body and feel its smooth, tanned texture. My mouth is sweating as I watch her back move with each soft breath. I reached for my phone as quietly as possible, I would dare wake her up.

My socials are barren, Tessa's been so busy with me and Timmy that she hasn't posted lately. The thought of him entertaining her makes my stomach turn. I'm not sure why. He was a good guy; I could tell from what I'd stalked of him. Tessa would be happy with someone like him. He had his life far more put together than I did. He wasn't on an allowance like I was, and he owned a damn business.

But here I was, in bed with her.

I put my phone up again and rolled on my side to face her. My lips drag gently across her spine, her skin is so sweet. Tess lets out the softest breath, and my body trembles because of it. She squirms against the sheets; my lips meet the spot behind her ear and I'm pressed against her body. "Good morning." I whisper against her, my hands roaming under the blankets.

"It's still dark outside." She groaned, her ass pressing against me in a stretch. My eyes roll back as I practically bite through my bottom lip to prevent a boner. "I'm well aware." I snickered. Normally, I'd be going to the gym with Brice, but I couldn't get myself away from her if I tried.

"Can I make you breakfast?" I asked, kissing her neck once more. I could taste her body all day. What was happening to me?

"Do you even know how to use the oven?" She teased, her lips curling in a smile.

"Yes, baby." My left hand snakes around to cup her breast and she giggles. It was a valid question. I used to cook with my mom. It felt like a hundred years ago now, but I knew how to make a damn pancake.

"Okay, then make me breakfast in like four hours." She groaned as my hands continued to grope at her body. "No, let's get up now." I press my bulge into her more as she lets out a comfortable sigh.

"No."

"Then I'm gonna go for a run." I groan, pressing myself into her again. I watch her body contort against me in enjoyment. "Can't we just lay here?" She groaned, rolling over to face me.

Her amber eyes are practically glowing in the rising sun's light. It would be probably another thirty minutes before I got to see her complete beauty. I move the loose curls from her face and exhale from my nose. "What is with you and wanting to lay around lately?" I teased her with a smirk, rubbing her shoulder. Her full lips curl into a soft smile as she stretches. Her body is warm, radiating heat that I want to wrap myself in. I could forget all my responsibilities, the drama with Brooklynn, my father, and just drown myself in her warmth.

It must be embedded in my face as I find myself distracted in her presence. "Come here." She smiled with innocence. "What?"

She doesn't reply and pulls me to lay on her. My body is between her legs, my head on her chest with my arms on either side. I can hear her heartbeat; it's like rain. Every beat seems to take an eternity, but just the same, they all come crashing down on me like an inescapable storm. Tess runs her fingers through my hair. I exhale again, my eyes struggling to stay open. But I'm not tired, I'm completely relaxed. Her hand leaves my hair, running mindless fingers down my back. I wanna moan, but not out of lust. Maybe out of appreciation. I've never had someone touch me this way. I want to cry.

"Reese?" Tessa's voice is hesitant, but I can't help but pick up the notes of curiosity. "Hm?" I mumble against her chest. "Why don't you ever talk about your mom?"

I grip the sheets on either side of her, my body tenses against her and she can tell. "I'm sorry." She held me a little tighter and God, did I need it. My body heaves with breaths, I turn my chin to rest on her sternum. I could tell Tessa was comfortable with me not answering as her kind eyes stared back at me. She wasn't someone trying to gain a quick buck off me, she was someone that wanted to understand why I was such a shitty person.

"She left me at Maurice's." I responded plainly. I watch her eyes turn from kindness to sympathy. "Left you?" Tessa traces a hand up my spine and I nod. It's hypnotizing, like I will do anything she says as long as she keeps touching me. "I was thirteen."

Every word leaving my mouth is carved with glass. I watch her full lips part in shock, her hands resting on my shoulder blades. All she does is nod. I feel so seen and heard with such a simple gesture.

"She worked two jobs, and I was home alone a lot. I didn't care, I could take care of myself, y'know?" I explained, leaving a kiss on her sternum. It's like a way to buy time, I'm dreading explaining myself to her. Her patience is my fucking virtue. "One day, I came home from school, and she had a suitcase packed for me. I thought maybe we were taking the trip down to Myrtle Beach that she'd promised me for years." I chuckle to myself, thinking about how we'd flip through different travel magazines, planning the perfect vacation.

Tessa giggled, moving a hand back to my hair, the other propping under her head. I swallow hard.

"We pulled into Maurice's driveway. I'd only been there once when we tried to have a family Christmas." I left out the part where he freaked and kicked us out after thirty minutes. There was enough unloaded already. I wet my lips.

"She told me I could get a better life with Maurice. That I needed to go to the door and tell him I was left alone." Thus, the downfall of any shred of happiness in my life began. I watch her expression fall completely. That big heart of hers had shattered.

"Don't look at me like I'm a puppy in those sad commercials." I joked, trying to lighten the mood as she squirms underneath me to sit up.

I fucked up. I said too much. My heart is in overdrive, stacking bricks back up. I was an idiot. I sit up, rubbing the back of my neck. "I'm sorry, I didn't mean to make you-"

She squeezes her arms around my neck before I can finish my sentence, crawling into my lap. My arms are at my sides, my brows furrowed in confusion. I'm enveloped in a heaven that is filling the void inside of me. If her grip wasn't so tight, I'd be looking at the ceiling and thanking God for my mom dropping me off at Maurice's that day.

I finally lifted my arms, moving them to her back and absorb her energy. "I'm so sorry you experienced that." Tessa spoke into my neck. Jesus, was I crying? I can only work out a nod against the lump in my throat. I had to pull it together. The way she sat in my lap, her legs draped off one side, I could cradle her like this forever.

"Have you talked to her since?"

I shake my head. I looked her up on Facebook a few years ago. She was married and not at all thinking of me. I'm too embarrassed to admit that. It had been seventeen years, and I didn't cross her mind.

Twenty-Six

TESSA

"Okay, my turn." I climb from Reese's lap, sitting with legs crossed. The air was thick, I could sense how heavy this was for him. "Huh?" he asked with a confused brow.

"Ask me anything." I smiled, pulling one of his shirts up off the ground. It smelled of expensive cologne. A woodsy, tobacco scent. "Don't put that on." He groaned, leaning forward to try and take it from me. "I'm freezing." I smirked, sliding it over my naked body.

"Then let me warm you up."

I let out a sigh as his hand stroked up and down my arm, leaving goosebumps behind. The way his touch felt, it sent chills across my body. It set my heart racing; every move was ablaze with a passion. It's like the world stopped turning for just a moment. And at that moment, I was his. "Hmm," Reese thought for a moment.

"What's your family like?" He smiled, the sun now shining light on the tiny freckles of his ivory skin. "That's a copout question." I groaned.

"Answer, please."

"My family is pretty boring." I replied, feeling guilty for what I grew up with. Reese nods, waiting for description. He doesn't appear upset or jealous in the way I'd expect. "How so?" His question is shocking to me. Like he genuinely cared.

"My parents avoid arguing in front of us. They have this concept of a perfect marriage, it's dumb." I rolled my eyes. Reese's hand moves to my hair, tucking it behind my ear. The feeling is intoxicating. "Jesus, that sounds annoying." He scoffed, eyes wide for a second. I nod in agreement, feeling more connected.

"They moved to Florida after Kelseigh graduated."

"Your sister?" Reese asked. I nod, noting the fact that he already knew that piece of information. I'm curious how long he'd been looking me up, but not enough to address it. "Yep, she's a real peach. Be glad she's not up here. I'm sure she'd be all over you." I smirk, resting my hands by my chin.

"That's a bad thing?" He teased, a devious grin growing on his face. "I don't share my boyfriends. Especially with my sister." My mouth falls open, realizing the words spoken. The color leaves his face as he clears his throat.

What an idiot. "I'm so sorry. I don't know why I said that." I hide my face behind my hands as he laughs. "It's fine, Tess." He uncovers my face. "There's uh, something I wanna talk to you about."

I put a finger in the air as my phone rang. "Hold that thought." I reach across the bed and see it's a call from Kayla.

"Hello?" I answer in my most normal voice.

"Where are you?"

"Home, where are you?"

Reese shakes his head with a laugh, laying on the bed correctly with his head on the pillows. He puts his hands on my hips, moving me to straddle his lap.

"Why are you lying? I'm sitting on your couch flipping through old Stripe magazines. Are you with Reese, you slut?" I could tell by her tone that she was smirking.

"No, I'm not with Reese." I ran a hand up his torso as both of his grazed my hips. His length twitches beneath me and I pull in my bottom lip to hide my smile.

"You fucking liar!" she exclaimed into the phone.

"Did you need something, Kay?" I asked with a giggle, Reese's hands grinding me slowly against his hips. I steady my breathing.

"Well, *it is* my dad's birthday."

Shit, I'd completely forgotten about breakfast. Kayla's mother had an anniversary breakfast every year on Jake's birthday. It was something Kayla enjoyed until her mom met Gary. He was a nice guy and all, but he wasn't her dad. He was also twenty years older than Rose. I know I would be the same way if it was my mother. I couldn't fault her. "I'll be home in twenty." I hung up the phone without a reply.

"Stay here." Reese groaned, trying to hold me on his lap. I could tell he was fully turned on at this moment. His length throbbing against my opening. "Reese, this is really important." I sighed, both hands running up his chest.

"So is this." His nails dug in deeper to my hip bones, my eyes rolling back. "Oh, god." I struggle to form a sentence as I wet my lips.

"This is really important to Kayla." I take his hands, moving them up to my breasts, still wrapped in his shitty t-shirt. I can't help myself.

"Fuck, Tessa." Reese groaned, his member begging to spring up inside me. "Real quick. I can get it done quick; I swear." He begged, his voice breaking into a whimper. There was no such thing as quick with Reese. We'd only slept together twice, and I've quickly learned he was one to take his time. "All you gotta do is ride me, baby." He exhaled heavily through his teeth. "I can't, Reese. I have to go." My hips slide against his length instinctively as he calls me baby. My need for him is flooding from my body. I just can't tell him no.

"Please, baby." His hands trembled against my skin. "Can't you just come to my place tonight?" I whined, battling with the angel and devil on my shoulder. "No, I want you now, Tessa." His back arched as I moved to sit on his thighs versus his hips. "Look."

I watch his length jolt to a vertical position, and my mouth salivates. Reese's hand slides over the sticky member and I'm literally pouting. "Come sit on my dick, Tessa Baby." He whined, stroking his hand over the tip. "I can't, Reese." I sigh, running my hands up his thighs. He sucks in a breath through a clenched jaw.

"Can I watch you get dressed at least?" He smirked, putting one hand behind his head. I roll my eyes standing from the bed and grab my new thong from Reese's pocket on the floor. I turn my back to him, slowly pulling it up over my thighs. "Fuck..." He groans, his motions sounding more wet from where I'm standing.

I turn to face him again, gripping his t-shirt by the bottom hem and lifting it over my head to reveal my breasts again. He wets his lips, resting his tongue in the corner of his mouth. This is so foreign to me. I've never done this in front of a man before. Reese pushed me to try so many things and I loved every one of them. I reached down to grab my bra and started putting it on. "Alright, show's over." I sighed, latching the back as he groaned. "If you don't mind, I'm gonna go take care of this in the shower." Reese smirked, placing a hand on the side of my face, his thumb still wet with pre-cum as it traces my bottom lip. "And when I come over tonight, I'm fucking the life out of you." He grinned, staring at my lips for a second before pulling away.

Twenty-Seven

TESSA

Every second of my drive back home was spent thinking about Reese. Every stroke of my makeup brush, I thought about his shower. When I got dressed, I thought about his soapy body, pleasuring himself to the thought of me. I wanted to be in there with him, dripping in bubbly water.

"I said I was sorry, Kayla." I groan, entering the restaurant behind her. "I would just appreciate it if you arranged your dick appointments *around* pre-existing plans." She furrowed her brows as I nodded. She had every right to be upset with me. It was her dad's birthday, something I spent with her every year since his passing. And I was too busy thinking about getting dicked down by Reese again.

At the table sat Kayla's mother Rose and of course, her boyfriend Gary.

"God, if you can hear me, strike me down." Kayla whispered, her eyes rolling back into her head. This was her worst nightmare.

"There's my girls." Rose grinned, setting down her mimosa. "Already with the champagne mom?" Kayla's condescending tone sent a chill down my spine. Not much had changed over the years. "Hi, Mrs. Lorne." I greeted, sitting beside Kayla. I notice an empty chair on the other side of me, my brows furrowed in confusion. "Sorry about that. Work call." Timothy's voice is like needles in my eyes and I grip the menu tighter. "Someone is looking better." He kisses my cheek as he sits down.

I feel my skin burn red as I smile. I feel like the biggest asshole. "Yeah, it's amazing what some sleep and an antacid can do." I giggle with my eyes pressed shut, I can't even look at him.

Kayla's brows furrow and I feel her burning holes into my body. "I didn't know you were sick." She folds her arms, no longer interested in breakfast. "Overnight bug." I mumble, glaring back at her, hoping she could read my mind. "I'm surprised you didn't sense it, Kayla." Tim snickered, regarding our strong friendship that was crumbling at the seams.

"Yeah, Tess just keeps us all guessing." Her tongue runs across her top teeth, and I turn my attention back to the menu. "Well, this is awkward." Rose uncomfortably laughed, sipping her drink. Gary, on the other hand, had no idea what planet we were even on. I'm sure Rose had to pick him up from the nursing home on the way in.

Not much had changed in this old restaurant. Maybe the furniture. The designs on the tables were different, yet the leather booths were still ratted and torn. The smell was the same, old coffee and stale menthol. I close my eyes for a second; I can see Jake, Rose, and their children. We're coloring on the mats; Timothy helps me with the maze as Kayla works the weekly crossword with her dad. Rose sips a coffee instead of a mimosa, watching Tim and I with a smile. She really didn't start drinking the way she does now until Jake died.

"So, you two got any plans today?" Rose asked, pointing her fork at the two of us, jolting me from my memory. "Hm?" I look up, unsure of who she is referring to. "Actually, I was thinking about doing some local shopping while I'm in town. Are you interested?" Tim puts his arm on the back of my chair, I'm frozen with my hands on my lap.

"I'm actually so behind on laundry, I'll be occupying my afternoon at the laundromat." I smile, my cheeks warm as I finally turn to look at him. He's wearing cream, cotton long sleeve, rolled up to his elbows. The top button is undone, and I find myself staring for too long.

"Alright. I can meet you when I'm done?"

Of course he would offer.

"That would be great." I smiled, wanting to rip the skin from my face. Though no one wanted to hurt me as much as Kayla. I could see it in her eyes, the way she cut her waffle, practically cracking the plate with her fork. "Can't wait." Tim smiled, grabbing his coffee cup by the handle with a wink.

Laundry was now on the menu for me.

I pulled out my phone, texting Reese.

12:02 P.M.
T- change of plans, doing laundry tonight.
R- Come do it at my place then.
T- can't. have to hang out with my boyfriend.
R- Lol. Call me when you're done.

He doesn't flinch when I call Tim my boyfriend. Him and I both know it isn't true. It was, however, Reese's favorite way to refer to Tim. My heart races as I tuck my phone in my pocket, the idea of sneaking around with Reese only turning me on.

I watch as Rose pulls Gary's wallet from his pocket, paying for everyone's breakfast. I guess it was quite the life to live. Gary seemed to have unlimited funds, keeping her lifestyle alive. This man was withering to nothing, and Rose was banking on it.

"Still going to the one on 97th?" Tim asked, opening the driver door to his Toyota. I nod, rubbing the back of my neck strenuously. "Perfect. Text me when you get there." He smiled, climbing inside.

I feel Kayla staring at me from behind. She clears her throat, her arms folded over her green, army jacket.

"Hey." I awkwardly smiled.

"Don't hey me. Are you fucking Tim too?" She was always so blunt.

I shake my head, a groan escaping. "No, I'm not fucking Tim."

"Look, I hate him too, but that doesn't mean you get to lead him on." She argued. The tone in her voice was serious, no longer that playful Kayla I'd known and loved. "I'm not leading him on. Tim is a great guy. He's kind and smart. He's known me better than anyone for a greater portion of my life." I sighed, walking to her car. Timothy was so reliable. He was the type to fix my flat on the side of the highway, take our daughter to dances, and teach our son to ride a bike. With Tim, there was a future. "But?"

But? My mind was reeling. With Reese, there was the present, the wild ride of the now. The never-ending thought of what next? "Reese is just... I don't know. There's a fire between us." My lips curl into a soft smile that I can't help. "Yeah, well, where there is fire, there are burns.

You know his reputation, Tess." Kayla's eyes softened as she put the car in drive. Only a few weeks ago she was pushing him on me. Maybe things were different with her big brother in the mix. I nod, taking it into consideration. Reese was notorious for partaking in things that I didn't want any part of, but I couldn't put into words just how good he made me feel. Physically and mentally.

"I know." I wanted to crawl under a blanket and sleep for years. It was a realization that I hated. Reese had slept with more women than residents I'd cared for. I can't get the picture out of my mind. Even the thought of his mystery 'Brooklynn' makes my stomach churn. "You need to make up your mind." Kayla ordered, pulling into my complex.

I have nothing intelligent to say. No answer for the way I feel. I'm a terrible person.

"I love you. Now get outta my car." She weakly smiled in my direction.

I dump my whites first, moving the basket under a table. "Wait, wait, wait." Timothy catches me off guard, opening the washer back up. "That was a close one." He pulled out a red bra, holding it comfortably like he bought it for me. "My hero." I snickered, taking it from him. Right place, right time. It was his legacy; Timothy was always there to help. I wasn't sure if I could say the same for Reese.

Did he even know how to use the washing machine? Let alone sort the colors from the whites?

"I wouldn't call myself a hero, but I won't stop you from saying it." Timothy teased, leaning back against the folding table. "You're an idiot." I smirked at his stance. He had this smugness about him that I didn't recognize. Like he was trying to put on an act for me. "How was your shopping?" I asked, digging out quarters from my purse.

The vending machine has carried the same snacks in it over the last ten years. Chips, candy, pretzels. Timothy stood close behind me as I sighed, deciding which snack to get this week. "Just get the Starburst, Kid."

I shoot him a playful glare. He did know me better than I knew myself. Where there were no gummy sharks, a Starburst would do just fine. I slide the quarters in, selecting A4. I turn back to the table, ripping the thick plastic wrapping.

"Damn, no reds." I sighed. Cherry was my favorite flavor. I loved everything with the flavor. Medicine, candy, drinks. I even earned the nickname Maraschino from my father growing up. As I was often caught in the fridge late at night with a jar of them.

My eyes watch as Tim crams his hand in his jeans, pulling out a dollar and some change. "Can't have that, can we?" He gave a lazy grin as the retro machine coiled, releasing my second pack of Starburst. "Thanks." I smiled, cracking the second pack. Two reds, out of twelve possibilities. "Damn, Tess. You want me to get a third? I just gotta run to my car." Tim pats himself down in search of his keys. "No, it's fine. I think I'll survive." I giggled, opening the candy. It was sticky and sweet, only a little stale, making my mouth salivate. Timothy snagged an orange flavor from the table. It made my brows crinkle with a smile. "A little old, huh?" He chewed with his eyes pinched shut as I nodded, struggling with the hardened texture myself.

"You never told me how long you're here for." I spoke with a wet mouth, swallowing my flavored spit as I sat on the counter. Timothy sighed, leaning back against the metal folding table. "I hadn't planned on staying too long. Until I remembered your birthday coming up." He smiled, grabbing another orange candy. My birthday was still weeks away, but I nodded. It was never a big deal. Kelseigh was born in November; we typically shared a party.

Timothy, however, made every birthday about me.

"What's on the agenda?" He looked up at me as I shook my head. "Work. Then probably sleep." I snickered. It was all I really had time for anymore. Had I really given up on a social life this soon? The most exciting part of my 'special' day was a complimentary latte at Starbucks. "You're killing me, Tess." Timothy groaned, his head falling back to view the ceiling. My head tilts to the side a little, enjoying the aerial view of him. It's as if I'm straddling him. The way his lips are parted, and his eyes are softly shut. I imagine the moans he'd let out, if they were the same as when we were young. Surely, they'd be huskier, manlier.

"Right?" His voice made me jump. I hadn't any idea what he was talking about.

"Right." I agreed to something I was unaware of. "Dinner it is."

"When?" I asked, curiously.

"On your birthday, dummy." His tone implies that I wasn't listening, which was true. His brows showed confusion as I nodded. "Oh, yeah. Duh, my birthday." I giggled, sheepishly.

It seemed like no time had passed until the washer buzzed. I brushed the loose curls from my face. My hair was at its most awkward length with the few strands that weren't long enough to reach my claw clip. "I'm gonna get a drink, do you want anything?" Tim asked, walking back to the vending machine. I shook my head, pulling my sopping clothes out and moving them to the nearest dryer.

When I turned back, there is a Diet Coke on the table. "I said I didn't want anything."

"You think I'm gonna fall for that?" Timothy grinned, making my heart flutter. Kindness was so thoughtless to him, he acted so nonchalant. Yet it was the sweetest thing.

My phone begins to vibrate, Reese is calling. I sent him to voicemail as I am actually enjoying my time with Timothy. "Can I ask you something?" I turn to face him, my legs crossed on the folding table. "Shoot." He replies with raised brows.

"How do you feel about Gary?"

I snicker at the deep groan Tim lets out. "You mean my step grandpa? God, the thought of him laying with my mom just grosses me out." We both laugh, like it's the way to cope with Tim's life. "Do you think she loves him?" The question falls out of my mouth, and I want to cram it back in like a genie in a bottle. He looks up at me, his eyes soft and I see the soul of the boy who got his braces off, sitting inches from me on his basement floor.

"I like to think so," Timothy sighed, a brief look of hesitation passed on his face before he continued speaking. "But love is just..." He trails off a bit, lost for words as he stares at my lips. The way his eyes meet mine again sends a warm feeling through my body. Like the soft brush of breath on my skin. Something about the way he stares at me makes my heart race, a flush creeping on the back of my neck.

"Love is a feeling. You just know it when you see it."

I nod, turning my attention back to the toppling dryer. My phone vibrates again, and I groan. "I gotta take this." I hop down from the counter and Timothy nods, clearing his throat.

"What?"

"There's no way you're still doing laundry."

"Reese, I've been here an hour." I sighed, pacing the broken tile flooring. "Just bring it here, I need to see you." He whined over the line; I feel my stomach flutter in the same way it does when I long for him. "I can't do that."

"He's there, isn't he?" I can hear the smirk on his face. "No."

"Yes, he is." Reese's laugh is low, as if he's being inconspicuous. "No, I'm alone." I look at Tim from the corner of my eye, he's watching the small box television playing reruns of Walker Texas Ranger.

"Then who's standing at the table you were sitting on?" His voice comes out in a growl, a twinge of jealousy in his tone. "Are you watching me?"

I jolted my attention out of the window, my lips parted in shock. "I had to make sure he kept his hands to himself." Reese chuckled, nodding his head from the Lincoln. I want to be mad; I want to hate him. "You're insane." I shook my head, using every muscle in my face to stop my smile. "Maybe." He sighed, wetting his lips and still looking in my direction.

"Jealousy isn't a good look for you, Mr. Finch." I reply, my voice dripping with sarcasm. "That doesn't change the fact that I don't like him around you." Reese shifts in the seat of his car as I roll my eyes.

"I have to go." I hung up the phone without waiting for his reply. I know I'll pay for it later.

Timothy is texting on his phone, and I let out a breath I didn't know I was holding. The last thing I wanted was for him to be suspicious. "Your clothes are done." His lips pulled into a tight smile, and I look to the basket of unfolded clothes. "You need help?"

"Nah, I'll do it later at home." I stretch before grabbing the basket by its handles. "Let me." He takes it from my grasp, and I sigh in relief. I truly couldn't carry its weight. "Lead the way, Daws." He grinned.

Twenty-Eight

REESE

I watch from my car as Timothy places Tessa's laundry in the back seat of her truck. The sun was near setting as I frowned, my headlights off to avoid suspicion. He stands so close to her; I want to run him over. I wet my lips, putting my right hand on the gear shifter. One wrong move and I'll fucking do it.

He opens the driver door for her, and I adjust my grip on the top of the steering wheel. My body is full of rage as her back is to the faded black paint and he stands toe to toe with her. I can't tell what they're saying, the nightlife is too loud. Tessa twiddles her fingers, looking mindlessly at her hands. I can tell she's uncomfortable. I put the car in drive, if he moves an inch closer, it's all over.

She looks up at him, her lips parted as he leans down and does the unspeakable. I watch her nervous hands move to his cheeks, and my chest burns. That should be me pulling her in for a kiss. I've never felt her lips on mine and now some other dude is touching her, tasting her saliva. It's not fair. I try to contain myself, but it's all too much. My rage burns bright as I clench the steering wheel harder, ready to do something to tear them apart. I want her for myself.

But if I make a scene, she'll hate me forever.

I sped past them, flooring it back to Tessa's apartment. I hope she got the message, my anger toward her. It's only minutes later when I receive a text from her.

7:13 P.M.
T- i'm guessing you saw that.
R- What do you think?
T- typing...

She doesn't reply. I hope she's relishing in guilt. My eyes are burning, am I gonna fucking cry? I wait upstairs at her complex. I wanna break the door down and destroy everything she owns. The temptation is more than I can bear. I put both hands on the door frame.

"Reese?" Her voice is soft and velvety behind me as I lift my leg. I'm frozen. "Were you about to kick my door in?"

"No." I blankly replied, caught in my tracks. I wet my lips, eyes darting around in embarrassment. "Can we talk inside, please?" She places a warm hand on my back sliding around to crouch between me and the door. "Not until you wash Timmy out of your fucking mouth." She keeps her back turned to me as one hand holds her basket against her hip and the other unlocks the front door.

"It was one kiss."

She's so nonchalant. I want to tear her down, call her names. "Yeah, I saw that." I wet my lips; my fists clenched. I could punch a hole in this dreary apartment wall, and no one would care. She places the basket on her kitchen counter and turns to stand in front of me. She pries my left fist open, tracing the lines in my sweating palm. "Deep breath." She runs her index finger across the longest line, and I inhale through my nose. I hate listening to her, but it makes me feel so good. *She* makes me feel so fucking good.

"There." She whispered, my right hand releasing by itself. "Let's talk."

I don't want to talk. I want to yell. I want to tell her how much she hurt me. Yet, I have no foot to stand on. If Tessa knew that I was up to my neck in shit with Brooklynn, I'd be the one getting screamed at.

She pulls me to her couch, sitting with her knees to her chest, her back to the arm. I stare straight ahead, my arms folded as I cannot set aside my anger. "Timothy and I kissed." She breaks the silence and I scoff. "Thanks for reminding me." My voice is attacking but Tess doesn't even flinch. "Our past is complicated." She continues.

I roll my eyes; I've heard that before. Hell, I've used that before. I open my mouth to speak, and she cuts me off.

"It's my turn to talk, Reese." I'm silenced like a dog who'd been hit on the nose with a newspaper. "I met Timothy when I was twelve. By 14, we were young, dumb and in love." She giggled. I wanted to be baptized in the sound of her laughter. "We dated all throughout high school, and only really broke up when he went down south for school." I watch her expression change, one that I cannot read. She's trying to hide it, but I know she's still hung up over it.

"Why?"

"I was still only going into my junior year. Long distance never works for kids." Tess pitifully laughed, and I found myself feeling empathetic to her situation. I'd never been in love. At least not in the way she had. I had love for my friends, and my mom wherever she was. But Tessa had felt real love, heartbreak and everything in between. I was jealous.

"So, you wanna be with him." I tried filling in the blanks, beating myself to the punchline. "I don't know what I want," She clutched her arms around her legs, her chin on her knees. "It was just a kiss." Tessa whispered, not feeling the magnitude of her words.

"It's not just a kiss, Tess." I scoffed, turning my body to face hers.

"I mean, you won't kiss me, so why does it matter if he will?" Her voice pushes the air from my lungs. I can't think straight. Won't kiss her? I wanted to *maul* her every second of the day. But kissing seemed so much more intimate than sex to me. So serious, so much more devoted. I just couldn't do it, not without ruining everything between us. "Yeah, you've got a point. Timmy's the perfect guy, isn't he?" I mocked, leaning back against the sofa once more. God, I hated myself.

I watch the color leave her face and I'm left with a stomach full of guilt. I wanted to drown her in kisses, lick the tears that were begging to escape. Now wasn't the time for that. I'd overstayed my welcome.

"I'm sorry, Tessa." I muttered, wanting to grovel at her feet. "I know." Her reply is a dagger. Not a single petty argument has ever been forgiven, only acknowledged. Tess wets her lips, a sniffle filling the silence as she stands to her feet. "Well, I have a basket that needs tending to."

She puts on the fakest voice, trying to hide her emotions. I've fucked up royally. I may as well prepare to raise the family with Brooklynn that she's blackmailing me for.

"Tessa," I groaned, following her back to the kitchen. "Goodnight, Reese." She waved her hand in my direction, avoiding my gaze. "I'm not leaving." My voice is broken, I'm trying not to cry. "Please go." She licked the tears from her lips. "No, not until you listen to me."

I clear my throat, desperately trying to rid myself of the lump that is obstructing me.

"What, Reese?" Her face is full of defeat. The anger burns behind my eyes in pools of tears. I don't deserve her, but neither does Tim. I feel like I can't breathe. "I have wanted to kiss you since I met you two fucking years ago." My cheeks turn red as the memories flood back to me.

"I even remember the scrubs you wore when you helped me move my dad's shit into his apartment. I remember how you introduced yourself to us. And all I thought was how beautiful you were. Hell, I could only stare at your lips the whole time you talked!" I run my hands over my face in defeat. She'd won, I'll fold every single time.

"If you want me to kiss you, I'll fucking do it, Tess. I'll *beg* on my knees just to feel your lips on mine."

The way my voice came out in a whine had to make me look pathetic. I'm a mess. But I didn't care, I'd do anything for her.

"I don't." She whispered. Bullshit, I knew her better than this. If she meant it, the door would be open already.

"Yes, you do." My voice was low as I took a step closer, leaving no gap between us. She wouldn't look at me, she'd cave if she did. I take her chin between my thumb and index, lifting it to my gaze. "Look at me, baby." Her big, doe eyes flicker to meet me and I'm star struck. I'm drawn in without warning and left stunned in her brilliance. I can't stop staring at her, the stars are aligning, and we are bound for eternity.

I watch her chest rise and fall in pattern, my hands moving to her neck and my thumbs on her jaw. I want to say something romantic, something to knock her off her feet.

"Kiss me."

The words fall out of my mouth, and she doesn't hesitate. She tastes as sweet as she smells, her lips are soft and smooth. I never want to come up for air. My tongue quickly finds hers as I push her against the front door. Her arms scramble around my neck, her fingers tangling in the loose curls at the base of my hair. I take this as my cue to grip her thighs from underneath, scooping her up and around my waist. The blood is pumping to every part of my body except my brain, I'm going to faint from the euphoria.

My lips break from hers. I trail down her neck, sucking and biting at the skin. I feel just how much she craved this as she takes my head in her hands, pulling me back up to meet her lips. "I fucking need you, baby." I moan into her mouth, her nails scraping the back of my neck.

Tess nods, unable to form any words. I'm so fucking weak for her. I could cum right now.

I tightened my grip around her before backing away from the door. I look down the hall, one way is the bathroom, the other is her bedroom.

If I make it beyond that door, I swear I'll change my ways, God.

Tessa crams her tongue back in my mouth and I'm fully accepting. I use my left leg, kicking the door open with one good jolt. We watch as the knob falls on the ground. I can't control my laughter as Tessa's jaw drops. "I still live here, you know!" She giggled through her words.

"I'll pay someone to fix it, just stop talking." I press my lips back against hers, only separating to lower her on the bed. I crawl to rest on my knees between her legs and we waste no time stripping our shirts. I let out a sigh, my voice shaky with anticipation. "You are so beautiful, baby. *Jesus fucking Christ.*" I kiss her swiftly before moving my lips down her jaw, then to her sternum. Kissing her is like a gateway drug. Now that I've started, I can't stop.

She responds in purrs and moans, and I know I'm doing something right.

"Reese," She pants, pushing me lower by my shoulders. I know what she wants. I'm the only man to do that for her. I could bet my inheritance, or lack thereof, on the fact that Timothy would never make her feel the way I do. I helped her lift her bottom from the bed, stripping her shorts down and off her ankles. Moving my shoulders between her legs, I run my nose against her thong as she moans. "Is *this* what you want, princess?" I snickered. Tessa claws at the sheets as I hold back my devilish grin. "More, Reese." She whined as I kissed the area between her thighs and underwear. I shook my head no, refusing her the pleasure that she wanted so badly.

Tessa hooks her silky legs around my neck, the smell of coconut and vanilla invading my senses. "Please, Reese." She was begging, desperate for me. The tables have turned. My eyes raked over her reaction, her back arching as my hands tugged the material off her hips. "I'm so obsessed with you. Everything you do, Tessa Ann." I teasingly kiss the soft skin around her entrance between my words as she groans. Her left hand is in my hair, I can feel it trembling. I spread her open, blowing cool air against her.

I run my tongue along her opening, watching her breath hitch from the best seat in the house. I lap over her clit, savoring the flavor. Her thighs twitch, tightening her grip around me as a loud moan escaping her lips. "Does he make you feel this good, Tessa?" I asked in a taunting tone, my jealousy peaking as I'm reminded of their kiss when I shut my eyes. She shakes her head 'no' quickly, unable to form words.

"Does Tim know where you like to be touched?" I slip my middle finger inside her, pumping in and out slowly. I relish the way her eyes roll back, her back arching. Tessa shakes her head again, but it's not enough for me. "Use your words, baby."

"N-no." She stammered out, gripping the bed sheets tighter. "Do you crave him the way you crave fucking me?" I practically force my ring finger in beside my middle, her walls are tight around me like a warm, wet, vice grip.

"Holy fuck, no." Her body practically jolts from the bed, and I move my fingers faster, leaning down to reward myself with the liquid lust that was flooding her. I pull her clit back into my mouth, growling and sucking as she convulses around my fingers. She can't take much more but I'm nowhere near done with her.

I retract myself, sitting back on my knees. Her body is lifeless, on the brink of expulsion. I smirk, looking at the shiny, sticky honey on my skin. I've never been more addicted to a taste. I suck them clean, and she looks at me with longing. "Do you know how fucking good you taste?" I asked, my voice low as her head shakes softly. I wet my lips, my chin still dripping with her. "Do you *want* to know?" My brow raised as I spoke to her with a curious whisper, almost like speaking to a lost puppy. My fingers slide up and down her wet, silky, skin before pushing back inside.

I am in awe when she nods. Never in my life did I peg Tessa as this type of girl. I'd slept with just about every single woman in New York. Not even one had this desire. My lips curl into a devious smile as Tess sits up, hands on either side of the bed. "Open up, princess. Taste how good I made you feel." She sucks my fingers clean, and my head falls back. "Fuck," My voice is weak, nearly a whimper as I unhook my belt with my free hand. I tug my pants down vigorously, my eyes struggling to open.

"That's my girl." I pull my fingers out of her glistening mouth. "I *love* when you do what you're told." I looked down at her, stroking my dick as her eyes were glossed with innocence. "Now lay on your stomach, baby."

Of course she does what I tell her.

I tightly grab her hips, pulling her back to meet mine as a whimper escapes her lips. I slide my length between her lips and my eyes roll back again. I have to stay focused.

Twenty-Nine

REESE

Focus. Focus. Don't finish yet.

It's so hard, watching her body contort to me, her stomach pressed to the sheets as her back arches to an angle. I can't believe it. I take her hand and wrap it behind her, pushing her into the mattress. My right hand keeps her in rhythm by the waist with every thrust. Our bodies are drenched in sweat, my heart is going to explode. I'm completely buried inside her and she's taking every inch like a champion. I don't even recognize her.

The sounds that fill the humid air are primal as I graze her cervix. She's everything I've ever wanted.

I want to tell her. Tell her how crazy she makes me. But I cannot seem to find words as my tongue hangs slightly out of my mouth. I'm so close in a matter of minutes. I pull her up against me with the hand I'm holding, moving my right that was once on her waist to her throat. I pinch slightly at the sides, just enough to weaken the blood flow for her pleasure. She's a puddle on my dick and I love every second of it.

"You're taking it so well, baby. Breathe." I whisper in her ear as her head falls back to rest on my shoulder. Our bodies are becoming one, glued by the perspiration exuding our pores. Her curls are wet as I move myself slowly, feeling myself release in her. "There you go, princess. Breathe with me."

She tightens around my length, finishing at the same time as me. We're connected in more ways than physically.

I pull myself out and she falls slowly to the bed. "That was-" Her body is still twitching as traces of me leak from her onto her sheets. I smirk, crawling off the bed and watching her gather her thoughts.

"Come on." I extended a hand for her to take. "Go take a shower, I'll get you some clothes and join you." She nods, allowing me to pull her up. I watch her head for the door, but not before my heart takes over my mind.

I grabbed her by the arm, turning her around to face me. My hands move to her cheeks, rubbing the glazed skin, my forehead inches from hers as I crouch to her eye line. I planted a soft kiss on her lips, with no intent besides showing her how much I wanted to change for her. A soft moan escapes her lips, her arms linking around my neck for a moment.

"Now you can go." I smiled, breaking our kiss and nodding my head toward the door. Her eyes glimmered looking up at me, I was one step farther than Timothy. I was still in the running for her heart.

When I returned to the bathroom, it's already full of steam. I pause, admiring the way the water beaded down her body. She hums gently under her breath, her eyes shut in tranquility. I quietly folded her clothes, setting them on the sink and smiled.

Tessa blushes, moving to cover her body as I climb in behind her. I don't understand why, she's the most beautiful thing I've ever laid eyes on. I spin her to face me, the water dripping down the back of her hair and drenching her curls flat. She looks so different with straight hair. I love it, but it doesn't compare to the mess I'm used to. Our smiles are childish, giddy even, as this is the most intimate I'd ever been with anyone. I can't help but wonder if she felt the same.

I kiss her nose, and her eyes shut. The water beads off her long lashes. The butterflies want to be freed from my stomach. When she opens her eyes again, the look of innocence is beaming up at me. I'm reminded of just how small she stands in comparison.

"Can I wash your hair?" Tessa asked with a loving smile, and I wonder what she's up to. I can't stop my brows from lowering in confusion. "Why?" I responded with a mild frown, as if I didn't really trust her.

She answers with a shrug, and I nod, turning my back to her. I tilt my head and feel her soapy fingers work into my hair. She massages and scratches my scalp. My lip quivers as I moan under my breath, a reaction I could never really hide from her. I close my eyes, consenting to letting her do whatever she wants to me. Her touch is intoxicating. I've broken all my rules of intimacy for her.

And I'm in love with her.

September 14th,

I'm sleeping so peacefully. I've never felt this type of relaxation. I can feel Tess's heart beating against my bare chest. She breathes softly through her nose as I become more aware of my surroundings. A vibration is coming from nearby. I crack my eyes; her leg is draped over me and she's cuddled under my right arm in the same position we fell asleep in. I can't hide my smile as my hand lazily caresses her side and rests on her hip. The smell of her shampoo lingers in my senses as I rub my eyes.

I lift my head a little, my phone flashes on the end table. I stretch for it slowly, trying to keep from waking her up as Brice's name fills my screen.

"What's up?" I whisper into the line, peering my head down to see she hasn't moved.

"Do you not check your messages, dude?" There's a sheer panic in his voice and it makes my brows furrow. "Hold on." I mumble, sliding my arm out from under Tessa.

Something in my mind tells me to look at her once more before leaving the room. As if I need to memorize the image of her tanned skin, wrapped in her white comforter. Her arm is still over my half of the bed. I take a deep breath, wanting to remember this forever.

I close the bathroom door behind me, putting Brice on speaker. "What the fuck are you talking about?" I asked, checking my messages. "Were you gonna tell me you knocked up Brooklynn?"

"What are you talking about? She's not-"

My mouth goes dry, I open the text image as he rambles. I can't hear him; the world is underwater. It's an image of Brooklynn and I outside of my car, grabbing a pregnancy test from the ground.

"I'm gonna be sick." I mumble. My chest is burning, my heart beating faster than I can contest. "Fuck," I place the phone on the sink, running my hands over my face. "Pull the picture." I tell Brice. I'm begging. My life is about to be ruined with the work of one person.

I wasn't crazy. I knew what I saw that night.

"You know I don't have that power, man." Brice's voice is sympathetic. I can't believe it. I've single handedly fucked myself over. "Brice, please." My voice cracks as I wet my lips. "She'll never speak to me again." A lump fills my throat as I feel my dinner trying to leave my stomach. "Who, Brooklynn?"

"Tessa."

Brice sighs. "The best I can do is hold off a few days." I nod, as if he could hear it. My mind is scrambling, leaping for any type of solution I can come up with.

"Give me until Thursday." I opened my bank app as I waited for his answer. After Brooklynn drained me of my last six hundred dollars, I was flat fucking broke. It's not the smartest thing I've ever done, but it'll have to do. Maurice. "I'll try, you know how my mom is." He groaned. Having mommy as his boss had its perks, I'm sure. But destroying his best friend's life was probably not one of them. I hang the phone up without another word and I'm shaking.

I turn the faucet on, splashing cold water on my face. It feels like needles against my skin, and I deserve it. I deserve to feel this shitty. The reflection of the man looking back at me is one I don't recognize. I feel like a loser. The biggest piece of shit on the planet. I should have been honest with her. She would have understood then. It was too late now.

The door creaks as I crack it open. I slide my jeans back on. Tessa is curled into a ball on her half of the bed as I climb in on top of her. I kiss her bare shoulders, then her neck, working my way to my new favorite place.

"Mm..." She groaned against my lips, trying to stay asleep. "I'm gonna take off, princess." I whispered to her, kissing her once more. Her lazy arms wrapped around my neck. "Stay." Tess pouted, finally opening her big, brown eyes. I hated telling her no. I would break my own leg if she asked me. "I can't, Tess." I smirked, leaning in to kiss her once more. I let my tongue casually drift in her mouth, memorizing the taste of her in case it's the last time. "Is everything okay?" Her voice is soft as she pulls back. I didn't realize my hands were still shaking.

I sigh, wanting to word vomit. Instead, I wet my lips and nodded. "I'm gonna go visit with my dad." Her eyes went wide, surprised that I would go see him without malicious intent. "Do you want me to come with you?" she offered, tucking a loose strand of my hair back. I wanted to collapse on top of her and stay in bed all day. I shake my head, kissing her forehead.

"It's your day off, enjoy it. Just not with Timothy." I teased with a wink. "Or there will be repercussions." I smirked, running my nose along the crook of her neck as she giggled. "You're an idiot."

"Yeah, I know." I climbed off her, grabbing my shirt from the floor. I watched her snuggle back in her sheets, without a care in the world. With the assumption that I was a good person.

Thirty

REESE

I held the handle to Maurice's apartment so tight my knuckles turned white, my right hand on my hip. Why was this so damn hard for me?

"Hello?" His voice is croaky, calling from around the corner as I step inside. I don't recognize him. His body is practically lifeless in the hospice bed. The moisture leaves my mouth, making its way to my eyes. My father was dying, and he wouldn't even look in my direction.

"Hey." I muttered, giving a subtle wave.

"I'm not giving you any money." He coughed between words, the sound like nails on a chalkboard. I cringed, knowing full well why I was here. "It's not for me." I rub the back of my neck, strenuously. "It's for Tess."

Maurice's attention turns fully in my direction, no longer to the black and white sitcoms on the muted television. "Is she alright?" He whispered.

"Her birthday is coming up." I sighed as Maurice clearly didn't care about hurting *my* feelings. "I want to do something nice for her." I sit on the small recliner, my elbows on my thighs as I stare at him. "You should have money in your account, Reese." He argued back, every sentence labored by death's rattle in his lungs.

"Yeah, well, I fucked up, dad." This was as far into my admittance as I'd like to get with him. I didn't owe him an explanation. "I already have a check for her birthday." Maurice pinched the bridge of his nose with what strength he had left, and I wanted to break his fingers.

"It's not enough. You know better than anyone that she deserves a damn vacation from this place." I retorted. I figured I'd skip out on the part where I was in love with her. It would only make things worse in his eyes. If he was younger, not by much, Tessa would be another prize. Just like my mother was. He would have her for himself.

Maurice stared at me for a moment, he knew there were no flaws in my logic.

He sighed, weakly pointing to his bedside table. "I'll fill it out." I offered, knowing the odds of him holding a pen at this point were slim. Maurice nods, reclining his bed again. I open the checkbook, the first one is blank, yet they are all pre-signed. I glance at my father whose eyes are shut. I could drain him of everything, and he'd never know. But I've got enough bad karma stacked against me. I address the check to myself, writing in an unnecessary, yet unalarming, amount. I want to thank him, but in my fucked-up mind, this is owed to me. He owes me everything.

I watch him fall back into his comatic sleep. I imagine I'm at his funeral.

I'm wearing black, Tessa is at my side. She's crying and I can't muster a single word. We stand around his casket as it's lowered into the ground. It's only us, everyone else is gone. I put my arm around her waist as she buried her head in my chest. My button down is soaked in her tears. I can't look down; I stare straight ahead. The priest mumbles some bullshit that no one cares about and Maurice sure as hell didn't believe in. And I don't feel sad. I don't feel anything for him.

I drove straight back to my apartment after depositing the check. I open my laptop, pulling up flights to an island in the Maldives. I'd been there with my friends in the past, it was secluded but not enough to raise concern. They were a decade behind as far as technology went, buying me enough time to explain myself to Tessa. I booked first-class tickets, and a bungalow overlooking the water, walking distance from the bar. She'd love it. Tranquility, solitude and relaxation.

I'll convince her to leave her phone behind.

There'll be no distractions or connections to the outside world.

I close the laptop and sigh, running my hands over my face. I am a bad person, but I'm doing what I have to do to keep her safe from my fuck up. I pull out my phone and check my bank account again, releasing a comfortable sigh at the number of zeros looking back at me. A notification drops down from Brice.

1:01 P.M.
B- I pulled the pic until Thursday.
R- I owe you.
B- Lunch?

I grab my keys, wasting no time. If Brice wanted caviar and wagyu for lunch, I'd be more than obliged. At this rate, I owed him everything I had left in my bank. Brice had covered for me so many times in life. He convinced his mom to pull several covers of the Stripe. I was a hot commodity, always out and about in things I shouldn't have been. His mom would have financially retired on the summer of my 21st birthday if it weren't for him. I was always moved to page six, but at least it wasn't the cover. His friendship lies deep. Third grade deep.

I sat at my desk, my bottom lip quivering as everyone dumped their school supplies in their new desks. Mom begged Maurice for help with back-to-school shopping. He gave her forty dollars and told her to leave before he called the cops. The problem was, my toes were beginning to grow out of my shoes, my jeans were now floods and I was wearing her coworker's kid's shirts.

Brice reached into his backpack, pulling out half of the rainbow in markers, crayons and colored pencils. "Here, man." He smiled, missing his two front teeth. I nod, closing my desk. My embarrassment was palpable, but Brice didn't even flinch. He understood my frustration without even knowing who I was. And from that day on, we looked out for each other. I beat up anyone who merely breathed in his direction and he answered my midnight phone calls when life was too hard for me to bear.

"So, she got an abortion?" Brice asked, cramming a wad of fries in his mouth. My eyes darted around the small burger joint, hoping no one heard his casual tone. I shrug, truly I didn't know the answer or how that works. She needed six hundred dollars to deal with this and I handed it over without any questions. I can still taste my vomit as she handed me the positive pregnancy test. "You don't know?"

"She said she was gonna take care of it. I trust her."

Brice nodded, looking at my untouched food. I lacked an appetite today. "She definitely didn't want the baby." I continue building my case for reasons I was unsure of. "What about you?" He asked.

I felt like I was being interviewed.

I scoffed at his question, though I hadn't thought about it before. "Of course not." I laughed, my mind dreaming at the thought of being trapped in a relationship with Brooklynn. I'm raising a baby with someone I only used for sex. The next eighteen years of my life are forced into a marriage, paying for college scholarships and sports. She'd end up with her mother's addiction and my arrogance.

It wasn't a dream; it was a nightmare.

"And Tessa?" Brice raised a brow, knowing that I wasn't sure how to fix that part of my problem. I let a sigh become my answer. "Why don't you just tell her?"

I snort, it would never be that easy. Tessa wouldn't understand, nor would she forgive me for keeping it from her. I shake my head, forcing myself to take a bite. I chew slowly, letting myself mull over a response.

"Tess is not the type of girl to take Brooklynn's pregnancy lightly. And I like her too much to fuck that up." I spoke with a mouth full, hoping the food dulled my anxious tone. "So, you'd rather lie to her and hurt her more?"

I rolled my eyes, that was a little far-fetched.

The last thing I wanted to do was hurt Tessa. "I just need to buy myself time." More like, secure her love for me before I drop the A-bomb on her. "You really like her?" Brice sat back, folding his arms with a grin. My interview had become an interrogation. Of course I liked her. I loved her. I thought of no one else. She made me crazy.

"Yeah." I nod, my stomach refusing another bite of my burger. Brice sighed, sucking his teeth. "Then I hope you don't ruin this, man."

Brice and I part ways, I close my car door. My head rests on the steering wheel, and I want to thrash myself against it. I pull out my phone, chewing the dried skin on my lip as I look at her name in my contacts. I can't do it. I can't tell her about this. I look at the flashing light of the mini mart up ahead. I need a fucking drink.

"You're Finch's boy, right?" the cashier asks. He appeared Maurice's age, withered and hardly hanging on. I simply nod, pulling out my card. "Just for you?" He questioned in a croaky voice, pointing to my handle of vodka. I nod again, avoiding his gaze as I wait for him to take my card. "I thought I recognized you from somewhere." He sighed, shaking his head as he placed my liquor in a brown, paper bag. He was definitely referring to my shining cover of the Stripe in 2018, one Brice couldn't move to page six.

I snatch the bag from the counter, my chest burning with anger, and begin walking the streets. The vodka goes down smoother than I'd like to admit. It's comforting like the chirping of birds in the morning.

The numbness seeps to my bones, and I feel my body relax The burn in my chest disappears, but my anger remains. I'm feeling dizzy as I peruse the streets; I wish I could turn my brain off. I don't want to think about her for five minutes. I'm begging myself to stop as thunder rolls around me. For a moment, my thoughts are muted.

I swig again, looking at the setting sun and envisioning its fading warmth as Tessa's love. I close my eyes, remembering the feeling of her laugh last night, wrapping around me tighter than any hug I'd ever received.

"Put me down!" She squealed, kicking her feet against my stomach. I carried her into her kitchen, setting her on the counter. "Not until you try this." I brought over the pot of my concoction sauce made with ingredients she had. "Please, don't make me do this." She laughed, covering her mouth. "Tessa, I worked so hard on this." I laughed back, placing the pot on the counter. I move both hands on either side of her bare legs. There was nothing sexier than when she wore nothing but my shirt. "Come on, baby. For me?" I smirked, rustling my nose against hers. "Fine." She covered her eyes, and I went for the spoon, ladling my mysterious red sauce up. I watch her lick the remnants off her lips and her face pucker. "Reese, I need you to never enter this kitchen again." She giggled, uncovering her face. I can't help but bellow in laughter, my face red and my stomach hurting. "It can't be that bad." I slurp myself some off the spoon and gag. Her laugh replays in my mind like a record stuck on repeat.

I almost had fucking everything.

"Reese Finch! Over here!"

I groan, hearing the yelling of paparazzi. His camera flashes in my eyes "Leave me alone, man. Please." I put my free hand up, shaking my head. "What's in the bag, Finch?" He asked, his camera in my face. "Just back up, please." I repeat more forcefully. I push the guy back and he stumbles. He's quick to mimic my actions and I drop my near empty handle. "Are you fucking kidding me?"

I grab the man by the shirt. "I told you to leave me the fuck alone." I growled through my teeth, raising my fist. Another camera flashes from my left, a punch meets between my eyes.

I land on my ass, blinking hard as blood rushes from my nose. The man says something, but Earth is spinning on a different axis than I'm aware of. Just another thing for my dying father to hate me for. My heart is racing, tears in my eyes as I'm left on the sidewalk, drunk and lost.

I'm finding it hard to breathe. I blink rapidly, feeling as though I'm about to explode, like my throat is closing on me. My lungs are empty and being squeezed like lemons, my breaths come in short gasps. There is a dagger in my chest. I'm about to lose control. I crawl onto the park bench, pulling out my now cracked phone.

"Hello?" Her voice is like a weighted blanket in my panic. It's warm and light, unsuspecting of my anxiety.

"Hey," I reply, my voice shaky and slurring. The line is full of static as she thinks of something to say. I'm staring at my lap, the keys to my hidden car rattling in my vibrating free hand. "Is everything alright?" Tessa asks softly, and I nod as if she can hear it.

"Reese?" My head lowers and tears fall.

Thirty-One

TESSA

"I'm here." His voice mumbles into the line, I close my laptop and sit up in bed. "Are you drunk?"

"Tess, you're the only good thing I've got in my life. And I'm sorry I fucked that up." My brows furrowed in confusion. My question is indirectly answered. "Reese, you didn't fuck anything up. Where are you?" I grab my keys and head for the door. "I don't know, baby. I'm just really fucking sorry." His voice is shaky, followed by heavy tears. I look up at the ceiling, praying for a sign. "What's around you?"

He sniffles, remaining silent. "A taco truck."

"Does it smell terrible?" I asked with a soft grin, already suspecting where he was at. "Like absolute shit." He cried, taking a labored breath. "Stay where you are." I sighed, hanging up the phone.

Soft raindrops turn to downpour as I fly down busy streets to meet him. I squint, my wipers in overdrive as I see him lying on a bench. "Shit." I mumble.

"Reese!" I call, though he doesn't move. I rush over to him as the rain drenches my curls. "Reese, come on." I pull on his jacket, but he is dead weight. "I said leave me alone, man!" He jolts from my grip. His angered voice makes me wince in fear. Someone had pushed him in some way.

"Tess? I'm so sorry, baby." He sits up sloppily, wrapping his hands around my waist so tight I can hardly breathe. "Reese, it's pouring. Let's go." I try to pull him up, seeing remnants of dried blood on his face as he shakes his head. "I'm sorry, okay? Can you just forgive me one time?"

I look at him with confusion. I had no idea what he was talking about. "Let's go." I lifted his head to meet my gaze. "Not until you forgive me."

"I forgive you. Now let's go, baby." I sigh, still puzzled about what he meant. Reese nods, rising to his wobbly legs. I open the truck door and he plops in. The entire vehicle reeks of liquor and wet clothes. I drive with my right hand, my left rests on the window sill and cradles my head. The only noise is his breathing and rain hitting the windshield. I occasionally glance back at him until we approach his apartment.

"Come on, big guy." I flash a comforting smile, the last thing I want to do is make him think I'm upset. I know how his relationship with Maurice is, I was in no position to change or try to fix it. We would talk about his visit in the morning. "You're the best girlfriend ever, you know that?" He slurred with a lazy grin and my eyes went wide. He'd never exchanged that label, nor was I sure that's what I wanted anymore. "Yeah, okay." I giggled, letting it slide for the evening.

I get him in the elevator, our clothes sopping wet as we go to his floor.

"Next time, get drunk in a nice, dry bar, okay?" I teased, bumping his shoulder before stepping off. "No kidding." He snickered, taking my hand to lead him.

I took his keys and unlocked the front door, curious of where he may have left his car tonight.

"I'm fucking freezing." He groaned, trying to pull his soaking t-shirt off. "Here," I sigh, grabbing it by the bottom hem and lifting it over his head. His raven hair is disheveled and beading water on the ends. I look down at his chest, covered in goosebumps down to his navel. I swallow hard. This was not the time to feel the way I did. "Are you cold?" he asked with a smirk. "Don't worry about me." I giggled, walking down the hall to grab both towels and dry clothes.

I pull out an old Ramones shirt, and a pair of old sweats for me to wear home.

When I return with clothes and an ice pack for Reese's nose, he's opening a beer from the fridge in only his tight, white briefs. I swallow again with more difficulty as he turns to face me. His length is exposed through the thin cotton, and I try to adjust my gaze back to his face.

"You do not need this." I smirk, wringing my hair with the towel and taking the beer from him. "Come on." I guided him down the hall, taking him to his bedroom. "Get in." I pull the covers back and point to the silk sheets. "You first." He deviously grinned, taking slow steps in my direction. His hands met my hips as he leaned into me.

"Not with the way your breath smells." I put my index finger to his chest, stopping him from coming any closer. Reese rolls his eyes, taking my hand and pulling it down toward his briefs. "I'm serious." I batted my lashes up at him, an annoyed expression taking me over.

"So am I." His voice was low, and I felt my body buzz. My mouth went dry as I took a shaky breath. "I'm going home. But I'll call you in the morning." I smiled as he climbed into bed with a husky groan. "Don't leave." I can see behind his douchey mood, he means it. There's a different story in his bloodshot eyes. I can't make it out, but there's something more than I know.

"Scoot over. No funny business." I sternly ordered. Reese pulls me by my hips so that I am against his body with a grunt. His head burrows on the back of my neck, his body is freezing.

I can feel him absorbing all my warmth and I'm okay with it. I am the flame, and he is the moth. His breathing slows behind me as our eyes become heavy. I can't think, I'm powerless.

September 17th,

I spoon up Maurice's dinner, pureed turkey and mashed potatoes. He smashed it between his gums, seeming no longer able to wear his dentures. "This cannot be good." I snickered as Maurice rolled his eyes. "Terrible." He weakly muttered. I was growing concerned. Maurice slept most days, only awake in the evening for dinner. The nurses requested I come in twice a week to help him with dinner, as he refused for almost everyone else.

"Reese is really turning his life around." I smile, spooning another bite. Maurice attempts a laugh but falls short in a cough. It makes my brows crinkle; did he not believe that Reese could change his ways and become a 'responsible adult' as he once put it? "He's really trying." I sighed as Maurice decided not to comment. His feelings toward Reese were becoming more evident to me by the second. To treat your own son with such dismissal, my stomach filled with dread. I was lonesome for him. "Want me to turn on your shows?" I offered, lowering Maurice's bed back down. He simply nodded, getting more comfortable. I sigh at the familiar Gunsmoke theme, keeping it on a low volume. "See you tomorrow morning, Mr. Finch." I smiled, taking one last look before exiting the room.

"There's my girl." Reese smiled, sitting in a chair in the hall. "What are you doing here? It's not Thursday." My voice was full of confusion, though I was more than happy to see him. "Your nose looks better." I snickered, taking his chin in my hand as I looked down at him. Reese's nose was slightly purple, clearly the effects of a right hook. His hands met my hips, his fingers rubbing softly against the material of my scrubs. "Are you ready to tell me what happened?" I asked with a smirk.

He shook his head 'no', a soft grin reaching his lips. "Keep it up and I'll give you a shiner to match." I winked, moving my hands to the back of his neck. "Gimme a kiss, Rocky."

His hands pulled me in closer and I leaned down to meet his soft, supple lips. They parted gently, his tongue searching for mine. "I'm on the clock." I whispered into his mouth.

"Yeah, for like the next five minutes." Reese groaned against my lips; his brows raised in a pleading way. He was right. Reese had learned my schedule with all the time we'd spent together. It was strange, after our fight about Timothy, Reese had become the most intimate person I'd ever met. He always wanted to kiss me, touch me, or do anything to be near me. And I was the same. The second we'd part; I was begging to see him again.

"Go clock out, I have something for you." He smirked with a soft slap on my ass, causing my heart to jolt. "A surprise?" I giggled, taking a step back and pulling him up. "Yes, a surprise. Now go." His expression stayed the same as he twirled me away. I don't think I've ever run faster.

Reese is already waiting for me beside his car, the trunk is open as I step outside. "What is it?" I asked, my voice full of glee and excitement. I sounded like a child on Christmas. He motions to the trunk, and I hurry to his side. "A suitcase?" I asked, puzzled.

"A suitcase." He appears nervous, anxious even as he dries his hands against his thighs.

"For what?"

"You." He rubs a bead of sweat on his forehead. "Where am I going?" I'm almost afraid of the answer. I've never been more lost in my life. "The Maldives, for your birthday. We leave tomorrow night." He wets his lips, his brows low and I watch him swallow. "I can't just pack up and go on vacation, Reese... I- I have work." I'm spiraling. The thought of the hot beach and white sand was amazing but I couldn't abandon my priorities. "Tess, please." He begs, taking my hands. I shake my head, looking up at his expression that barricades the sun from my eyes. "You don't understand. I have bills and my residents need-"

Reese cuts me off, putting a calloused hand over my mouth. Not in a rough way, but in a gentle *please shut up* kind of way. "What do *you* need, Tessa? If you don't give yourself the break now, you never will." Reese speaks softly, leaning down to meet my gaze as I exhale through my nose.

His eyes are about to water, the whites becoming red as the tears cling to his dark lashes. "It's all paid for. All you have to do is say yes." He whispered, removing his hand slowly.

I stare at the beige and gold suitcase, running my fingers across its elegant designs.

"It *is* really pretty." I sigh, watching him move to stand behind me. "Let me give you what you deserve." He whispered against the top of my head before planting a kiss. "I don't even own a swimsuit." I lied, causing a smirk to bubble up. "Perfect. I'll pick one out for you." He teased, taking my hand and dragging me to the passenger door.

"What do I even pack?" I ask, sitting on my bedroom floor, surrounded by scattered clothing items as I prepare for the trip. Reese is on his side on my bed, his hand propping his head up as he grins at me. His smile was infectious, I always found myself mirroring it. Reese just had that effect on me, making me feel confident and attractive. "Whatever you want, baby." He says, his tone laid-back and casual. "That doesn't help me." I can't hide my pout. I hadn't been on a real vacation in years. Florida didn't count. We would stay at my grandma's beach house in the Hamptons every so often. And sure, I went to

California with Kelseigh once. But flying across the globe with Reese? That was so foreign.

"Well, I don't plan on keeping you dressed very much. So, it really doesn't matter." He shrugged again, giving me a wink. I throw a sandal in his direction, he ducks, and it hits my end table. "You're an idiot." I forced a scowl, turning back to my suitcase. "That's what I've heard." He rolled to his back and sighed. "You've got a whole day to pack. Why are we worried about it now?"

Men just didn't get it. I needed to pack now, so I could repack tomorrow. If I had known about this a week ago, I'd be on repack number three. "You wouldn't get it." I shake my head, choosing to save him the explanation. "You're right. Come get in bed." He ordered, pulling out his phone.

I ran my tongue over my top teeth, admiring the way his left hand rested under his head and the right held his phone against his sternum. I climb in the bed, moving to straddle his lap. He quickly locks the phone, tossing it to the side. "Do I have your undivided attention, Mr. Finch?" I giggled, feeling like a true priority to him. "Always, Ms. Dawson." His hands slid up my thighs, toying with the hem of my spandex. "Good, because I'm hungry." I snickered, taking his hands and interlacing his fingers with mine. I can feel his length flexing against my bottom as he tries to stay focused. "I can fix that."

"With food, I hope." I spoke sternly, hiding my creeping smile. "If you insist." Reese wet his lips and smirked. He didn't seem to think straight around me, and I loved that. I watched him shut his eyes as he thought. "P-Pizza?" He fumbled with his words, finding himself weaker than I suspected. I nod, leaning forward to kiss him teasingly. My mouth opens only a little, my tongue grazing his. Reese's back arches, his hands quickly finding my thighs.

"I'll be in the shower." I pull away and kiss his nose before climbing off him. "Get your ass back here." He rolled to his stomach, watching me walk to the door. His face is flushed, his bottom lip practically quivering with need. "Don't sound so needy, Reese. It isn't a good look for you." I winked, seeing the flames of lust and desire burning bright in his crystal eyes. He groans, grabbing his phone.

I've never showered faster in my life.

"Thanks, man. Have a good night." He shut the door as I walked into the hall in just my towel. "Can I wear your shirt?" I asked softly. His brows furrowed in confusion as he gave me a look of disbelief. "It's dirty."

I always took clothes from his closet when I slept over, but right now, I was craving his scent. His body, his cologne, the smell he left behind on his clothes– I wanted all of it. "Please," I begged, my eyes batting over long, thick lashes.

"I hate when you look at me like that." Reese sighed, reaching his hands behind to pull the shirt over his head. The image makes me breathe out of sync for a moment. "What?" he asks, his hands on his hips as I admire his trap muscles down to his navel. "Nothing." I pull my lips in to stifle a smile and spin on my heels down the hall, clutching his shirt so tight I could tear through the fabric.

Reese hands me a plate with two slices on it, and in exchange I hand him a diet coke. He nods a 'thank you' as we walk to the couch. I wasn't lucky enough to house a dining area in my tiny apartment. "What's your favorite food? And don't say something douchey. I wanna know what you crave at 3 A.M. on a Monday." I sit on the sofa, my back to the armrest and my knees up. Reese scrolls through *Netflix* aimlessly as he thinks. "You don't wanna know what I'm craving at 3 A.M. on a Monday." He smirked, avoiding my gaze as I stretched my foot to kick him. "Fine, probably just some really cheesy garlic bread." He nodded with a big grin. It was such a simple choice, lacking all pretentious filters.

"Oh, I fuck with cheesy garlic bread." I snickered, taking a bite of my pizza. Reese nods, chuckling under his breath. "What about you?" He turned to look at me.

"Definitely my mom's chili. Weather like this makes me miss it so much." My answer comes out more dramatically than I'd like. Reese nods, unsure of what to say to something so pathetic. "We could always vacation in Florida instead?" He smirked, knowing how repulsing that idea was.

"I'd rather rip my eyes out, thanks." I nudged him again with my foot, smiling at just how perfect my life was.

A knock startles the both of us, causing our eyes to meet. "Answer it." I demanded.

"Fuck you, this is your apartment." He spoke in an anxious tone as I pushed him to stand up. "Yeah, but I'm just a girl."

Reese groaned, swatting my hand away from him as he walked back toward the kitchen. The knocking gets louder, turning to pounding. "You owe me, Dawson." He scolds, opening the door. I can't see past his frame.

"What the fuck are you doing here?"

Thirty-Two

TESSA

Tim.

My stomach drops as I spring from the couch, eying Reese as the steam spews from his ears. "I wanna talk to Tessa." He slurs and I look to the ceiling, asking God why the hell I attract drunk men.

"She's not fucking talking to you." Reese went to slam the door, but he was met with resistance from Timothy. Tim was built like a specimen from a goddess's canvas. Even though he was intoxicated, he had the muscles of a titan. He clearly kept up with his workout routine from high school. "Tim," I interjected, my hand grazing Reese's back as I crept around his tall figure.

"Tess, I gotta talk to you."

His eyes are bloodshot, his normally perfect hair is disheveled and untidy. I don't even recognize him like this. It's like one of those movies where the prom king is now a washed up has-been. Reese looks down at me, his bare chest and face flushed with heated anger. He gives me a look that says *'say the word and I'll beat the snot out of him.'* I put my index finger up, softly shutting the door on Timothy.

"Wait here," I start to leave, and Reese grabs my arm, his grip surprisingly tight. "You're not going out there with him, he's fucking wasted." He ordered.

"So were you only a few days ago." I spoke calmly, somehow being the one to keep the peace between the two 'roided out men. "That's different." He spoke in his clenched jaw, practically breaking his teeth. I wanted to explain the flaw in that theory, but it was of no use. "Trust me." I replied, keeping my eyes on him so he knew the severity. "Tess," He groaned, shaking his head. I put both hands on his face, standing

153

on my tiptoes. "Please." I whispered, his jaw relaxing as he looked from me to the door.

"If he lays a finger on you," His voice was a low growl, the edge of jealousy as sharp as a knife. His gaze turned to laser focus, the mere thought of Timothy touching me was the most important thing in his mind. "I'll... I'll..." His voice trails off and I imagine he's running through a Rolodex of different ways to kill Tim. "Forget it." He sighed, stepping back and waving for me to go. "Thank you." I breathed cautiously, feeling like I had just broken up a fight between two street cats.

As I walk out, Timothy is sitting against a wall, playing with the fake flowers by my door. "What are you doing here, Tim?" I asked softly, sitting beside him. I've never seen him look this way. His eyes are bloodshot, his clothes a mess. Dream Tim was falling apart before my eyes. "You never called." His face was puffy, telling me he'd been upset for quite some time tonight. "Call?" I asked in curiosity.

"We kissed, you said you'd call me. And you never did." He avoids my gaze, his words slurring and falling out of his mouth. I did say that. And then Reese came along just like every other interaction I'd had with Tim lately. "I know, I'm sorry." I stretched my legs out in front of me with a loud, exaggerated sigh, resting my head on his shoulder. I feel the repercussions of my actions.

"Come back to Seattle with me."

I stare straight ahead; my ears feel like they're underwater. I can't lift my head from his shoulder, it weighs a thousand pounds. Why was everyone always trying to leave me and this state?

I was suddenly twenty-three again, waving my parents and sister off to Florida. Or worse, I was sixteen and watching my soulmate be hauled away to Texas Tech with no real closure. And just like that day, I could never leave the place I loved most.

"You're drunk." I whispered, finally lifting my head to look in his defeated face.

"Not that drunk." He blinked slowly, struggling to keep his gaze off my lips.

I shake my head with a pitiful smile; I was loyal to everyone in my life. Even myself. "I'm not going to Seattle, Tim." I wet my lips, preventing myself from the tears that dared to escape. Tim looks straight ahead again, nodding slowly as he drunkenly scoffs. "Because of him, right?" He points lazily at my door, and I shake my head.

"This is my home."

Tim's head rests against the wall, he squeezes his eyes shut as fresh tears spill down his cheeks. We're in a teenage heartbreak once more. "Right." He weakly chuckled, the sobriety beginning to set in. He was still hurt; everything was so fresh. "You've never changed. You know?" He opened his eyes, still avoiding my gaze. "Is that good or bad?" I elbow his side, trying to lighten his spirits.

"It's perfect." He sighed, wetting his lips and looking at me with more love than I'd expect after breaking his heart. I have to stop him from feeling more. "Do you need me to call you a cab?" I offered, hoisting myself off the ground and extending two hands to him. He groans as I use all upper body strength I have to lift him. "Nah, Kayla is downstairs waiting for me."

My brows furrowed in confusion. "Kayla brought you here?" I asked, my words coming out rather annoyed. Tim nods, cramming his hands in his pockets and walking down the hall. I'm lost as to why she would do that. Maybe it was to force me to decide, I can't say that I blame her. This was the finale I needed.

Timothy stopped in his tracks, turning to face me. "I'm leaving Friday."

"You finished your business here?" I asked, my head tilting to the side.

"You were my business, Tessa." Timothy shrugged, his arms stretched out with a smile, and I felt someone sledge hammer my heart. My jaw slacks as he smiles, stumbling back down the hall. I rest my head against the door, no longer able to hold my tears back. I'm sobbing, losing my breath in devastation for the man that I have broken. I can't restrain the cries that come from deep in my tattered soul. Timothy was never meant for New York.

And I, single handedly, received the closure I needed after all these years.

Thirty-Three

REESE

Tessa closed the door behind her, her head hung low. I can tell she was crying, I want to beat his face in. I nearly pulled the door from its hinges to be met with an empty hall. It's then I realize I'm focusing on the wrong things. I look back over my shoulder, Tessa's hands are on the counter as she quietly sobs to herself.

"Tess," I sighed, turning her to face me. My index and thumb lift her chin slowly and her tears are illuminated by the light. "What did he say to you?" I want to kill him, rip him in half. She shakes her head as I use my thumbs to dry under her eyes. Her body twitches in hyperventilation like she can't catch her breath, I don't know how to help her. I scramble, my eyes scanning her body. "Tell me, baby. Let me make it better." I lean in, kissing her salty cheeks. I listen as she attempts to breathe through her nose with closed eyes. My lips traced her jaw, then her neck, knowing the comfort it gave her in the past. I'm absorbing the salt against my lips as it smears across my face. Her arms tightly wrapped around my neck, and I run my hands under the familiar material of my shirt and against her back.

"Just breathe, Tessa." I have no idea what she's going through. Loving Timothy for a greater portion of her life but choosing me, it doesn't even sound real. I have won yet I feel like the loser. I can't comfort her; I've claimed her for myself and I don't even know what she needs from me.

"Talk to me." My voice cracks, I struggle with the idea that she regrets her choice. I pull back from her hug and look down at her. She's broken. I want to get on my knees for her, tell her how much I love her.

She looks up at me like she's expecting me to say it. She wants me to confirm she's done the right thing by choosing me.

My jaw is slacked, I can't get myself to spit it out. "I just want to go to bed." She spoke with her bottom lip quivering. "Done." I scoop a hand under her thighs and on her back, carrying her close to my chest with ease. Timothy may have been muscular, but I wasn't someone to be fucked with. And neither was the girl I was in love with. Her damp curls drip on my bare chest as I walk to her bed. The soft pastel covers are still so nicely placed as I lay her on them. Her trembling hands pull them back and climb underneath.

I lean over her, kissing her forehead. The smell of her shampoo is all I'm going to get as a reminder of her tonight. I can't help but hover for a minute, still hooked on the idea of her changing her mind. "I can leave if you need." I whispered, pushing myself back off of her. Her nails dig into my arm, causing me to look down.

"I don't want to be alone." Her eyes are pleading, my heart is pumping. "Okay." I nodded, motioning for her to scoot over.

Tessa climbs on top of me, my hands meeting her back. Suddenly, I'm nervous. I feel like we're strangers, in the best way. We're starting over with no middleman, no obstacles. Her head rests on my chest, and I hope she can't hear my heartbeat going wild. I trace my fingers against her skin under the shirt, in the dark, with only the sound being the New York traffic below us.

September 18th,

"What the fuck is this?" I'm awoken to a copy of the Stripe, colliding with my face. I rub my eyes, sitting up. On the cover, the infamous photo of Brooklynn and I. "Tessa, I can explain." My heart is leaping from my chest, I crawl across the bed to the floor, following her as she walks off. "You're a liar. And I *hate* liars." She won't even look at me.

The air in the room is cold, so cold I can see my breath. "Let me explain, baby."

I scramble, the tears already falling. I can't, nor will I, attempt to hide them. "You need to leave." She's so angry, her entire body is freezing me out. "I'm not-"

"Get the fuck out." Her brows are lowered, I don't even recognize her voice. I shake my head, my chest heaving as I sob. "Tess, please." My bottom lip quivers as my eyes lock on to hers. "I- I love you." I wipe my eyes with the back of my hand. I'm reaching for her, but she feels so far away. "Well," She begins.

"I don't love you."

I take a huge gasp, opening my eyes with Tessa shaking me. My side of the bed is drenched in sweat and tiny beads cover my bare skin. My eyes are tearful and afraid as I dig my nails in her arms, coming back to reality. "Reese, hey. It's me. You're awake."

I can only imagine my expression as she looks at me with worry. "What?" I begged for her to repeat herself. It was like she spoke another language. Her eyes are so sympathetic, and I realize I was dreaming. "You had a bad dream." Tessa strokes my cheek and I place a trembling hand over hers. It wasn't real, none of it was. She still had no idea about Brooklynn.

My head falls back to the pillow as I sigh, out of breath. Tessa kisses my chest and I move my arm back around her. I'm covered in a cold sweat, but she seems not to mind. "Are you okay?" She whispered against my skin as I shut my eyes. "Yeah." I wet my salty lips and tried to regulate my breathing. "Sorry if I woke you." I cock my head to kiss her forehead as her hand runs over my torso.

"I was already up. It's about time for me to go to work." This would go down in history as the closest I've ever gotten to acceptance from her. She kisses me again, each one softer than the last. The thumping in my chest mellows with my hand tracing her shoulder. "I'll drive you."

I pull the blankets off us and sit with my legs off the bed. I rest my elbows against my thighs, replaying my dream. That cold, blanketed stare. I was terrified.

Tessa crawls behind me, her legs on either side of me as she wraps her arms around my waist.

I let out a comforted sigh as I rubbed her arms with one hand. My head still hangs low, I'm nauseous with myself. "Do you wanna talk about it?" She asks me, her warm cheek resting against my spine.

"You don't have to worry about me." I don't want to tell her, I can't. "Not when we have a vacation to prepare for." I craned my neck to see her smile. It was worth more than anything I could ever receive. Tessa's eyes brightened before she quickly climbed off the bed. She sat on the floor, cross-legged and looked around at her mess of clothes. She'd already forgotten about my nightmare. "I have so much to do."

I can't help but snicker, watching her find her groove while packing the last of her things. "I'm gonna take a shower." I kiss the top of her head as she nods, not acknowledging me in any other way. I shake my head playfully, leaving the room.

When I return, Tessa is dressed. Her hair is pulled back in her infamous clip and I'm drooling over her. "I hate when you wear those." I shook my head as I pointed to her scrubs, cramming my foot in my shoe. I throw my dirty shirt back on, feeling drunk at the scent of her overriding mine. I take a quiet inhale, hoping she doesn't notice.

"Why?" She rolls her suitcase over to me to handle and I laugh, watching her fold her arms with a pout. "I wear scrubs every day, Reese."

"Not those." I waved my finger over the tight black material. The pants were a size too small, at least for my liking and the top was a V-neck, cutting right above her cleavage. Every curve on her body was accentuated in ways only I should see. And she knew it.

I watch her cheeks flush and a smirk appears across her face. "I'm just saying, I have no problem kicking an old man's ass if he puts his hands on my girl." I step closer to her, placing a lazy hand on her lower back to pull her to me. She moves to her tiptoes, and I smile into a kiss.

"Alright, let's get you to work. The sooner I can get you on that plane and into bed the better." I winked, preparing myself for the slap that was bound to come. She didn't let me down as I rubbed the now red, tender skin on my arm.

"You know, we're missing your responsibility lesson this week. You *should* be working today too." Tessa folds her arms as we pull into the parking lot. "I understand that, but I still have shit to do." I smiled, lifting my sunglasses up to rest on my head. Tessa's eyes follow my actions, focused on the way they sit. She softly wets her lips, and I can't help but smirk.

"I'll pick you up at 4. Be ready." I move my hand to the back of her neck, pulling her into a kiss. My tongue pries her lips apart, eclipsing in her sweet saliva. She softly moans against me, and I'm instantly a puddle of a man. "Get out of my car before I drag you in the back seat." I groaned, putting the car in drive. "See you at 4." She smiled, her hands on my window. I could tell by the look in her eyes that she was beyond ready to leave New York, if only for a few days.

I pulled my car into the *Target* parking lot. I'd never been, but Tessa always told me it was her favorite store. My livelihood was beyond a discount store like that. Fortunately, I'd adapted a new outlook on life with her by my side. I walk in and grab a basket, looking left and right. My brows are scrunched, I'm not sure where to start. There are people everywhere, families, single women, I could get lost here. I follow a sign towards the food, passing a white dress on a mannequin. I stop, my head leaning to the side in thought.

The dress is knee length, white and thin, with a little ruffle on the sleeves. It's cut low, showing off just enough of the chest. I take a minute to envision her tanned skin against the fabric. I feel my dick twitch as I adjust myself. *No, she'll hate it.* I make my way to the snacks, grabbing her gummy sharks, sour ropes, and *Doritos*, something I'd never had before I met Tessa. They were now my midnight snack *because* of her.

I turn back out of the aisle; the dress catches my attention again as I try to keep my gaze off it. *Soap. Maybe I should grab soap.* Anything to keep me from buying her that dress. I didn't want to make it weird. Sure, I'd bought her a thong in the past, but that was owed to her.

I look over my shoulder at the mannequin, a woman stands close by. She would know. She was older than Tessa by at least fifteen years, but she seemed to have decent taste. I groan, looking at the fluorescent lights in the ceiling. "Jesus Christ." I grumble, making my way over.

"Excuse me, miss." I awkwardly tapped her shoulder; she jumped, turning to look up at me. I pulled out my phone, going through my camera roll to find a picture of Tessa and I that she took at the ice cream social. There's a dollop of whipped cream on my nose and some smeared on her cheek. I restrain my smile as I flip the phone to her. "Do you think she would like this dress?"

I point to the mannequin, and the lady glances between the two. "I think so." She smiles, turning to grab a size that looks appropriate for Tessa. It's then that I can see the salt and pepper grays that fill the woman's hair. "Girlfriend?" She asks, handing me the dress. My jaw slacks, I'm unsure how to answer. We'd slipped up in the past, but was it *official*? "Yes." My lips curl into a tight smile and she giggles, finding humor in my reaction. I can feel the warm sensation of embarrassment on my cheeks yet I'm okay with it.

"Reese?" I'm walking to the register when a voice calls to me. I stop in my tracks, spinning on my heels. "I didn't know you even knew what Target was." Brooklyn mumbles with a soft grin. I take a step back. I don't want to be seen with her. "Did you... You know?" I ask, my demeanor now stoic as I keep a safe, friendly distance from her. Brooklyn nods softly.

"Yeah, I did. Don't worry." She tucks a dead strand of bleached hair behind her ear, and I sigh in relief. "Well, an article's gonna drop about it tomorrow. So just prepare yourself for that." I sighed, my basket resting at my hip. Brooklynn's face turned gray, processing the way her life could be flipped upside down. Her face was blurred in the photo, chances are she wouldn't be identified. But the world was a mysterious place now, technology had come so far.

"I guess I'll see you around." Her tone was hopeful, like this accident would have only brought us closer. But I was happy with Tess. I was obsessed with her, and I wasn't going to let Brooklynn get in the way of that.

"I don't think so, B. Take care of yourself, alright?" I mean it in every way it could be taken. Brooklynn nods, turning down an aisle, and I bolt for the registers.

I am never fucking coming back to Target again.

Thirty-Four

TESSA

I come barreling out of the front doors, unable to contain my squeal as Reese leans against his Lincoln. He's wearing a black button up with the sleeves rolled to his elbows and his top four buttons undone. I can see the small silver chain that drapes around his ivory skin. His jeans are cropped, tightly rolled to above his ankles. His glasses sit perched on top of his head, the sun revealing his crystal eyes that sparkled every time he looked my way. A few strands slipped past the barrier of the glasses frame and fell down his forehead. Light freckles dot the ivory skin across his nose and cheeks, while his lips curl in a smug smirk as he looks at me.

I stretch my arms around his neck as I stand on my tiptoes. "Ready?" he asked, his hands creeping under my shirt and against my back. I nodded, kissing him quickly and going for the door. "Wait, I got you something." He opens the trunk, pulling out a red and white bag. "You went to Target? *Without* me?" I asked, my eyes practically falling from my head. I never thought Reese would be caught dead in a store like that. "I wanted to be a little seasoned before my first time with you. And I wanted you to be comfortable on the plane." He winked, pushing me away with the bag. "Go put it on."

I nod, running back inside to the bathroom. I pulled out a white sundress and smiled. Not only did Reese go to my favorite store, but he thought about me while he was there. I pull it over my figure, feeling it glide against my tan skin. I twirl around in the mirror, admiring the way the dress makes me look, feeling more feminine and delicate than I have in a long time.

When I step out, I feel the gentle heat of Reese's gaze, radiating on me like a comforting sun. My cheeks are warm as his lips part lightly, and his tone is one of amusement as he speaks.

"Tess," He chuckles, his attraction to me evident in his voice. "I look stupid, don't I?" I cross my arms over my stomach, feeling the slightest bit self-conscious, even if his tone is playful. "You look beautiful, baby." He continues, noticing how insecure I seem to be. His tone was filled with so much care, like I was the most precious thing to him.

"It's just so strange to see you like this. I love it." The corners of his mouth curl up to a smile. "I have shoes to go with this in my suitcase." I hand him my purse, and he buried his head in the front seat. I dig in the trunk for my brown sandals so I can look the full part. "How's this?" I ask, taking my curls down from my clip and pointing to my feet. Reese stumbles back from the car like I've caught him sneaking out of his bedroom. "Hm? Yeah, you look hot. Ready?" He smiles, his mouth closed in a tight smile.

The departing planes come in closer and closer in view, and my gaze starts to wander from Reese's driving and towards the window next to us. My sense of wonder and awe return as I watch the planes soar through the sky like birds, the sheer size of them bringing childlike wonder to me. "If you would have asked me two months ago if I would be in a car with you, let alone on vacation, I would have laughed my ass off." I giggled, taking in the beauty of the skies and the feeling of the cool wind blasting through us with the windows down.

"You and I both." Reese lazily grinned and took my hand, gently linking his fingers with mine, kissing the back of it. The gesture felt like I was a princess. And he was the knight that came to rescue me, hiding in plain sight behind his stupid jokes and arrogance.

Reese parks the car, and we grab our things. I check my purse; I have my passport, my wallet, my essentials. "My phone... Shit, I think I forgot it at work."

Reese stops, arms still on his suitcase in the trunk. "There's no time to go back, Tess." He glances at the airport and back to me. He's right, we'd miss our flight. I didn't want to ruin our vacation already. "I- I don't know what to do." I felt my eyes well with tears. This was so unlike me; I was always so organized. "Hey, it's alright, take a breath.

How about this," Reese quickly drops his suitcase on the ground and comes to my side. "I'll leave my phone in the car. We can disconnect from everything and everyone. Just you," He takes my hand once more.

"And just me."

He places it on his chest, and I focus on his heartbeat against my palm. It was such a simple, romantic solution. "No one knows where I am." I forgot to tell anyone about the trip in the chaos of Tim and work. Reese nods, running his tongue over his top teeth in thought. "What's Kayla's number? I'll shoot her a text with where we'll be staying and how to contact us." He smiles so confidently; I already feel at ease again. "Okay," I give him the number and he goes silent for a moment.

"Done." He smiled, turning his phone off and tucking it in his trunk. "Just you and me, baby." He smiled, wheeling both of our suitcases.

"Wait, what about pictures?" I stopped halfway into the airport. "Tess, they sell cameras on every street corner." He snickered. I hadn't thought of that. Reese always thought of everything, I hated that about him. Or maybe I didn't. "And what happened to disconnecting?" He teased as we approached our terminal. "I'd like to document this. It very well could be the last time I'm ever seen again." I teased, handing the woman my ticket and driver's license.

Our flight boards almost immediately, I find myself anxious and clammy in the seat. I've never been on a flight this long. "Are you comfortable?" Reese asked, placing his hand over mine on the armrest. I lie with a quick nod and unsure smile.

"We're gonna be here awhile, so just let me know if you need anything."

He kissed my cheek, and I stared straight ahead, waiting for the impending turbulent take off. I've never been comfortable with taking off. I shut my eyes, hoping I could just sleep my way through it. "You're gonna be fine. You've flown before, Tess." Reese chuckled, catching me in my mental meditation. "Never for eighteen hours." I shoot him a glare, exhaling quickly through my nose as the attendant tells us to be buckled.

"Want me to distract you?" he asks, squeezing my hand tighter. I nod, my eyes shut so tight I begin to see stars. "Have you ever heard of the *Mile High Club*?" He was practically giggling. "I hate you." I whisper in a mousy voice, even though his words make me smile. "I heard they're accepting new members." He jokes again as the plane begins to stabilize in the air, the turbulence beginning to calm. My breathing returns to normal, my blood pressure back to steady rates. This would be the longest ride of my life.

The captain's voice comes through the overhead speakers, informing the passengers that they are free to roam around the cabin for the remainder of the flight. I let out a sigh of relief, my stomach tightening with a nauseating feeling. "I need to use the bathroom," I quickly unbuckle my seatbelt, feeling like I should vomit. "Right," Reese replies with a smirk, his tone playful and teasing. I look at him with squinted eyes, confused but decide not to ask.

About three minutes later, I heard a soft knock. "One sec!" I use my most chipper voice, as if I'm not gripping both sides of the tiny sink with my eyes shut. "Let me in." Reese whispers.

"What?" I whip the door open to see him with that goofy grin. "Do you need the bathroom?" I ask with a raised brow. "Wha- No. I thought that was code?" He replied with his arms up in a puzzled way. My jaw slacks and I realize what he is implying. "Reese, please go away."

"Come on, I'll be quick." He whined, looking down at the cabin aisle. I rolled my eyes, shutting the door on him. He was never quick. I loved his thoroughness with taking care of me before he even dared to care for himself. Hell, I think half of what turned him on was the ability to get me off so fucking fast and so often.

While washing my hands, I'm distracted by our past rendezvous replaying in my mind. The way his muscles flexed with every thrust, his sweaty hair, his full lips and tongue tucked in the corner. My god, I was losing it an hour into our flight. I needed to do something, but sex in this small bathroom wasn't it.

I shimmy out of my thong, tucking it into my hand before leaving the bathroom. I walk back to my seat, very nonchalant and poised. I've done nothing wrong. No one knows a thing. I clear my throat, sitting back at the window seat. "Don't talk to me." He fakes pouts, looking away. "I'm sorry, pumpkin. Hold my hand?" I ask in my most velvet voice, he can never resist. He turns slowly, his face skeptical as if trying to read me. Reese lays his hand palm up and I link my fingers with his, my thong rolling into his grip. Reese sucks in a breath between his teeth and shakes his head with a scoff.

"I hate you." He groans, adjusting his length through his pants. I smirk, knowing I'd achieved my goal. Reese rests his head against the headrest and exaggeratedly sighs. "Get your ass in the bathroom." He whispered through a clenched jaw. "No, we get dinner in thirty minutes. I don't wanna miss it." I scolded, pulling out my book from my purse. "Tessa Ann, get up." Reese adjusts himself again, rubbing the lace material of my underwear at his side between us. My chest is burning hot beneath this dress, I need him. His tone is like he owns me, and I worship it. I wish he talked to me this way forever.

"No, Reese. You must be patient. It's only another 17 hours." I gave a sassy smile as he breathed heavier. His eyes were dark, glaring at me in frustration.

He trembles his way through a decent airplane dinner, grilled chicken, asparagus and a salad. As soon as the attendant comes back for the dishes, Reese stops her. "Could we get a blanket? We were up very late last night and would like to get comfortable."

He smiled so politely, hiding all tension in his body.

The woman nodded, pushing her cart further down the aisle. I continued with my book, avoiding him. It was getting darker, now 8 P.M, our time. "Here, I'm sure you're cold." Reese offers, draping the blanket over us. I can't read the tone of his voice. It's sneaky, almost suggestive. He was right, my body was covered in goosebumps from the stale plane air. "Thanks." I pull my arms out from the blanket, turning the page to my book. "Yep." He mumbles and I briefly look at him. That was a very unlikely response.

The other passengers began pulling their sleep masks down, their seats as reclined as could be to get comfortable. My reading light illuminated our section, everything else seeming like the bottom of the ocean. My eyes felt heavy, but I was determined to finish this book before I went to sleep. I had only six chapters left, I could do it.

That was until I felt Reese's hand creep onto my thigh, tracing mindless circles under my dress. "What are you doing?" I whispered, my book close to my face. "Just be quiet." He hiked my dress up to my hips, my legs instinctively spreading for him. "Reese," I whispered, my jaw slacking. "Shh." He spoke into my ear, and I nodded. His fingers parted me, tracing and sliding lazily on the wet skin near my opening.

"I knew you were my good girl." He whispered. I swallow hard, trying my best to be silent at his teasing. I look over the words on the pages, they're lifting from the paper and forming new languages. His middle finger enters first and I hear him exhale loudly through his nose, like he's longed to feel me this way again. My eyes roll back as my breath hitches.

His ring finger joins, stretching me before really giving me what I need. His thrusts are slow, hooking and curling right where I need to push me to a fast and aggressive climax. He makes my skin crawl in the best way. His head is in my neck, breathing against my ear heavily.

I moan against the pages of my book, and he pulls out.

"I told you to be quiet." He softly ordered; I can't see his face but I can feel that he's grinning.

He's getting a kick out of this. If I had half of a thought, I'd be stroking him as payment. But I'm lost for sanity. My right hand quickly slides under the blanket, and I force him back between my legs as Reese laughs. I felt like an idiot, but I was already high up. I couldn't fall this hard. He enters slowly again, pumping gently to build my climax. "That's it, princess." He whispered against my skin, his nose nuzzling to the sensitive spot behind my ear.

I've never had a thing for big hands, but they were godly in a pinch like this. I bucked my hips softly against him, riding his hand like this flight was stopping at the pearly gates. My legs tremble as I have my most silent orgasm ever.

September 19th

I open my eyes and stretch, muted sun peaks through the bottom of my blind. My body is heavy. Sleepily, I turn my head to see Reese. He rests against my shoulder, his mouth slightly agape as he breathes so softly. I use my free arm to crack the blind. The clouds rush past, and I see we are over water. I wish I had my phone, only eight hours to go.

I can feel Reese's breath rising and falling next to me as he sleeps, making me smile, even though I was trying not to. There was something about him that was very innocent when he was asleep, even if he was an asshole when he was awake.

I could see the faint traces of his stress lines and tension melt away as he slept, making me feel like I was protecting him somehow. I let my fingers drift to his hair, touching his locks as his breathing grew deeper and the tension in his body decreased.

I couldn't wake him even if the plane was on fire.

Thirty-Five

REESE

Finally, land. I want to kiss the ground as we step off the plane. Next time I fuck up, I'm taking her close to home. We are surrounded by blue waters and greenery. Her face is worth every penny spent. "Oh my god." Tess whispers, pulling her sunglasses up on top of her head.

As much as I'd love to relish her reaction, I need to find a bed. My body is stiff, every muscle tense and locked away.

I smile, pulling her along to the gentleman handling everyone's luggage. "I also rented a car, to get around the island." I mention casually, as if we'd need the vehicle. Tess may have taught me about responsibility, but she had a lot to learn about vacationing the Finch way. "How'd you swing that?" She asked with a smirk as the man handed me a set of keys.

"I have my ways, darling." I chuckle, flashing her a cheeky and playful wink before gesturing to her to come with me. I use the fob to light up a classic '67 baby blue Mustang convertible, the old school vibe instantly catching her attention. Tessa looks over the car, her jaw dropping and the sparkle in her eyes becoming even more radiant. "Holy shit," she chuckles, her amusement and awe clear on her face as she takes in the vintage presence.

The interior is neat and clean, with no visible messes or imperfections. The dashboard is a vibrant white color that contrasts beautifully with the blue leather seats. It's a capsule of a time gone by, when cars were made with care and class.

"Should we take her for a spin?" Tess asks, her face beaming with excitement. I opened the door for her and put our luggage in the backseat before hopping over the front myself. I don't think I've ever seen her so happy. As I start the engine, the rumble of the exhaust vibrates in my chest. I can't help but feel a sense of accomplishment and relief.

The wind rips through her hair, laughter bubbles around us as gravel pings underneath the car. Tessa puts her hands up, letting the breeze flow through her fingers. I smile, admiring her through my sunglasses. Her curls flow like silk ribbons, her hands hold her dress against her thighs. The scent of her perfume tickles my nose, warm vanilla and amber.

It's as if the world stops spinning and time stands still as she turns to look at me. She tucks a curl behind her ear, her delicate fingers brushing lightly against her cheek. She's so effortlessly beautiful, I can't take my eyes off her. I watch the slightest flush rise in her cheeks, and my mind runs back to the first time I ever saw it. The day I moved my father to Brindlewood, she helped me make his bed. I snickered, watching her fight to case a pillow. It was almost half her size, and I couldn't help but laugh as she wiped the sweat from her brow. I took it from her grasp, my hand grazing hers briefly.

There was that same blush, those rosy cheeks and big, brown eyes.

I'm not sure when that switch happened between us, when I became so angry inside and frustrated with her. Everything she said was like nails on a chalkboard; her tone, the way she spoke to me, all of it made me feel like she was intentionally pushing my buttons. But now I understand that my anger was misplaced; I was angry at my father, not her. That anger inside me was a result of my childhood, and yet I was taking it out on her. And she was always so patient.

I love her more than I've ever loved anything in this world.

We reach our beach hideaway, the small bungalow perched at the end of a dock. The sight of the ocean beneath and the white sand spread out in front of us. Down the beach a mile or so, is a small bar with cheap drinks and terrible music, but it's the perfect location for a secluded getaway. I grab our bags, watching Tess walk in front of me, the gentle breeze blowing her hair as she moves along the pier.

I pull the key from my pocket and hand it to her, watching as she takes a deep breath.

The door opens to soft neutral tones, a California king and a tub below the bay window overlooking the ocean. The walls are painted a soft ivory color, and the furniture has a vintage vibe to it, the wood pieces gently weathered from the sea-spray and humidity. Small touches of color are dispersed throughout the space, such as throw pillows and area rugs. I dropped our bags at the door, floored that I even pulled this off.

Tessa runs her hand over the comforter before walking to the balcony doors. As much as I want to follow her, this bed looks so fucking comfortable. I face plant into the mattress with a guttural groan. My hands grip the blanket as my eyes roll back.

"Tired?" Tessa begins untying my shoes from my feet that dangle off the bed. I nod, pulling the pillow under my head. "*Really* tired?" I can tell she's smirking as she massages my feet. She rubs up my calves through my jeans and I groan again. "Tess, I'd give my left nut to bend you over this bed. But I am so fucking exhausted." I sighed, hoping she wouldn't get mad. I'd never denied her anything, but I knew how other women were in the past.

"Okay." Tessa crawled across the bed to curl up in front of me. I kiss the back of her head, wrapping my arm around her small frame that leans into me. My head nuzzles behind her neck and in seconds, I'm unconscious for the first comfortable sleep in two days.

The sound of water running makes my brows crinkle. My jaw is still slacked, I hope I'm not drooling. I open my lazy eyes as the water shuts off. "Hi," Tessa blushes in the tub full of bubbles. It covers up to her shoulders, her curls pulled up into a messy bun.

"Hey," I smile, sitting up slowly and stretching out the kinks that I've accumulated from the last few days of traveling. My fingers move along my muscles, gently massaging as my eyes slowly take in the candlelight setting the intimate moment. My eyes wander across her body and when I see her lean back in the bathtub, I feel my breath catching in my throat. "I didn't mean to wake you." She smiled, causing me to chuckle. She was always so concerned for everyone else.

"That's okay, how's the water?" I asked, moving to stand at her side.

"Fine. I could live in a bubble bath." she giggles, shifting her legs together slightly. My eyes follow the gentle curve of her shoulders as she shifts, my focus slowly straying lower. My tongue runs across my bottom lip as I pull up a chair. "You know you could join me." Tessa offered as she leaned over the edge, folding her arms on the porcelain. I shake my head, quicker than I'd like to admit. Something about the intimacy was almost nauseating. I couldn't explain it. We had showered together before, but the candles and bubbles seemed to be too much. My mind is racing with excuses, and I feel guilty and angry with myself.

"I'd rather watch you." My cheeks were hot with shame and embarrassment. Tessa picks up on this and nods without appearing upset. "Fine, then you can read me my book." She giggled, shutting her eyes as she got comfortable. My eyes linger over the scattering bubbles as her body is revealed to me.

I grab the weathered copy of the Great Gatsby and make a look of pure annoyance. "You cannot be reading this." I ask with wide eyes, stifling my laugh. Tessa splashes me, her brows furrowed. "I'm a sucker for the classics." She argued with a smile. I roll my eyes, opening the book to her bookmark. She was nearly done, only ten pages left.

"So, we beat on, boats against the current, borne back ceaselessly into the past." I closed the book, raising a brow to her reaction. Tessa stares into the ceiling, clearly chewing the inside of her cheek. "What do you think that means?" She asks me. I scoff, I'd never read it.

Beyond the last ten pages, I wasn't sure what had happened in this book. "Hell, if I know." I sighed, leaning back in my chair.

"I think it's about regret." Tessa broke the silence, her arms resting on either side of the tub. I nod, letting her explain further. "Like, no matter how hard we try to forget and move on… It's always there, you know?" She should teach, I could listen to her debrief literature all night.

"I do." I feel like she's speaking to my soul, to every lingering ghost of my past mistakes. "Do you have regrets?" I blurted, feeling my embarrassment after. "Everyone has regrets, Reese. It's how you choose to grieve for them." She winks, pointing to her white robe, provided by the lodging, and takes her hair down. I want to tell her about Brooklynn, it's on the tip of my tongue.

And as I go to speak, she steps out from the water and my mind goes blank.

"Wait, let me look at you." I smile, holding the robe open. I stare down at her slowly, my eyes taking in her figure. She was so short but curved in every way I worshiped. The delicate lines of her body and the way the bath suds cover every inch of her skin. The sight was surreal, her body was a map to my obsessions. "Weirdo." She giggles, catching my eyes and my hesitation. "I…" I wanna tell her.

Tell her you love her, you dumbass.

Tess looks up at me with her amber-colored eyes, the depths of which I could easily drown in. When I talk, I find myself stuck on the words that we both want each other to say.

"Are you hungry?" I asked her, tying the robe as she nodded.

"Burgers? I'll go pick some up."

I'm eager to get the hell out of here.

Tess's eyes squint curiously as she realizes what I'm doing in my efforts to avoid the actual conversation. "Yeah." She giggled, making me let out my breath I was holding. I lift her chin, kissing her softly. "Get comfortable, I'll be back in ten."

She nods, grabbing her pajamas and disappears into the bathroom. I wait for the door to lock and grab my phone from the safety zipper of my suitcase. My texts are blowing up from friends about the article. It's trending on all platforms at home. I have a notification on Instagram, a follow request from one Kayla Lorne.

@kklorne517: where the fuck is my best friend?

@kklorne517: does she know you've got a baby on the way??

@kklorne517: did you take her phone?

Hell no. Not today. I turn my phone back off and hide it away, practically leaving a cartoon dust cloud behind me as I close the door. Maybe I shouldn't have grabbed it from the trunk when Tessa turned around. I almost would have rather not read that. My guilt is through the roof again. But I can't think that way. I have to remember that Brooklynn doesn't exist here. I'm a normal fucking person with a normal fucking life.

Thirty-Six

TESSA

"I fucking love food that doesn't come from an airplane." I moan as I chew my food. My feet are crossed on the bed as Reese sits beside me. "Hey, that was first class." He pouted, teasing as his mouth was full. While he was right and it could have been worse, there was nothing better than a greasy cheeseburger.

Reese takes fries from my tray, cramming them in his mouth. I playfully fold my arms when I notice him doing it. "Don't you have your own?" I ask. But he just grins up at me, the whites of his teeth stark in contrast to the slow dripping grease on his chin. My stomach flutters at his primal side and I realize I'm staring at his lips for a little too long.

"Yeah, but yours taste so much better." He winks, licking his lips clean. Reese leans in even closer, his lips almost touching mine now as our breaths mix. I can see the light glistening in his eyes as he stares into mine, his breath soft and even. My heart is beating in my chest as the tension mounts, the anticipation nearly igniting. His lips part close to mine, only for him to cram another fry in his mouth with a laugh. "I hate you." I sigh, pushing him away.

"What's wrong?" He snickered, sliding our containers to the side. "Don't be so pathetic." Reese took my hands, pulling me toward him as he laid back.

"Pathetic?" I asked with my head cocked. "I think you know *all* about being pathetic, Reese." If he wants to play this game, I will win. "What's that supposed to mean?" Reese moves his hands to my hips as I straddle his lap. My fingers trace up his arms and I can feel the hair standing.

"It means, I can have you begging me to fuck you in two minutes. *That's* pathetic." I smirked, knowing it was the fact. "Maybe you'd have to prove that theory." Reese dug his hands into my hips, this was going to be easy.

He was so weak; it took literally nothing for this man to spark a boner. I sigh in preparation, leaning down to kiss his neck lightly. It was just enough to raise goosebumps. My lips trailed to the notch in his neck, and I can hear his heartbeat from this angle.

I sit up to unbutton his shirt the rest of the way and he tries to sit up to meet me. "No, no. You don't get to participate." I smirked, pushing him back down. "Is that so?" He chuckled, a strand of hair falling between his eyes. I nod, sliding off his hips and propping myself on his thighs. I kiss his navel, inhaling his cologne on my way down. I could bathe in his essence.

"Ready to beg?" I asked, my fingers toying with his belt buckle. Reese lifts his head from the pillow and groans, shaking his head. "Fine." I want to die of laughter, watching him struggle between pants of lust. I've never had control over a man, it was the ultimate power move. I undo his bottoms, my hand snaking over his length that pulsed against my grip. "Ready?" I asked again, I moved my hands to the hem of his underwear, slowly and teasingly pulling them down.

Reese sucks in through his teeth, his back arching for a split second. "God, no." He stammers. I shake my head with a smile, his length springing from the briefs. I work my hand up and down the shaft, stopping only to gauge his reaction. Reese watches with his jaw slacked, his stomach muscles flexing as he focuses on not finishing. "Tessa…" He groaned deeply, his hands tightening on the sheets.

"All you have to do is beg, Reese." I purred before an idea struck my mind. Something I didn't have much experience in. But something about him made me ready to open that door.

I slide my tongue from the base to the tip. "Oh, fuck." He moaned, sucking in a breath with his jaw completely dropped. Reese looks down at me again, in awe of what he'd just seen. "I'll do whatever, as long as you do that again." He whined, his voice up an octave as his hands trembled. One sat perched on his forehead while the other gripped the sheets. "I told you." I winked, climbing off his lap and sitting beside him.

"Where are you going? You can't leave me like this." Reese whimpered, his body twitching for more. "What do you mean?" I asked in annoyance with a dramatic sigh.

"Please baby, I- I need it." He finally begged, his hand gripping my arm tightly so I couldn't get any further from him.

I was caught red handed, I was a damn good actress but there was no way I could fit him inside my mouth. My eyes darted from his length and back to him. "I can't." I blushed, feeling inadequate to the other girls he'd slept with. I'm sure none of them passed up the opportunity.

"You can, princess. Just go slow." Reese's hand met my cheek, wiping off the insecurity spewing from my pores. "I'll guide you through it."

I took a deep breath and nodded, sitting between his legs.

His fingers comb my hair back and lock it into place. "Take a little at a time, okay?"

I nod, my mouth sliding over the tip as he moans. I take about three inches in; its salty taste isn't anywhere near as intense as I'd imagined in my head. My eyes flicker up to watch his expression, his face is a tomato as he takes deep, sporadic breaths. "Oh, fuck, baby. Can you take a little more?" His voice is weak, practically burning for me. I push him in another two and the grip on my hair tightens. "That's it, you're doing so good for me."

My head bobs, my saliva covering his length as I test my non-existent gag reflex.

"Tessa, holy shit." He growled, my mouth taking in the final three inches to the back of my throat as my eyes watered. I'm now all the way to his hips and Reese is about to convulse. His hand guides me back up and down for his pleasure. "You're so fucking good, baby."

He spoke through a tight jaw and I'm feeling powerful. I'd never seen him so weak, so lightheaded. "I'm so close, Tess." Reese stuttered out. Of all the times Reese had tasted me, it was time to get what belonged to me. His legs trembled, his stomach tightening as he let out a loud moan.

I swallowed the release, something even Reese wasn't prepared for as his head lifted in shock. "Jesus Christ, Tessa. You... How long have you been hiding that from me?" He pants, seeing stars as he focuses on the ceiling. I shrug, wiping my mouth on the back of my hand. "I've never really done that before." I admit, laying down beside him.

"Bullshit." Reese laughs breathlessly. "Never?" My eyes meet his as we face each other on our sides. His hand traces up and down my arm, leaving chills in its place. "Well, I did it for Tim once, but I didn't really like it."

It was true, I'm not sure what I didn't like about it. I know I was young, dumb and trying to impress him. But I was nowhere near ready for that level of intimacy with anyone.

Reese nods, pulling me up close to him. He looks down at me, taking deep inhales. "But you liked doing it for me?" he asked, softly brushing the hair from my sticky face.

Liked it? I *loved* it.

I nod, my eyes feeling heavier with every brush of his hand. "Was it good for you?" I sleepily asked, cracking one eye to listen to him. Reese only smirked.

"No one has ever fit my entire dick in their mouth so quickly, so yeah. I think you did pretty fuckin' good." He chuckled, kissing the top of my head. I'm sure the heat is radiating from my body at his comment. "Okay, shut up." I covered my face with the blanket, feeling the aftershock of what I'd done. I felt dirty, but in the best kind of way.

Thirty-Seven

TESSA

September 20th

Reese sighs, frustrated by my hesitancy, as he holds his hand out to me. I shake my head no, refusing to take it and deciding my fate regarding the water. "What if something touches my foot?" I pout, digging my feet deeper into the white, hot sand. "Tessa..." Reese sympathized, taking a step closer to me as he raked in the sight of my pink bikini and bare legs. I feel my arms wrapping around my body instinctively, shielding the world from my vulnerability and lack of confidence.

My heart is pounding and I'm feeling increasingly anxious as Reese's patience with me wears thin. The ocean looks different than at home, the water so clear and crisp, the fish swimming in the depths are visible. I step back, my hands wrapped tighter around my body. "I can't," I whine, feeling like an idiot for making such a fuss about something so simple.

Reese stares at me with a look of annoyance, but that quickly turns to a mischievous grin when he assumes the position to chase after me. "Don't," I say, pointing my finger at him as I back away. "You've got three seconds, Dawson." He smirked, sulking out of the water, like a cheetah on the move for its prey.

"One... Two..."

His arms are around me before he can say three, his body is so cold it takes my breath away. I kick my feet in the air with no hope as he walks us into the ocean.

We're shoulder depth when Reese finally lets me go. I pump my feet to stay up as he shakes the water from his raven hair. "I hate you." I lie with my brows crunched. Reese's smile glimmers off the sun's morning light. "You can't tell me you'd rather wake up any other way." Reese turns to watch the sun as it takes its highest place in the sky. I don't respond, I only watch for myself. It warms the water and my wet skin. I shut my eyes, basking in its glory. I'm grateful to have this opportunity and I'm even more grateful to have known Reese in this new light.

"I can't believe I'm in the Maldives." I laugh, breaking the silence between us as Reese pulls me to wrap around his body. He chuckles, giving me cold, playful kisses on my neck. "I'll take you anywhere you wanna go, Tessa." He smirks, my arms tightening around his neck as we float. "Vegas?" I ask with a raised brow.

"I can't promise I'm not banned from most of the casinos but yes, I can take you to Vegas." Reese's nose grazes mine and I smile at his sense of humor. There wasn't a doubt in my mind that his face was plastered on many 'do not serve' lists out west.

"Grand Canyon?"

"Anywhere, Tessa." He reiterates, his lips grazing mine in a slow kiss. I feel his tongue creep in, it's a feeling I'm now so familiar and comfortable with. He was my green light at the end of the dock, always reachable yet ever illusive. Reese was real, he was tangible. He was someone I could have and have it all with. But he came with his own set of complications and issues. It was a double-edged sword, and now I was stuck between wanting him and the problems that could come with that burning desire.

We spent the rest of the day there on the beach, both of us enjoying the warm sun and the calming sounds of the ocean waves. I relaxed in the sand, working on my tan as Reese watched me from nearby.

I tried to keep his hands off me as he tried to find any excuse to touch me, even in the innocence of daylight. In essence, we were two people trying to pretend that there was nothing going on between us, when in fact the tension was so palpable that we could cut it with a knife. I knew the second he got me inside, I was done for, just like every day before.

As the sun began to set, the golden hour faded away. Music and laughter could be heard coming from the bar nearby. I shifted myself upwards, propping up on my hands as the thought of people excited me.

"Let's go!" I smiled, filled with energy and a desire for new stimulation. As much as I liked Reese, I was growing bored of our same conversations the last two days. But he didn't seem to feel the same way, shaking his head and laying back down on the sand as he let his arm rest behind his head.

"No, lay back down." Reese groaned. My heart skips a beat as he grabs my upper arms and pulls me on top of him, the sand scuffing between our bodies. He then strokes my back gently, doing his best to convince me to stay on the beach with him instead of going to the bar. I can tell that he's determined, as well as being very persuasive with his charm. After all, it had always worked on me before. "Please, there's a band." I whined. I could feel my body getting weak with every gentle touch. "Just lay with me." Reese smirked, as if he would win this battle.

With the last of my last feministic strength, I push off him.

"I'll just go by myself." I smirked as I knew his possessive side would come to the front at the mention of me leaving alone. "Fine, go right ahead." He scoffed, not giving me a second glance. Sure enough, I was right on the money with the sound of sand kicking up behind me only a few minutes later. He was too easy to manipulate, and I couldn't help but feel a little proud of myself for it. I continued walking, a slow, graceful sway to my steps as I headed towards the entertainment of the evening. "You're so fucking stubborn." He groaned, walking into the bar behind me.

I tie my sheer coverup a little tighter around my body as Reese guides me to a table from behind. "Let's order food and go." He looks over his shoulders as if he would run into someone. "What's wrong with you?" I snickered, looking at the menu. "What? Nothing. This is just not my scene." He groaned, rolling his eyes at the old couple dancing to the 1970s cover band. "Oh, please. You're at the club with your friends every weekend." I sighed, annoyed with his attitude as I sip the water dropped off by the waitress.

"*This* is not a club, Tessa." Reese stifles a laugh as the elderly man in a Hawaiian shirt twirls his wife in a matching dress. My lips curl into a smile without my permission and I struggle holding my anger with him.

I order a salad, Reese sticks with his water. I can tell he'd like to be anywhere but here.

The singer of the band sports a blowout, the lengthy locks ending just past his shoulders. His shirt is unbuttoned at the top, just enough to reveal a bit of his chest hair, while his pants are covered in sequins and sparkles. He moves about the stage with a sway of his hips, singing the songs like we'd traveled back in time. I giggle at his erotic dances as Reese only cringes, sliding down in his seat.

"For this next one, I'd like you to grab that *sweet*, sweet lady in your life. And tell her she's *so* much more than a woman." The man winked as my eyes went wide.

"Reese, do you know what this means?" My cheeks hurt; I was smiling so hard as *More Than A Woman* by the Bee Gees began. Reese shook his head with a groan. "That it's time to fucking leave?" He sighed, playing with the straw wrapper. "I love this song. Just one dance, please?" I pouted, standing from my stool. I pulled on his hands, trying to get him up from the table. "Hell, no. Let's go, Tess, please. Fuck the salad." Reese whined, throwing his head back.

I wasn't leaving here without my dance, whether it was with Hawaiian guy or him.

Thirty-Eight

REESE

I shake my head, standing my ground. The music was, indeed, shitty. The crowd was lame. But as Tessa pleaded with those big, brown eyes, I could not help but feel my resolve cracking under the onslaught of her cuteness and innocence. My anger dissipated quickly as I was lulled with her innocent gaze and her simple, yet adorable, request.

Tessa folds her hands, pleadingly and pulls in her bottom lip with a smile.

"One fucking song." I grumble as she squeals and pulls me over to the dance floor. I take her hand, twirling her so she's facing away from me, and I gaze down at her swaying hips against mine. She was like a serpent being charmed from a basket, moving in seduction. My hands grip her hips, sliding against her coverup and guiding them along with the beat of the music. The tanning oil fills my senses, making my breath catch in my throat.

"You don't know anything about this move." Tessa smirked as she turned to face me, a hand on her hip as she pointed with her index on her free hand. It was a playful taunt of the *Saturday Night Fever* look, filling me with a mix of amusement and confusion. It was goofy, but it was also incredibly sexy. I'd never seen her so carefree.

Her curls were full of sand, her body covered in tiny grains that made her glisten in the twinkling bar lights. She was still in that bikini that left little to the imagination.

It was the most honest version of her that I've ever seen, as if she was willing to cast aside the mask she wears and embrace her true self. I was falling victim to her without much restraint.

I took her hand, spinning her so she was facing back towards me and pulling her closer, as if I couldn't stand not touching her. She looked so beautiful. There were no other words to describe her, I could read a thousand novels and never have the right words. She was so soft in my grip, and I wanted to hold her closely for as long as possible.

"Tessa, I love you."

She freezes, an expression I can't read. The words I'd only ever said to my mother fall out, unbidden and unexpected, the intensity of my emotions overwhelming me. It comes out faster than I anticipated, finally acknowledging that I'd kept it hidden deep down inside. I couldn't control the words as they spilled out of me.

"And... I don't want you to say it back. I just *really* had to tell you."

Tessa continues to look up at me, her eyes the size of the moon, as I begin to panic. "What was in that water, Finch?" She seems to think that I am making it all up, like I would lie to her about something so serious. Regardless, she looks as if something is wrong with her or maybe she's just joking around. My brain is too foggy to think clearly, so I keep staring back at her until I finally clear my throat.

"I'm serious." I moved my hands to her cheeks.

"You're tired." *Tired?* I was wide awake. Tessa sighed, her eyes darting between both of mine, the song is ending, and I have nothing left to say. I could hear a bit of frustration in her voice, as if she didn't understand why I was telling her this. My words may have been simple, but the feeling behind them was anything but. "You just don't get it, do you?" I scoffed, the blue stage lights covering our bodies.

"I'm not fucking with you." I looked down at her, my cheeks sore from the stupid grin plastered on my face. "Okay." She smiled, still not believing me as her arms returned around my neck. The band slows with an *Eric Clapton* hit.

"I'll just have to prove it, won't I?" My eyelids lower lazily as I smile, swaying her side to side.

"Just take me back to the room, Loverboy." Tessa moves to her tiptoes to give me a kiss and I feel like a schoolboy. I felt a tingle all throughout my body, and all I could think about was how good it felt to be so close to her. I didn't want this moment to end, I didn't dare pull away first.

During the walk back to the room, I listened to Tessa's pleasant ramblings while I mentally planned for tomorrow. A candlelit dinner on the beach would have to prove to Tessa just how much I loved her. Maybe she'd say it back. In truth, I was horrified at the idea of her never saying it back. "Shower?" Tessa asked, grabbing two towels. "You go, I'll catch up." I smiled, grabbing the camera we'd bought from the gift shop in town.

Inside, are photos of mainly Tessa. I'd been to the Maldives with Brice and Christian a few times. I didn't need more pictures. But I couldn't pass up an opportunity to photograph her, she was an enigma. It became almost an obsession, the need to document her in different spaces and situations. I snicker to myself, stopping on a picture of us, my tongue on her cheek as she cheeses hard.

I look up, listening to her soft hums from the shower. With Tessa in my life, everything was suddenly falling into place. I lived my life feeling unlovable and unworthy. My childhood was turbulent at best. I'd been alienated and outcasted, a stranger in my own home. Yet here I was, completely and utterly in love with a girl who didn't care about any of it. I had found the person I was meant to be with, my missing piece.

"Thank you for dancing with me tonight." Tessa smiled, crawling onto the bed in one of my t-shirts. I was glad to have packed her favorites. She claimed they smelled like me. I didn't have the heart to tell her that I always loaded them with my cologne before I saw her.

I roll my eyes, shaking my hair against my towel. "Yeah, you owe me." I winked, loosely gripping the one around my waist as I combed my hair back in the mirror.

"I do?"

My back is turned to her, yet my body twitches at her voice.

All the hair on my neck stands, as if my spidey-senses are tingling. I know that tone. I *love* that tone.

When I face her, her knees are to her chest, her legs parted with an evil smirk on her face. I let out a heavy sigh, my focus shifting to the missing underwear from the equation. The lack of clothing was nothing new, but the smirk was what really gave me the impression that the evening would be filled with something much more interesting. My eyes flicker to meet hers and I don't bother getting dressed. I know our agenda for the night.

September 21st

My body is aching. Although Tessa didn't say those three words, there was no denying the sounds she made, the cries of my name being enough justification on their own. I lift my head from the pillow, she's curled up to me like a puppy. I smile, brushing the bedhead from her eyes. Her mouth hangs slightly agape, unresponsive to my touches. I decided to leave her be. We'd leave for New York tomorrow and I owed her today. There was nothing but doom for us back home.

Tessa sleepily stretches, sitting up to look at her surroundings. My hands trace up and down her back, helping her become more aware. She rubs her eyes, rolling away from me. "Are you not ready to get up?" I snickered, pressing my body against hers.

"I'm sore, don't talk to me." She groaned, pulling the blankets up further.

She had always been dramatic in other areas of her life as well, so it wasn't really a surprise to see her being dramatic about being sore. I made a mental note to tease her about it sometime later. I had to admit that it was sexy, knowing what I could do to an innocent personality. For now, I was just going to let her rest.

"I'm gonna go for a run." I kiss her cheek and she nods, her eyes still shut. I walk to my suitcase, quietly pulling my phone out and a blue Giants cap. "Your ass better be out of bed when I get back." I scold as Tessa flips me the middle finger.

When I'm a safe distance down the beach, I turn my phone on and prop myself under some rocks. I catch my breath, scrolling through my newest messages from Kayla. All of which are relatively the same. I decide its time I make myself known to her.

@finch_reese: Tessa is okay. She'll be home soon.

It was late in New York; I hadn't prepared myself for a response.

@kklorne517: how could you lie to her?
@kklorne517: she's never gonna talk to you again.
@finch_reese: I know.

I close the app, there's no use in that conversation.

Thirty-Nine

TESSA

"How was your run?" I stretched in bed as Reese let the sunlight through the door. My eyes are burning, like I didn't sleep last night. Which is easy to do when you're sharing a bed with a man who doesn't know how to keep his hands to himself. I couldn't complain, Reese knew every part of my body inside and out. "Get your ass up." He snickers, sitting in an armchair and untying his shoes. I can't help but roll back over, getting comfortable once more. I'm not sure if it's the inevitable dread of returning home tomorrow or the island relaxation, but my motivation is nonexistent.

Reese unzips his suitcase as I try to fall back asleep. "Oh, no you don't." He rips the blankets from the bed as I groan. I want to lay here forever. "Get up." He smiles, crawling on top of me, kissing every inch of skin peeking out from the t-shirt.

"You smell." I squirmed, pushing him away from me. His aroma of musky sweat is one I could get used to. "Then come shower with me." Reese's hand slides up my mid-thigh and rolls me to lay on my back. It's then I see his backwards hat, his cheeks burnt from the sun and droplets of sweat on his glossy face. I've never seen him wear a hat; I was sure my dad had the same one. The Giants won the Super Bowl in 2012 and *everyone* bought that hat. I stretch my arms above my head with a lazy smile. "I'm not the one who smells." I giggled as he changed our positions.

He props my legs on either side of him, bending them at the knee and caressing up toward my hips. His hands could swallow me whole. "Yeah, but it's so hot when you wash me."

I lift my foot and push it to his chest with an eye roll. "You're a freak." I snickered as he massaged my feet. "I can show you a freak."

Reese winks and I jump from my skin. "Reese, if you put my foot in your mouth, I'm getting on the first plane out of here." I firmly spoke, laying my boundaries on the line.

He only chuckles as my cheeks burn brighter than his sunburn. "Relax, I was only joking." He moves my leg back out of his way, now hovering over me.

"I've got plans for us tonight." He kisses my neck, and my arms are instinctively around his neck like a bike lock. "You *will* be leaving this bed." He moves to the other side. I want to glue my back to the bed to prevent my arch as he kisses me again. "So, let's get up... Make our way to the shower..." Reese's hands move to the hem of my shirt, and I sit up slightly to help him remove it. His lips graze my sternum and move down to my abdomen. I take a sharp breath.. "And go to the beach." He moves down lower and I'm shaking.

I groan as he stops at my navel, looking up at me to gauge my reaction. "Come on, princess." He smiles as he tightly grips my hip, leaving red fingerprints in its place. There's no coming down from this high, not without release. "No, I don't want to shower now." I pouted, trying to link my legs around his shoulders. "As much as I'd love my dessert first, I need breakfast." Reese kisses both of my inner thighs delicately enough to make me whimper.

He lets out a soft laugh as I am practically crying for him. When did I become so dependent on him? "You're such a baby." He smirks, crawling off the bed. I'm left with his lingering aroma.

I followed him into the shower, eager to give him exactly what he wanted. I take my time, letting the suds ripple against his muscles, massaging his back, and caressing every inch of his taut frame. His muscles are tight as I take in his physique and appreciate every inch of its perfection.

His breath hitches as I wash his chest, making it clear exactly how much he's enjoying the moment.

I can feel him flexing under my touch, and my fingers continue to explore his body slowly and thoroughly. I take my time rubbing every inch of him, paying special attention to his most sensitive and tender areas. Reese drops his head back with a moan, leaving his lips parted. "You're so tense."

I sigh, moving to kneel in front of him. "Don't… Please don't sit down there." He stutters out, looking down at me.

"I'm just gonna rub out your quads." I snickered, running my hands up and down his left thigh. I try not to focus on his length that I'm so hungry for. My stomach is growling for him to fill me up. But I'm staying on my best behavior as he leans against the walk-in shower wall. "Oh, God. Yes…" He grunts, running a hand through his hair as I rub the knots from his muscles. I move on to the right leg and Reese lets out a sigh. Exercise is his way around going to therapy, it shows in how vigorously his body is overworked. Rather than discuss his feelings, he would run miles at a time.

"Fuck, Tessa." He places both hands on top of his head as he watches me, and I giggle. "It's just a massage, Reese." I smile up at him, working my way down his calves as he lets out a laugh that seems to vibrate in his throat. "Yeah, in the shower while you're completely naked in front of me." He snickered as I rose back to my feet. "Hmm," I sighed, turning to get my hair wet. "Yet, you won't do anything about it." I raised a brow, daring to prove him wrong. I didn't recognize myself; I was a cat in heat. His confession from last night has corroded my brain. I want to hear him say it again. Over and over. *I love you, Tessa.*

Reese washes my hair, shaking his head at my comment. "Tess, I would love to fuck you in this shower, but I already told you I have plans for us tonight." His denying me only made me question myself. Had I broken Reese? Was he the man Maurice wanted him to be or was he just trying to make me work for what I wanted?

I pout, dropping my shoulders with a sigh. "Stop whining." He grips my hair tight, pulling me back against his chest and I giggle. The heat of his breath fills my ear, as his voice is low and husky. Reese kisses my cheek, his grip lightening up.

"Should we take the car?" He points to the time capsule parked out front.

I shake my head no. We'd grown up in New York, walking was in our blood. The car was beautiful, something straight out of a movie. But I loved to walk, I loved to hike. Being in nature was my safe space.

The year my family moved to Florida, Kelseigh and I took a trip to California. It was our first, and only, time alone at that point. We hiked through Yosemite for three straight days, sleeping under the stars and reminiscing on past fights.

"It all seems kind of dumb now, don't it?" Kelseigh asked, pulling her smoldering marshmallow off the stick with her teeth. I nod, my gaze fixed on the orange flames. It's as if I can see my past through them. Every track meet, every school dance, every bad Kelseigh break up. "You know you don't have to go with them." I replied, poking the fire. It was almost like I was trying to convince her to stay. Like I'd be lost without her. "Are you kidding? I can't wait to get out of New York."

My heart sinks, my whole family is ready to abandon ship.

"Right, well… You can always visit me." My offer is met with a nod and nothing else. Deep down, I think them moving away pulled us closer. She was no longer down the hall, two doors away.

She was states and a phone call gone.

Reese groaned, following me up the hill while carrying the bowls of fruit we picked up from the local market. "I don't see why we couldn't just sit at the beach." He huffs behind me.

"Reese, that's all we've done for two days. It's our last day here, I'd like to try something new. Besides, you have the evening planned." It was only fair. Reese decided everything about *my* birthday trip. I deserved one thing. I adjust the backpack on my shoulders and pause, listening to the sounds amongst the trees. "Do you hear that?"

The noises of rushing water fill the distance, and Reese raises a brow like he's confused. I smile at his expression, finding his surprise comical. It was something so simple and normal, but it was a part of his charm. "You know, for someone who posts about his travels online, you sure know nothing about hiking." I folded my arms as Reese groans.

"I ran two miles this morning, Tess. The last thing I wanted to do was hike." I snicker at his complaining, turning to walk backwards through the trees. "I promise it'll be worth it." I smile, taking a second to admire his unbuttoned shirt.

We had rounded several corners, following the trail and passing through densely wooded areas. And as we took the final turn, I could see the sight in front of us. The hidden waterfall was like paradise, a secret treasure tucked away in the lush greenery of the forests. The waterfall was small but beautiful, splashing against the rocks into a small pond. The sound of its cascade filled the air, the water reflecting the glimmers of sunlight that had managed to worm their way through the canopy.

"Holy shit." Reese laughs. I wasted no time stripping my jean shorts and t-shirt, jumping in. "What are you doing?" He asks, cocking his head to admire my body. "Swimming." I kick my feet, staying afloat as my hands work at the knot on the back of my swim top.

Reese pulls a towel from the backpack and sits, opening the container of fruit. "I see that." He grins, popping a pineapple chunk in his mouth. The juice drips down his chin as he licks the sticky texture from his lips. "You do?" I threw my top on the towel, seeing if I could hook him back into our morning events. "I may be easy, but I'm not that easy, Tess." He snickers, sucking his fingertips clean. God, I wish he was sucking on my skin. Maybe I needed therapy.

Forty

REESE

My breath hitches as the black bikini top splashes me on its landing. Though I was a sucker for pink, the black was just as nice. Tessa sinks down to her nose in the water as I close the fruit back up. "I'm gonna get you in touch with a priest when we get back." I pull the blue gift shop shirt from my freshly loosened shoulders, my shorts following close behind. Tessa's eyes loom over my dick and I painfully laugh. This was the longest day of our lives.

I felt like sticking pins in my eyes at the thought of having to keep my hands off her. The need to touch her, the desire to hear her sighs and moans. Tessa was beautiful, she was intelligent, and she was funny. Her skin was so soft, she fit so perfectly against my body. I've thought about every time we've had sex in a fast forward loop after she threw that top at me. *Tonight, would be worth it,* I reminded myself. Tonight, I would give her every ounce of my strength, my affection and my love.

I get a running start, cannonballing into the clear blue water. When I come up, I grab my hat that's drifting away, placing it on Tessa's head. I shake the hair from my face, put my hands on her waist and lift her up without any trouble. Her arms loop around my neck, squeezing just the right amount. The sound of the waterfall fills our ears, engulfing our senses, and it feels like the soundtrack to our life together.

It was loud, and at times overwhelming. We were the rocks beneath the water, trapped under the pressure of the outside world and the judgment of what was back home.

I hold Tessa close, feeling the heat from her body against mine, and I breathe in the scent of her, wanting nothing more than to just hold her and never let her go.

"I love you." I smiled, my fingers toying with the strings on her bottoms. "That's what I heard." Tessa wet her lips as I moved a hand to the back of her neck. She wasn't ready. I still had tonight. "I want to stay here forever." I sighed, my grip now cupping her breast. Tessa leans back slightly, flipping my cap backwards on her head. "In the waterfall?" She questions, her eyes struggling to stay open. My thumb rolls her nipple, and she shutters, I needed to give myself a *little* fun before tonight.

"No, with you." I speak against her neck as she moans. "Stop teasing me." She whimpered, her lips beginning to turn blue at the water's crisp temperature. Tessa looks into my eyes, causing my heart to race. "If you're not gonna fuck me, then let me go, please." She smirked as I erupted in laughter at her vulgar mouth. I always knew she meant business when she spoke that way. I was the best she'd ever had; I can tell by the way I made her tremble with every touch and hot breath.

"I'm not gonna fuck you, Tessa. Not right now." My hand drifts down the front of her bottoms, sliding across her opening through the nylon fabric. She was so desperate for me, and I knew behind that desperation, was all the love that I needed. The thought crossed my mind to fuck the love out of her, right there. It'd be so simple, no interruptions, no secrecy, just us.

For a second, I'm leaning into it. I kiss down to her collarbone, my hand working into her bottoms for both of our pleasure. I'm practically growling against her skin. We didn't have a lot in common, but what we did have was pleasure. Tessa bucks against my fingers, bobbing up and down in the water on them. Her hands tighten around my neck as she moans.

Focus, Finch. Focus. I retract my hand, and she exhales, resting her head against my shoulder to catch her breath.

"Why'd you stop?" She pouts as I stare through the canopy of trees, asking God the same question. "I told you; I'm saving myself for tonight." I let her go with a smile and we drift apart, swimming in the small pond.

"There's got to be something we can do to occupy our time that doesn't involve sex." Tessa runs her tongue across her top teeth, softly pushing herself off the bottom of the pond every so often. The water goes up to her chin but stops at my chest. "We could always just talk?"

I give a lazy grin as Tessa's brows rise. "About what?" She swims in a circle around me.

"Anything. Ask me anything."

"Who's Brooklynn?"

The question makes me queasy. She'd been sitting on that for a while. I should have known it would come up. "Brooklynn. She's uhm, well... She's someone I used to sleep with." I swim closer to her, but she keeps her distance. "Did you sleep with her after you slept with me?"

"No." I answer honestly without hesitation, Tessa nods. "What's she like?"

"Why does it matter?" I ask, once again trying to get closer. "I'm just curious. You know all about my ex." Tessa's tone is soft, but she holds a callous resistance with me, as if she's insecure. "She's not an ex. I went to high school with her. She's a year younger than me. Her parents cut her off after a picture of her being tossed around a party went around in the paper. She's a good girl, but she's always been mixed up in bad shit. And when I'm with her, I get into the same shit." I sighed, annoyed with my honest rambling. I'm hopeful that it's enough to appease her.

"Like that day when I wanted my wallet?"

It wasn't.

"Yes. That was the last time I slept with her."

She nods, coming to terms with there being nothing between Brooklynn and me. I feel my heart return to its original state. "What about you? Did you sleep with Tim?" I asked with a grin, already knowing the answer.

"Oh please. I hadn't had sex in like two years." She scoffs, swimming to the edge of the pond. "What?" I scoff, following her out.

She puts my blue button up over her shoulders, leaving it undone so I can fantasize about the curvature of her breasts peeking through. I throw my shorts back on and sit beside her on the towel. "Tessa, I basically took your virginity." I snicker, tightening my shoulder for the punch I'm about to receive. "We can't all be New York's hottest playboy." She teases, opening the fruit and pulling out a watermelon slice. I watch her lips suck out the juice and I zone out.

"Right, well, I wear my crown with pride." I roll my eyes, grabbing a strawberry. "I haven't slept with *that* many women." I sighed, feeling embarrassed at my reputation. Was it a lie? *Yes.* Did Tessa know that? *Unfortunately.*

"Reese, you know way too much about a woman's body for me to believe that." She giggles, grabbing another slice and laying her head in my lap. "That counts as a compliment." I wipe the juice from her lips as she looks up at me. "I meant it as one."

The hike back is excruciating. I'm tired, wet and sandy. But I'd do it again. "Remember, this is a special night. So, dress the occasion." I smirked, taking her chin in my hand and pulling her into a kiss. I glance at the freshly made bed and sigh, thinking about our last night together. She disappears into the bathroom, where she'll be for the next two hours I assume.

I grabbed my phone from my suitcase and check my texts. There was nothing more from Kayla, I'd appeased her by knowing Tessa wasn't dead and buried in the sand somewhere. I sigh heavily, seeing a missed call from Brindlewood. I knew Maurice was getting worse. He was eighty-three.

That's what happened in the circle of life. I didn't need an update, though I would be thanking him for being so cruel to me, as it led me to her. I tucked the phone away and lay on the bed, reviewing my plan.

After she finishes in the shower, it's my turn. I'm quick, nervous and eager to get to our dinner.

"That was fast." She snickers, applying her makeup as I walk behind her. I grip my towel with one hand, the other turning her face to kiss her cheek.

I gel my hair back, leaving one strand to fall in my face like Tessa loves. My hands tremble as I button my cream shirt halfway, tucking it into my khaki pants. I decided against the penguin suit, as it just wasn't me. It wasn't us. Tessa hums in the bathroom, indifferent to the knock coming at the door.

"We've got everything set up for you down here, honey." The old woman from the bar smiles and I sigh in relief.

"He's got the music?" I asked, putting my watch on with shaky breaths as she nodded excitedly. "Thank you for doing this." I give a half smile, watching her walk away. Everything was falling into place.

I'm tying my shoes in the armchair when Tessa opens the door. Her hair was styled into a pony with a white ribbon, her curls giving her a soft, airy look. Her dress was a light shade of blue, almost gray, floating around her upper arms and off her shoulders. It ended at her mid-thighs, just enough to be both flowy and free. The material was so light, I was completely speechless. She was angelic and so foreign to me, so innocent.

"Is it too much? I brought another one." I stand from the chair, slowly as if I'll wake up by moving too fast. "Tessa..." I whisper, kissing her hand as she blushes. "What?" She rolls her eyes playfully, as if she's incapable of seeing herself the way I do.

"You've never looked more beautiful." My voice is almost too serious, I can feel the lump growing in my throat. I'm so scared of losing her. I exhale slowly as she looks up at me over her thick lashes. "You look really nice too." She giggles, I can feel the heat radiating from her cheeks. My thumb rubs over her knuckles as I can't stop looking at her eyes. Whatever iridescent glitter she has on them has hooked me like a siren.

"So, what's this *special thing* you have planned?" Tessa sighs, taking my arm as we begin walking down the dark beach. "I know I've told you I love you, but you've given me that same damn look every time. Like you don't believe me. So, I wanted to show you that I'm not just saying it."

We approach the decorated set up and I watch Tessa's face brighten, her jaw slacked in surprise. "You did this?" Her eyes glimmer in the fairy lights strung up in a square, a small table and two chairs in the middle. She turns to look at me. "Reese, I..."

"With some help." I smile, she's as speechless as I am about her. On the table is a bag of gummy sharks and a glass of red wine for the two of us. On a stool, the old man in his same Hawaiian shirt, strums his guitar while his wife stands beside him. "Reese..." She repeats my name like she's having a stroke. "Dance with me." I extend my hand and she's hesitant. "You hate dancing."

I playfully roll my eyes and smile. "Please?" I watch her brows go up in weakness and possibly in love. I fold her hand in mine, my other on her lower back. I'll respect her boundaries this time, keeping myself above her hips. She plays with the curls at the back of my neck, and I'm transported to the first time we danced together at Brindlewood.

"Do you recognize the song?" I quiz while the woman sings *At Last* by Etta James. She's a touch out of tune, but Tessa doesn't seem to notice between her sniffles. I've thought about this song at least once a day since then. She moves her hand under my arm and on my back to rest her head on my chest. "Your first class." She giggles.

"You threw me to the fucking wolves that day, you know? You challenged me to be a better man. To be someone that could make a difference. I've never been the same since that day. I've thought about you from sunup to sundown."

I lift her chin to look up at me.

"I *love* you, Tessa. And I mean it." I smile, tears daunting an escape. She stares at me for a moment, the words are on the tip of her tongue, but she doesn't say it back. Instead, she pulls me down by my neck, kissing me slowly.

Forty-One

REESE

"I can't believe you'd go through all of this for me." Tessa giggled, laying on the blanket beside me. She lay on her side as I caressed her arm with my index finger. Her silhouette is intoxicating in the moonlight. The old couple had left, we were alone once more. I propped myself up on my hand, admiring her. "I'm not gonna repeat myself again." I snickered as she grabbed a gummy shark from the bag. "Not until I know you feel that way about me." I tap the tip of her nose and she blinks slowly.

"Well, I think I feel that way." She smiles.

"Think and know are two different things." I sighed, biting the shark before she could. I wish I could just force it out of her. "Yes, but they're just words." She gave a witty smirk. It was true, but they were sacred. "Then just say them." I teased, rolling on top of her. Tessa's breathy laugh fills my senses as she wraps her legs around me. My elbows are on either side of her head as I stroke her pulled back curls. "Tell me you love me, Tessa." My thumb moves down to her cheekbone, then her bottom lip.

"Not here." She sighed, her hand rubbing my forearms up to my jaw. I want to pout. I want to kick my feet and cry. "Where?" I ask, trying to bury my whine.

"Come on." She smiles, motioning me to climb off her.

We walk back to our room for the last time, in silence. I'm feeling defeated, like I'll never hear those words. She doesn't love me, and all of this was for nothing.

Tessa runs the bath, pouring an excessive amount of bubbly mixture.

She steps out of her sandals and turns around for me to unbutton her dress. I don't even have to be told; my fingers are already put to work. At every button, I stop to kiss the skin that is exposed.

The dress falls to her feet, and she steps out in just her thong. She turns to face me and I'm swallowing hard, feeling the adrenaline build up. She removes my shirt first, then unbuttons my pants. "I want you to take a bath with me." She orders as my body is covered in chills; my stomach tied knot after knot. I needed to do this for her.

There's an undertone in the room. Like we both understand that things won't be the same when we return home. So, for tonight, I will give her everything I have.

I pull my khakis off, taking her hand to help her in the bath. I step in after, easing my way to sitting. The water smells of cherry blossoms and I'm feeling more relaxed by the second. Tessa moves to sit between my legs, leaning back against my chest. I rub her shoulders as she lets out soft breaths through her nose. This wasn't as bad as I'd imagined. I feel more connected to her, more present. I take a deep breath, my head resting against the porcelain. Her hand creeps from the water to hold mine on the tub's ledge.

"The last time I told someone I loved them was years ago. I'm sure you already know who." She giggled and my blood ran cold at the thought of Tim. *Please don't tell me you still love him*, I thought. "But with you, Reese... I just..." She turns to face me, and my heart is jumping from my rib cage. "I'm so free and myself. I thought I could push it down... Or convince myself you were lying, but I can't." Tessa straddles my lap, the water pushing around us as her elbows rest on my shoulders. I pull the ribbon from her hair, watching her curls fall over her sudsy shoulders. She was an angel.

My very own angel.

I rub her back, lightly scratching the wet skin, her hands in my sandy hair. I'm withholding a whimper as my jaw slacks; I know it's coming.

"I love you, Reese."

My lips meet hers fast and hard, so fast the water shifts around us again. I want to be gentle, but I've been starved of those words from everyone in my life. Her hips softly grind against my dick, and I moan into her mouth. "Say it again." I whine, running a hand to her throat softly.

"I love you."

I fight back my own tears as I run my thumb over her bottom lip. "Again." My free hand positions my length beneath her, allowing her to sit down on it the way we've craved all day. I've missed her vice around me, allowing me to stretch and deepen her in the way only I was allowed to. She was mine, and I was officially hers. "Oh, fuck..." She moans, her eyes rolling back as she loses sight of reality. "Tell me, Tessa. I have to hear it again, baby."

"I... I love you, Reese." She whispers, her lips trembling and her body slowly bouncing on mine. I sit up, our chests together as the water splashes onto the floor like needles. "I fucking love you, Tessa." My hands dig at her back, hungrily. We're conjoined, out of breath already. All the tension of waiting is melting in this bath water. "Fuck, yes... Just like that. More, baby." I moan, my arms under hers and hooking her shoulders to pull her down completely. I hit her cervix, knowing I've gone as deep as I can. I pepper her chest in kisses, sucking and nibbling on her breast. Her head falls back, hands never leaving my hair. "Reese, baby... Oh my god." My name, holy fuck. *Reese, Reese, Reese.* I wanted it on repeat.

The bath is nearly empty, her movements getting more sporadic. My hands are trembling. "I want to be in bed." She moans, stopping her motions. I nod and with a quick swoop of my hands, she's being carried to bed, dripping water across the wood floors.

I lay her down, crawling on top of her. I wet my lips, now nervous, as if it was my first-time having sex. I kiss the space between her breasts before sitting back on my knees.

I stroked myself, lifting and parting her legs a little more. "I want to feel you, I want you to give all of yourself to me. No holding back. It's our last night here and I want to act like it." I stammer out, trying to stabilize my breathing. She blushes.

"I'm already yours, Reese Michael. Do what you want with me."

Green light. I have the green light. I push my length back in, slowly. "Yes, Reese. More..." Her back arches. As much as I wanted to give her that light passion, I needed her to feel me everywhere.

I force myself all the way in, my head buried in her shoulder as she cries in ecstasy. My grunts are primal, My jaw hangs open and I'm afraid to open my eyes. Her nails draw blood from my back, the bed crashing the wall with every thrust. I can't slow down, I can't stop. Her legs slide up my sides and I have goosebumps. "That's my girl. Does that feel good, baby?" I look down, her skin so soft, her face glowing with sweat. Tessa nods, wetting her lips and unable to speak.

"Use your words, princess." I pull myself back as she opens her mouth and slam back in. "Yes, oh fuck yes." She wails, her back nearly snapping. "There you go, you can take it."

Her legs began to shake, she was about to orgasm. I wasn't ready. I pulled back. "Did you wanna cum, baby?" I asked in a coy voice. Tessa whined, nodding quickly as her hands searched my body anxiously. "How bad?"

She looked like she might cry, my thumb slowly circling her clit enough to build her back up. "S-so bad." Tessa whimpered. "Beg for it." I demanded as if it were even necessary.

"Please, please let me cum, Reese." She cried, sitting up to pull me down on her. "Wait for me, Tess. I want you to cum with me." I winced, feeling myself build the tension. My breath was ragged, my body beginning to ache.

With one last thrust, I collapsed on her. Our bodies drenched, our heads throbbing. Tessa laid star-fish underneath me.

I kiss her forehead, rolling off. She blinked slowly, practically falling asleep. I wasn't ready to lose her just yet. "You still love me?" I asked, resting limp on my stomach, trying to catch my breath. "Of course." She kisses my shoulder, looking over her markings on me. "I've branded you after all." Her index finger traces my fresh, stinging scratches. *Branded.*

Reese Finch, bad boy, playboy and everything in between,

I was now branded by the woman that loved me.

Forty-Two

TESSA

September 22ⁿᵈ

I've never been happier to be back in New York. The smell of pollution, cheap pizza and expensive perfumes hits my senses as we exit the airport. "Shit," Reese wets his lips, speaking under his breath. We're met with a circle of paparazzi, preparing for war. I cling tightly to his arm as we're blinded by flashing lights. He pushes through the chaos, sparing no violence. I've never seen him this way, so aggressive with everyone. They all shout amongst one another as Reese drags me to the car. Whatever the topic is, it's important. Reese had been with me since Wednesday, what damage could he have caused before he left? I can't understand what they're saying as I press my eyes shut, begging to be anywhere else.

Reese slams my car door shut, quickly throwing our bags in the trunk.

"I'm so sorry, I have no idea what they're here for." He runs his hands over his exhausted face. His demeanor is off. His hands are sweaty and he's quiet. He wets his lips profusely and looks all around.

"I'm not sure either, you don't have a mug shot about to air, do you?" I tease, toying with the strings on my gift shop hoodie. Reese ignores my comment as he pulls out of the airport. I don't give it much thought. Even though we'd admitted our love, we had only spoken to one another for several days. The conversations began to lull, we had nothing left to say. We were in dire need of a break from each other's company.

"Do you think we could stop at work to look for my phone?" I asked, crossing my legs in the passenger seat. He looks at me out of the corner

202

of his eye. "Let's get our shit back first." Reese rubs his forehead with one hand, his other on the steering wheel. He isn't his charming self; I'm feeling new tension. It makes my stomach hurt, like the impending dread of a test you know you failed.

I'm quiet the whole way back, thinking of what I could say and what I should do. Reese was barely replying to me, his silence making me feel uneasy.

I'm continuously met with a nod or a simple "Mhm." I was being avoided. Maybe I didn't fix him. Maybe he had something to prove with me. How long it would take me to fall for him, I was his challenge.

Now that he'd completed it, he didn't need me anymore.

I let out a breath I didn't know I was holding at the familiarity of my apartment complex, all of its chipped bricks and weathered windowsills. I turn to Reese, his face pale like he could vomit or faint.

"I love you." He mumbled, looking up at me.

I didn't know what to say. I wanted to call him a liar. If he loved me, why had I felt so invisible in the past hour?

"I love you too." I decided reassurance was my best option. Maybe it was insecurity I was feeling from him. The reporters were a trigger for him. I knew of his past; he had nothing to feel ashamed of. "Promise?" He whispered, pulling the keys from the ignition, never leaving my gaze. I nod softly, feeling my unease returning.

"Go upstairs, I'll grab the bags." He orders, looking down at his feet as I open the car door. I look over my shoulder before entering the building to see him sitting in the same position. His vision fixed on the steering wheel, as if contemplating on leaving. I shake my head, going upstairs.

I don't turn the lights on, relishing the moonlight that illuminates the place. The smell of my apartment is comforting, vanilla and apple. My mother has sent me the same candle every fall from a woman in Florida. She was an older woman, the mayor's wife. And coincidentally, my parents' neighbor. She made candles as a hobby and gave me this one for my birthday the first time I visited.

I ran my hand across my bed, remembering the much larger one I shared with Reese. My hands go numb, tingling at the memories of him wrapped around me. The way his back flexed against my hands, the way my body arched to meet his. Our moans, his warm breath, the lingering in my body still from Saturday. It seemed like weeks ago now.

Reese turns the living room light on when he enters, I can see that not a thing is out of place. "I found your phone. It was under the seat." His tone is still so soft, almost cautious. He places it on the counter and stands back beside my suitcase. "It was?" My brows rise in confusion. That just didn't seem like me. I didn't even remember taking my phone out of my purse. I don't question it; I just want this day to be over. "Thanks."

I hum down the hall as I walk to my bedroom, plopping on my bed as I wait for my phone to turn on. Reese doesn't follow.

My phone dings repeatedly, missed calls, voicemails, texts, direct messages, every form of communication from Kayla. She asks me where I am, if I'm okay, if I've read the Stripe. I'm confused, my mind tramples over thoughts faster than I can process them.

10:50P.M.
T- i thought Reese told you we were going out of town?

She's quick to respond. Always has been, and always will be.

10:51P.M.
K- He's a fucking liar. Where are you?
T- i'm home, what's going on?
K- Thank God. He got her pregnant.
T- who?
K- Brooklynn.

I'm confused. I watched Reese text her. I feel like I have wool over my eyes.

I sit up on the bed, my stomach in knots. I'm going to puke. I quickly logged onto The Stripe's website and sure enough. Reese is on the cover grabbing a pregnancy test off the ground with Brooklynn. She's tall, blonde and everything I'm not. Even on her worst day, she was gorgeous.

I'm breathing so fast; I can't read the article behind my tears. Reese is in the same spot where I left him.

"What is this?" I ask calmly, trying to keep a steady tone. The lump in my throat grows, I can't breathe. He knows, his eyes are red. "I didn't want to hurt you." Reese sighs, running his hands through his hair. "You got her pregnant?" I'm surprised with the tranquility in my voice. I want to scream; I want to rip him in half. But I just can't. I feel sorry for myself.

"It was a mistake. You have to understand-" He takes a step toward me, and I back up. I don't recognize him. I shook my head; I didn't want to understand. "She took care of it, Tessa. She told me."

My eyes grow wide as the tears fall. He didn't even have the courage to go with her. "You made her go alone?" I ask, my pity now focused on her. I can only imagine the way she felt, in that room alone while Reese was with me.

"I didn't know what to do! I just didn't want to fuck this up with you, Tessa. Please, let me just explain from the beginning." His voice cracks, taking my hands. I try to pull them away, taking shaky deep breaths as I cry. I need him to leave.

"Tessa... Come on, baby. I *love* you. Let's talk about it."

"You lied." I look at the ceiling as Reese gets on his knees. I can't look at him. "I asked you about her. Why didn't you tell me?" I cried. "I wanted to; I just didn't know how. I knew you wouldn't speak to me again." He kisses my thighs, gripping his arms tightly around my waist as he sobs. "I'm sorry, okay? I'm so fucking sorry."

There were so many things for him to be sorry for, where did I begin?

"I'm not even mad about that, Reese." My hands meet his hair, caressing and pulling at the hair so delicately as he soaks my skin in salty tears. I have to stand my ground. I'm so weak for him. I weep for the boy inside, losing the only other woman to love him. "You stole my phone. No one knew where I was." I try to push him from me and he squeezes harder, practically pushing the air from my body. "I'm a bad person. I'm so fucking sorry." Reese claws at the material of my shorts, trying to get as close to me as I can.

"I just wanna be alone." I wipe my eyes, trying to even my breathing. He shakes his head against me. "No, I'm not fucking leaving. I'm not leaving you, Tessa." He argues. In truth, I wanted him to hold me. To cradle me while I cried. It wasn't fair for him to cry; I was the one betrayed.

"Please, Reese. I need you to leave." I pull his glue-like arms from me, and he stumbles back to his feet. "Let me stay. I can fix this." He puts his hands to my cheeks, leaning in for a haphazard kiss. My cheek instinctively turns away, I'm repulsed at the idea. "No, Reese." I sigh, placing my hands on his chest. He whines, begging to come closer. I feel like his mother, the day she left him outside of Maurice's. How sad and scared he must have felt. "If you love me... If you *really* love me, you'll walk away."

His eyes dart between both of mine, his cheeks are stained in tears. "This is what you want?" he asks softly. *No, hold me. Kiss me, never let me go.* I nod, taking one last labored breath. He runs his thumb over my bottom lip. "I love you." His bottom lip quivers and I can see the depth in his words.

"I know."

September 23rd,

My phone reads 5:31 A.M. I still haven't slept. I want to text him; to let him know I just need time. But it would make me weak. I'd be an idiot. My birthday trip revolved around keeping a secret.

I revisit the article on my phone, reading over the insane title a thousand times before clicking it.

Has Spring Come Early? Baby Finch on the way!

The writers paint her in such an awful light, that she was the *Pretty Woman* of New York. It displayed several photos of her with other men. At clubs, leaving fancy hotels. But she was a person, hurt by the same man I was.

My stomach churns thinking about her. How was she holding up during this? Had Reese even checked on her? I open Instagram and search Reese's followers until her name comes up. Brooklynn Davis. She had one post, a picture of her standing on a balcony with a ton of supermodel esc women. She was so gorgeous in her birthday sash. She had so many friends, all of them looking at her in such admiration. Thirteen thousand likes, she really was a socialite. I decided to take a leap, sticking my nose where it doesn't belong.

@tdaws93: this is going to come off weird, i'm not sure how to say this. but i hope you're alright.
@bdavisxo: Let's sit down for coffee sometime.

I'm quick to set a time for today after work. I could get away with working for half a day. I just really needed to see Maurice and let him know that I wouldn't be helping Reese anymore. I couldn't bite my tongue, I had to be blunt in my explanation. Reese was going to die the way he'd always been. Selfish.

Forty-Three

TESSA

"Good morning." I smile at the nurses as I walk down the hall. Everyone evades my gaze, and I'm feeling just as I did with Reese. I waved to Francine, and she gives a sympathetic smile in return. My chest is burning, the thought of anyone being upset with me is excruciating. I've done nothing wrong; I know that. So why do I feel this way?

"Mr. Finch!" I knock softly on Maurice's door, entering with a bright smile. "Maurice?" I called again, rounding the corner to his bed. He's full of different wires and tubes, my brows sink. There's been so much change in the few days I've been gone. No one wanted to tell me. I didn't do anything wrong; they were afraid of hurting me. I let out a heavy sigh, picking up his chart and pulling a chair up to his bedside.

I scanned the writing, ultimately finding him to be nearing the end of his time with us. "Oh, Maurice." My eyes are wet, I let out a soft sob. I want to call my mom, she would know what to do, what to say.

"I'm sorry, Maurice. I... I couldn't do it. I was so close but... He'll never change." I place a hand on his arm, it flinches at my touch. He turns his head slowly, looking at me. I know he's listening. "I love him but... He'll always be the same old Reese."

Maurice blinks slowly, engraving every word into his mind. "I'm so sorry." I apologized again. His eyes told me everything I needed to hear. *You did everything you could.*

I sat back in the chair, my hands running over my face. Everything else in life had suddenly stopped mattering compared to Reese... My education, the arrangement, all of it. I was consumed by him. It wasn't fair. He made me fall in love with him, and now I was determined to hate him.

I watch Maurice drift back asleep, his breathing is labored and rattled. His hands are purple, his skin gray and dry. I know he's close. I couldn't help but wonder what exactly was keeping him alive.

Was it the idea of his son becoming something great? Or simply being miserable in his old age. The way Reese described; Maurice was always miserable. So, I think I'll stick with that. I couldn't imagine the feeling of growing up with a father like him. Handing me money just to get out of his sight. As much as I want to hate him, my heart hurts for the boy who endured more than he needed.

I continue the rest of my shift, popping in on Maurice every so often. No change in condition, I guess I'll go meet my fate.

Across the street, a few buildings down, was a coffee shop. Not the one Tim had introduced me to, but one that was well known by just about every New Yorker. The interior was dated back to the '70s. Whoever the owners were, had preserved its memory over the decades. I often come here on my lunch breaks or days off. The food was decent, the coffee was about the same. But the smell of weathered furniture and stale Marlboros was comforting like my grandma's house.

Kelseigh and I spent several summers with her growing up. Her house in the Hamptons was full of nicotine-stained furniture and as many sweets as we wanted. We'd spend all day in the sun, only to return to a home cooked meal every night. When we got older, Kelseigh made friends and went down to the parties, meeting boys and doing God knows what. But not me. I stayed with my toes in the sand and my head to the sky.

I remember my grandma sitting behind me, brushing the sand from my hair and braiding it back. "You are just as wonderful as her, Tess." She spoke so warmly.

I was jealous. Kelseigh was perfect. She was blonde, beautiful, and the talk of our family. Wherever we went, she was the star of the show. I hid behind my humor and my respectful personality. Kelseigh's beauty was the most important thing to everyone.

"Right, that's why everyone loves her and tolerates me." I rolled my eyes, taking a bite of the sandwich she brought outside for me. My legs are crossed on the patio sofa, I listen intently to the sounds of the ocean. She only sighs, resting her weathered hands on my shoulders. "Oh, honey. I hope you don't really feel that way." She whispered, squeezing my shoulders gently. I felt guilty. Kelseigh hadn't done anything to me, yet I had so much jealousy toward her. I wanted to be her. I wanted her laugh, her carefree mentality. She was a dream that I'd burn myself out trying to reach.

I walk into the cafe, looking around to find Brooklynn already sitting at a table, scrolling on her phone. Her hair is down and straight, a lot like Kelseigh's.

Her makeup was flawless, looking nothing like I'd imagine after having a procedure like that. "Brooklynn?" I pointlessly asked. She smiled, motioning me to sit.

"You can call me Brooke." She smiled, putting her phone in her pocket. "Tessa." I extend my hand for her to shake as I sit down. She refuses and waves me off. "I know who you are, hon." She even laughed like my sister. I could feel the pit of jealousy grow in my stomach. No wonder Reese liked her. She was so tall and skinny, her skin not bearing a single imperfection. What the hell did he see in me?

I don't even know what to say. Our eyes dance around the room. "So, you must be the girl that Reese dropped me for." She teased, her expression telling me that she wasn't serious. "Not for long." I chuckled under my breath, suddenly feeling like I could vomit. "Did he talk about me?" I want to punch myself for asking.

Brooklynn shakes her head, looking down. "But there were signs." She weakly smiled.

"Signs?"

She nods, rolling her eyes with a smile. "There's always signs when a boy likes a girl." This time I find myself laughing, like two old friends catching up. "Reese Finch has had Instagram since it came out and has followed the same five people. When I saw that number jump up to six, I knew something was suspicious." Brooklynn gives a playful smile and I feel my cheeks warm. I push away the thought, shaking my head. "And then I caught him in Target last week."

We laugh and tease about the idea of Reese trying to shop like a normal person. Brooklynn seemed as normal as it gets, she was nothing like him. She was kind and genuine, with no shell to crack. Almost like she was searching for acceptance from someone. She asks me what happened, why we didn't work out.

"He told you he loved you?" Her face is practically ghostly, the shock of that four-letter word being used by him almost killing her. It was almost a look of hurt. God knows how long she waited for him to say that to her. I nod, sipping my latte. "It was a lie. He just wanted to cover his tracks with you." I sighed, setting my mug back down.

"Right. Well, I did take care of that." She smiled, placing her hand on my forearm. I didn't know what to say, I wanted to hug her. I could tell she needed it. "Yes, alone. I'm *so* sorry he wasn't there for that." I place my hand over hers and for a second, that smile cracks. She deserved an apology. If not from him, then from me.

Brooklynn takes a deep breath.

"It was nothing, really. We were both irresponsible." She gives a playful wink, dismissing her trauma. It makes my stomach hurt. She grabs her purse; it's been a sensitive subject, I'm sure. "It's been nice meeting you, Tessa. Some advice?" She smiles, throwing her bag over her arm. I nod, standing to my feet.

"Forgiveness."

I raise a brow, needing an explanation.

"I know you think he's lying, but Reese has only ever told one woman he loved her, and it wasn't me." Brooklynn takes a soft exhale through her nose. "Goodbye, Tess." She pulls me into a hug, reminiscent of saying goodbye to a friend at the airport. I inhale her perfume, taking in its velour fragrance. Forgiveness wasn't in my cards yet; I could barely stand saying his name.

I wait for Brooklynn to be a safe distance away before I leave. I kept an eye out for him, my awareness of everyone around me heightened. The city was only so big, and it would be impossible for me to hide forever. This was my home, and yet I felt so uneasy. I hated this feeling, like I didn't belong here, and I needed to leave. I was beginning to hate New York, a place I used to beg everyone to stay in.

I pull my phone out, scrolling to the bottom of my contacts. I exhale dramatically, trying to wave a cab down as my breathing harmonizes to the dial tone.

"Hey, kid."

"Hate me yet?" I mutter, the sound of his voice making my throat close.

"I could never hate you." He gives a husky chuckle.

"What's Seattle like this time of year, anyways?" I wipe my eyes, hiding all interference of my tears. Tim's laugh is deep, I can almost hear him sit up in his chair, his tongue running across his top teeth. "Well, it's about 70 degrees out, the sun should be shining in a few hours." I hear him take a drink. I forgot about time zones. "I didn't interrupt anything did I?" I ask, walking down the block a little further.

"No, never. It's still early here. Shouldn't you be working?"

"Half day."

Tim lets out a chuckle. "I don't think I'll ever understand your schedule."

"You and I both." I snickered, memorizing the cracks in the busy sidewalk. Reese knew when I worked. Hell, he even knew when I took my lunch breaks. I push the thought from my mind. "Listen, I can get you a ticket for next weekend. Say… the fourth? We'll call it a belated birthday gift." Tim knows something is wrong.

Can I blame him? I gave a big speech about not wanting to leave New York and here I am a week later, trying to get the hell out.

I take a second to think, turning my back to look up at a tall city building. "Can I have a few days to think?" I can hear Tim's sigh. "Of course, kid. Gimme a call if you get lonely." He smiles into the line, and I nod as if he can hear it.

"Of course, Timothy."

Forty-Four

REESE

September 25th,

I lean back in my chair; my vision is lazily focused on the women carrying trays of drinks. Brice stares into his Jack & Coke. He claims to have met someone, not wanting any part of this endeavor Christian has brought us on. I just want to lay in bed. My body is aching, and I can't seem to get enough sleep. My lungs are heavy, every breath I'm forced to take is deeper than the last.

I check my phone for anything from Tessa. It's been a few days, neither of us making the first move.

Tomorrow is Thursday, *our day.*

I silently battle with what to do as Christian groans. "Where are my friends? Are you guys in there?" He loudly scolds over the music. Brice hasn't looked up from his phone in twenty minutes, his fingers tap against the screen rapidly like it's an emergency. He's always been this way when he falls for a girl. Brice was ready to put it all on black with the drop of a girl's panties. It always worked for him, every girl saw him as the sweet and sensitive type. But when I put everything on the line for Tessa, it left me in a shitty club with my two dumbass friends.

I roll my eyes, standing from the table and making my way back to the bar. I order a vodka soda, resting my elbows on the counter and looking down at my feet. "Very classy order." A feminine voice pulls me from my trance as my head shoots up. It's her, in those tight black scrubs. Her curls pulled back into that clip, full lips in a smile as she looked up at me.

"Chelsea." She extends a hand to me, and when I blink, she's gone. A raven with dark makeup and a dress thinner than my patience stands before me. She's at my height, her green eyes looking into mine. She was pretty, but very clearly drunk. I rub my eyes in exhaustion, giving a fake smile. "Reese." I nod and motion for her to order, throwing a twenty-dollar bill on the counter. I wasn't going to be able to give her what she wanted. The least I could do was buy her a drink.

"Did you come here with friends?" she asked sweetly, in contrast to her dark makeup. I nod again, pointing my glass toward Christian with his arms folded in a pout and Brice smiling at his phone. "You must be the life of the party." She giggles, forcing a smile out of me as she couldn't be any more incorrect. I would rather commit arson than stand in this godforsaken place any longer. "Something like that." I take a large gulp, letting the vodka burn its way down. Its taste is reminiscent of my life before Tessa. When things were simple, and I didn't worry about whether I'm going to hell or not.

"Well, you can always come and join us." Chelsea points to a group of girls, all thin and sporting about the same look as her. Christian would go nuts over them, foaming at the mouth for an opportunity alone with at least one. In high school, he was known for collecting three girls at a time, taking them upstairs to his parent's bedroom. Of course, they crashed the party twenty minutes later. He still won't tell us what went on up there. It wasn't until the last few years of my adulthood that I achieved something like that.

I nod, not having much else to say. Merely standing with Chelsea seems morally wrong. I loved Tessa, and I was gonna be sure she knew that. I pull my phone from my back pocket, ignoring Chelsea's drunken ramblings.

8:19P.M.
R- What time would you like me at work tomorrow?
T- typing…

I cram the phone in my pocket before she responds, I'm terrified at the rejection I could face. My heart is racing. When I tune in to Chelsea, she's waving her hands and talking about something of irrelevance. I catch the words 'part time retail and 'east side.' It's all I needed to hear to determine my fate with her. There was nothing wrong with her career, but I had a hardworking woman waiting for me to figure my shit out. I nod along, tuning out as I wait for it to be over.

8:22P.M.
T- you're off the hook.
R- What's that supposed to mean?
R- Hello?

She doesn't respond. I hang my head back; Chelsea's voice is a soft hum to my pounding temples. I should have called; it would have meant more than a lousy text. But this stupid fucking music is so loud, she would have assumed I'm drunk. Hell, maybe I am. Am I drunk enough to take Chelsea in the bathroom?

No, no, I'm not.

I take a deep breath before interrupting her. "Chelsea, was it? It was great talking to you. Maybe I'll see you around." I weakly smile, stepping away before hearing her response. It was probably better that way; I could feel her eyes burning a hole in my back. I'd been called every name in the book, it didn't matter.

Christian's smile gets wider the closer I get, thinking I'm gonna come back with good news. "I'm gonna take off, man." I set my glass on the table, Brice looking up for the first time.

"What the fuck happened to my wingman? You are whipped over some pussy." He scoffed, putting his hands in his hair. I shake my head; he doesn't know shit about me. If I was whipped, I'd wear that title with pride. "I was actually thinking about heading out too…" Brice mumbles, tucking his phone in his jacket. Christian laughs dramatically.

"I cannot believe this. Remember this at my funeral, the time you *both* abandoned me." He shakes his head, pushing Brice. In truth, Christian wouldn't have any trouble finding a bed tonight.

Brice rubs his shoulder, feeling the ghost of Christian's aggression. "It's Wednesday, dude. I have work in the morning." I wasn't sure how he always stayed so calm. I'd beat the crap out of Christian more times than I can remember, and vice versa. We were the type of guys always looking for a fight with no one to challenge but each other.

I put my arm around Brice, walking out as a duo. He shakes his head, in the same boat as me on being out on the town. Brice was never a night owl. With his mom as his boss, it was hard for him to even find the time to be out.

"Talked to Tessa lately?" He asks as we make our way down the sidewalk. I shake my head, avoiding the embarrassment of her not texting me back. Brice only nods, knowing not to pry. "She'll come around." He politely smiles, reaching his car. "I wouldn't be so sure, Peterson." I scoffed with a pitiful grin. Tessa was stubborn, hard-headed and everything in between. I was dead to her.

I close the door behind me and stare at the phone for a second. A missed call from Brindlewood. I swipe the call from my notifications and dial her number. It rings twice before being declined.

> *"It's Tess. Leave a message after the beep. Unless you're a bill collector."*

I laughed at her stupid voicemail, knowing she wouldn't have answered.

> *"Hey, it's me. I just wanted to tell you that I'll be in tomorrow. And every Thursday after that. I'm not gonna let us end like this, Tess. I'm gonna make this right. Sleep well. I love you."*

There is no hesitation in my voice, I meant it. I hung the phone up and make my way home.

September 26th,

"Thank you, miss." I set Tessa's coffee in my cup holder, put the car back in drive and pull off. My hands are trembling as I think about seeing her again. She never returned my call, but I know she got my message. Knowing her, she's replayed it a hundred times. I turn on the radio to drown out my thoughts, *Lover* by Taylor Swift is roaring in my ears. It was all the signs I needed. I'd heard Tessa blare this song everywhere. The truck, my car, the shower. Hell, she even hummed it while writing in her journal. I knew this girl like the back of my hand, and I was determined to get her back.

I've overdone it with cologne and I'm in her favorite shirt, a brown, corduroy polo. I check my hair again as I pull into the familiar parking lot. I look down at the daisies in the passenger seat with a dramatic exhale. *"I'm sorry, I love you. I love you, I'm sorry?"* I rehearse my lines as I push open the doors. Francine, the receptionist, stands from her seat. "Good morning." I grin, thankful to see a familiar face. Though she doesn't reciprocate the same emotion.

"Mr. Finch, did you get our phone call last night?" She asks, walking out from behind her desk. Her hands are folded in front of her anxiously as I furrow my brows. The calls were pointless and always the same. Maurice is running low on supplies, call Uncle Arthur. Maurice is declining, call Uncle Arthur to finalize affairs. I was purely the middleman. It was on rare occasions that I took their phone calls anymore. "No, I didn't. Is everything alright?" My head tilts to the side, a brow lifting in thought. She looks down at the bouquet as if there's no way to answer.

"Francine?" I pull her from her daze, and she locks eyes with me again. "Tessa is upstairs." She smiles with her eyes wet. I feel my chest get tight as I turn down the hall to the elevator. I play the voicemail left behind.

"Hi, Reese. This is Janis, the third shift nurse, over at Brindlewood. I was calling to let you know that Maurice is not doing well. We find it important that you come in at your earliest convenience. Thanks, bye."

My brain rots with different ideas of what could have caused this.

Had he fallen out of bed? Stopped eating? I know I haven't visited in a week or so, but he was managing. I chew the inside of my cheek in the longest elevator ride known to man. I adjust my weight from my heels to my toes repeatedly.

The doors open and the activity room is empty, the unit is cold as if every window is open. I turned my head down the hall to Maurice's room. Tessa's back is turned, she's talking to a tall man. My jealousy flares briefly as I make my way to her.

"Tess!" I called with a nervous smile. The two turn to face me and I see the man is in his fifties. His thick glasses are on the tip of his nose and he's filling out a clipboard. Tessa's face is red, she's been crying. "What's wrong?" I ask, ready to pummel anyone who stands in her way. "Are you the son?" he asks in a monotone voice. His demeanor is casual, as if I'm not the first stop of the day. Tessa looks down at the flowers and coffee, then back up to me. I turn my head to Maurice's open door, locking eyes with a stretcher and several paramedics.

My head darts back down to hers. My chest is hot, rising and falling rapidly. "What the fuck is going on?" I feel my eyes burning as Tessa lowers her head. Her hands moved to my chest, trying to push me away from the scene.

"Let's go talk somewhere." Her voice is trembly, as if trying to stay strong for me. I shake my head again.

I'm stronger than her and she knows. My grip is so tight, I've popped the lid off the coffee, spilling its contents on the beige carpet. I look down only for a second, I can't focus on anything. My vision is blurry, I'm blinking faster than I can process. I'm gonna pass out. "Reese... Reese, look at me." She tried to hold my face, but I jolted away. I watch the paramedics hoist a sheet-covered Maurice onto the stretcher.

When I was sixteen, Maurice and I got in a fight, but not the usual kind you'd expect. I came home from a party with Brice, drunk and probably high. The memory is foggy today as I try to recall it. I'd sell my soul to watch it on tape. We strolled in around three in the morning, giggling and tickled with the memory of girls we'd just hit on. I'd made it to first base with Yvonne Sawyer, a senior that was way out of my league and would deny it come Monday.

"Dude, she's so hot. No one's gonna believe you." Brice laughed, his braces reflecting in the dimly lit hallway. "Trust me. No one forgets Reese Finch." I teased, popping my collar. The living room lamp flickered on, Brice and I froze like two super spies on the hunt for the hope diamond.

"Who won't forget you?" Maurice sat in his robe and pajama pants. I rolled my eyes, ready to catch the irrational scolding headed my way. His arms were folded as he stood from his chair, his white chest hair peeking through the thin silk.

If Brice wasn't there, I'd surely have been smacked around. But he loved to keep that side hidden. "Yvonne Sawyer." Brice piped, his head down to the ground. I shot him a look, furious for ratting.

"Do you know what time it is?" Maurice asked, his tone much firmer than a few minutes ago. "Yes, sir." We mumbled in unison. "Take your asses upstairs and get to bed." He scolded. Brice quickly nodded and left a dust cloud behind him. I followed shortly after, confused in the punishment I'd received. "Oh, Reese?" My dad called out. "Hm?" I stopped with my hand on the railing.

"A man is only as good as his reputation." He flashed a quick smile, sitting back in his chair. I'd never seen one before, not directed at me anyway. "I know, sir." I nodded, taking a few steps.

"Goodnight, son." I felt the stolen liquor making its way back up my stomach. It was the first and last time he'd genuinely called me 'son'. To this day, I wasn't sure what it meant. Was he trying the nickname on for size? Or did he view me as his in the early hours of the morning?

"Reese, baby…" Her voice is calm and soothing but it's too late. I can barely hear it, like it's miles away. I'm a bull and I see red. Destruction is in my blood, it's in my path. "Where are they taking him? Where's he going?" My voice is loud, and I can tell it scares her. I try to push past, but her heels dig into the carpet.

Tessa shakes her head, gripping my arm. The mortician takes a step back, giving us some space as he enters my father's room. I'm suddenly picking up every detail of this hallway. The seven ceiling lights, the way they flicker three times in one minute. The chipped, white doorway, the flowers on the entry table. I could count every petal in ten seconds.

"Why didn't you tell me, Tessa?" My throat is closing, my words are coming out scratchy and broken. Tessa's hands are in my hair, pulling me down to her. I drop the flowers, swallowing her entire body in my embrace. I can't do this. I'm gonna blow.

Forty-Five

TESSA

I'm holding him up with every muscle in my body. "I should have been here." His knees are buckled as he sobs. My shirt is soaked in salty tears, but I stay in this position as long as he needs me. His hands dig into my top, clawing my back with every wail that escapes him. "Shh," I ran my hands through his hair, absorbing the stinging of my skin and looking at the crushed daisies on the ground. I wet my lips, fighting back tears of my own. It wasn't my turn, it was his. "I was going to call you, Reese. I promise." I'd been at work all of thirty minutes before finding out myself. Reese was the first thing on my agenda.

His heaves against my chest weigh me down as he's practically on his knees. "Let's sit down." I try to guide him to a sofa as he pulls back quickly.

"I gotta get the fuck out of here."

My brows furrowed in confusion as he wiped his eye on his forearm.

"What? No, you just got here. Come on." I reach for his hand, and he jerks back, licking the tears from his lips as he places both hands behind his head. I see him, the little boy being left at his father's doorstep. He was now an orphan. "Reese,"

He shakes his head, sniffling as he turns around. I can't get myself to chase him, I've known Reese long enough to know he needs his space.

I was sent home for the day, the nurses ultimately decided I should take the day to grieve. Thursdays, my once happy days, were now full of heartache and grief.

My apartment is dark and lonely, I need Reese now more than ever. I call his phone, listening to his voicemail on repeat. He turned his phone off and I can't say that I'm surprised by that.

I could go to his place, but if he wanted that, he'd tell me. Instead, I lay in my bed, drifting in and out of consciousness.

I dream of the Maldives, and dancing with Reese. I dream of him telling me he loves me, the way he plays with my hair, his laugh. Though arrogant and boisterous, it was *his*. Reese was an anomaly to me, ravishing my brain with the thought of how could someone like him be real?

He was a dick, making my life a living hell the last two years. But in a month, I'd fallen head over heels for him. I'd changed him, at least I believed I did. The Reese I knew before would never cry for his father. Hell, the Reese I knew barely *referred* to Maurice as his father. He was different. I feel like a failure, unable to comfort him.

I was the person who fixed everyone, the person who held everyone while they cried. I put them back together with whatever pieces remained, giving bits of myself away. And I'd failed with the person who mattered most.

Or so I'd thought.

My eyes rustle open at the sound of my window sliding open. I prop myself up on my hands, trying to adjust my eyes to the moonlight. "Reese?" I whisper, as if I'll wake the responsible part of my brain. He doesn't respond, kicking his boots off. I watch him strip down to his briefs, a view I'd normally be melting over. He slowly crawls onto the bed, his muscles taut as he pulls the blankets back. His face is wet against my chest, he smells of vodka and cigarettes, maybe. My arms shield him from the world as he sighs. I ran my fingers through his dirty hair.

"Are you drunk?" I whispered; his face buried in my neck as he denied the obvious answer with the shake of his head. He reeked; I was catching a buzz just being near him. But I was too lonely to argue. "Okay." I held him close, giving him all the mothers love I could.

September 27ᵗʰ,

He was gone, without a word or a note. My chest burns with anger. Wasn't I worth a lousy goodbye? I did what I was supposed to. I held him all night, while he cried and slept. I want to cry but I'm too angry.

It will only make everything worse. I could hear my father's voice in the back of my head like I was twelve years old, scraping my knee during a track meet. It felt like fire, making all the hair on my body stand, yet his tone was always the same.

"No use in crying about it, T."

And he was right.

I yank my phone from the nightstand, dialing the only person who would understand.

"What?"

"Are you still mad at me?"

"I was never mad at you, Tess." Kayla sighs into the line, and I feel my bottom lip quiver. Her and Tim were more alike than she'd ever admit.

"Really? Because I feel like I'm just fucking up, time after time."

Kayla takes another deep breath; a thick moment of silence makes my stomach cramp. She was the type of friend to serve tough love on a silver platter. No matter how much I tried to prepare myself, I knew something would be headed my way. "Get dressed, I'll be there in ten." She hangs up the phone without another word. I look down at the call log on my phone, my brows raised in delightful confusion. Kayla was turning over a new leaf.

I can't bring myself to leave the bed, not even when Kayla's key rattles in my door. I'm mindlessly scrolling through the internet in the dark, subjecting myself to picture perfect lives that don't involve me. My friends from high school are all at such different stages than I am. Marriages, babies, home owning. I feel so stuck, so trapped. What did I have going for myself? I only briefly had Reese; my apartment was shitty. My truck was a safety hazard. All I had was my job. My underpaid, underappreciated job.

"Tessa?" She knocks softly on my door, pushing it open with her knuckle. I lock the phone, lifting my head from the pillow. "Jesus, who lives here? Dracula?" She scoffed, laying on Reese's side of the bed. She faces me, a sympathetic look on her face.

"Hi." She breathes softly, her simplicity causing me to smile. Her voice is gentle and so uncharacteristic of her. Maybe someone was changing her in the way I tried with Reese. "Hi." I whisper, any strain on my vocal cords feels like razors, slicing the emotion from my body. She rubs my upper arm, my eyes closing out of habit as I imagine her soft, feminine hands to be him. "Maurice died." I admit, feeling my eyes sting. "I'm so sorry, honey." Kayla holds me closer. Finally, it's my turn to grieve. I let my tears out on the one person who understands it was deeper than a resident or my job. I grieve for the failure I am. For Maurice, a father who never got to see his son become the man he was destined to be. For a son who never lived up to the potential or received a parent's love. Maybe if he had, Reese would have been different.

We would have met in a coffee shop on my lunch break, or in the airport before leaving for Florida. We would have gone to the movies and took walks in the park. We wouldn't have argued every chance we could or kept secrets from one another.

Kayla strokes my hair in the same way I do Reese. I can still smell him on my sheets, and I pray she doesn't mention it. "It'll get easier." She rubs my cheek with her thumb, swiping the tears that remain. I nod, I've lost many residents in the past. "I don't just mean Maurice."

I shut my eyes, hydrating them from the burning sensation. "I know." I lied. I didn't know. Does it *really* get easier? I wanted to be angry at him, but all I could remember of him now was the look on his face when he stepped off the elevator. I could never hate him.

"Let's go get some greasy breakfast. It'll make you feel better." Kayla smiled, gently shaking me by the shoulder. I groan, rolling on my back. "Can't we just order takeout?"

Kayla hits me with a pillow, causing us both to laugh like we're seventeen again. "It's nine in the morning, we're not getting takeout."

Who said Chinese for breakfast was a bad thing?

I sat down in a booth with Kayla, ordering pancakes and a coffee. "So why aren't you mad at me again?" I asked, curiously.

"Because you didn't do anything wrong. You followed your heart, and I could never blame you for that." Kayla pulls the plastic straw from the wrapper, blowing it at me. "Reese is a prick. Taking you out of the country without telling anyone was not only dangerous but stupid. Did he really think the article with that slut was gonna disappear?" She scoffed, shaking her head as she put the straw in her lemonade.

"She's not a slut. I think she really liked Reese." I grab the straw wrapper from my hair and twirl it around my index finger. "Why do you think that?" Kayla's brow raised, as if suspecting what I was going to say. "Well, we met for coffee."

Kayla runs a strenuous hand over her face with a groan. "You just love to stir the pot, Tessa Ann." She snickered and for the first time in what felt like months, I laughed. My genuine, real, laugh before I ever got entangled with him.

Forty-Six

REESE

Tessa is breathing so steadily, her arms lazily resting over my body. I don't want to wake her. This isn't how I wanted to say goodbye. I wanted to sit her down, explain to her that I loved her but needed time to collect myself and figure out how in the hell I was going to take care of things.

But as usual, I went out last night, drinking away any sense of a brain I have left. Her window is open, which means I scaled the fire escape versus using the front door like a functioning member of society.

I gently slid out from her grasp, grabbing my shoes and clothes. I don't leave the way I came; it'd be too much noise. Tessa doesn't move, her arm lays over the spot where the sheets crinkled with my presence. I look to the ceiling for a second, as if asking my father to fix this. Fix us, fix me. If Tessa couldn't do it, maybe it was a job for someone above. I want to use every sense I can to engrave her into my memory. I know it will fade as soon as I leave the room, I'm still fucking drunk.

My jaw drops at the sight of my car, the driver side scraped and smashed all to shit. The mirror is cracked and all I can do is tug at my hair in disbelief. I hope I didn't hurt anyone; I have no recollection of even being behind the wheel, let alone getting to Tessa's.

I've gotten into several accidents. I've gotten arrested. It's never made me feel the way I do right now. I'm embarrassed. A growing pit of shame bubbles in my stomach as I pray Tessa doesn't look out of her window. She'd be so ashamed of me.

I climb into the car quickly, not wasting another second. I take the easiest route to Christian's body shop. He's gotten me out of every pinch I've been in. I'll never hear the end of it, but it was the price I had to pay for free labor.

My last accident, the infamous DUI, was not my proudest moment. I'd gone out with Christian, Brice and Jody to a club just north of Jersey City. I was the honored designated driver. Only every time I used the bathroom, I bought shots for myself and a bachelorette party across the club. I've done a lot of stupid things, but when I watched the bride, dressed all in a white body suit, letting men take shots from in between her breasts, I knew I'd ended up in the wrong crowd.

I told the guys what I'd watched and as we drug Christian from the scene; I climbed back behind the wheel. My hands at ten and two as I took a deep breath, my mouth tastes reminiscent of vomit, had I thrown up in the bathroom? "You good, man?" Brice asked, pulling me from my trance. "Yeah… Yeah I'm alright." I smiled sloppily. Brice nodded, being sure to put his seatbelt on. I placed my right hand over the passenger seat, looking behind me as I put the car in reverse. Only, it was in drive. And I had just hit the only Hoboken squad car out that night.

Christian hightailed my car to the body shop while I sat in holding for the night, waiting for Maurice to bail me out. It didn't cost me a thing, just some cheap weed and to get removed from Brooklynn's blocked list.

I pull into the body shop and Christian comes out wearing that stupid suit he always wore to work. His arms are folded, and he shakes his head with a laugh. "Rough night, Finch?" He scoffed, running his hand down the dents on the side of the car.

"Let's skip the shit today, okay?" I drop the keys in his hand and his laughter fades to background noise while he gives the keys to the mechanics. I take this time to check out the cars he has for sale, stopping at a '69 Mustang. Almost like the one from the trip, only it's painted black, sparkling like the sun reflecting on the ocean.

I push the thought from my head as Christian approaches me with a clipboard. His expression is tight and the way his eyes flicker up to mine, tells me that I'm in for a treat. "It's gonna be like $15,000 to fix this thing, man." He sighed, running his pen over the paper. I have five grand left to my name. "Just fudge the bill, Chris. You've never charged me in the past." My face is red with embarrassment and pleading. I'm groveling for a handout. I thought I couldn't get any lower.

"That was for minor shit. Scratches, small dents... Reese, you definitely side swiped another car last night." Christian continues, flipping a paper on the clipboard as I cringe.

"Left head light, the fender, front and back driver side door all need work... And that's not even getting to the cosmetic damages." Christian runs his hand over his perfectly styled hair. He was so put together, I'm sure I looked like a fucking homeless person about now. I was hungover, my body cold and sweaty. My hair disheveled and greasily pushed back. My eyes dart to all the cars I can't afford, foreign imported and muscle cars fill the lot.

A row of bikes caught my eye, the *2018 Ducati Panigale* marked down to $11,000. It's sharp and aggressive, the type of thing you'd see in *a Jason Statham* movie. It's painted black, matted with only a few silver embellishments. "What's up with those?" I point, feeling my gears spin. "The Ducatis?" Christian laughed. "I can't fucking get rid of those things. I thought they'd be a hit." He groans, shaking his head. "I've got five grand on me right now." I offered; it was more than he'd get from anyone else. Italy was a lot farther ahead of the sports bike trend than New York.

"You're insane. The only people who buy these things are guys in midlife crisis, or guys who just got dumped." His words made my throat tighten, I wasn't dumped. Maybe I was, maybe it was mutual.

"My dad died." It was a card I didn't know I had in my hand. Christian's expression fell, a sense of discomfort in the air. "Right well... Five thousand and get me Brice's sister's phone number."

"Five thousand and I'll take you to lunch next week." I combatted, knowing Brice would have my head on a stake for doing something so evil. Christian groans. "Five thousand and I'll take the Lincoln." I'm sure he thought he could flip it. Maybe he could, I didn't know shit about cars.

"Done."

I was now the new owner of a midlife crisis.

I took everything I needed from my car, telling Christian to scrap the rest as he inspected the bike for the sale. I didn't care what happened; the Lincoln didn't bear any memories worth saving. If anything, it brought more harm to my mind than good. I could still see Tessa's phone flung under the seat and helping Brooklynn out while she held the pregnancy test when I closed my eyes. Good riddance.

I climbed on the bike, revving the engine as it vibrated between my legs. Christian handed me a helmet. "Complimentary, so you don't spill your brains on my property!" He called over the roar. I slid it over my head, the visor shading the world as I pulled it down. I kicked the bike into gear, nodding a last time to Christian before peeling from his shop.

That feeling, the rush of adrenaline and excitement as the air hits your body, is unforgettable. It had been about three years, maybe longer, since I was last on a motorcycle. Yet the sensations are still fresh in my mind as the wind rips past me. I'd need more gear for sure, but right now I had other fish to fry.

I rode to Maurice's estate. Normally a drive that took every bit of two hours, cut in half with the ability to swerve in and out of traffic. I felt alive, free of all things weighing me down in this world.

I parked the bike at the end of the long driveway beside Arthur's car, kicking the stand down and resting my helmet on the handlebar. He was probably prepping things for the funeral. So many memories were held in this house. The sun faded paint sheds light on my past, keeping my ghosts forever engraved in its chips and cracks. The first girl I'd snuck in, the parties I threw when Maurice was away on business, the day I stood up to Maurice.

Sure, I'd gotten a little mouthy, but it was nothing he couldn't handle. I held my ear to the office door as he met with colleagues. He told them stories about my mom being a whore, someone that he'd bent over his desk just to clear his mind. I can hear their laughter as all their questions about me were answered. I'd had enough, stooping to his level when they left.

"My mom isn't a whore." I sneered, my chest puffed out and my chin up as I looked up at the old man. I clenched my fork, wanting to stab him with it. He was in his sixties, but the man had seen enough war and blood in his day. I knew he could take me. I'd been with him all of three months, speaking only when spoken to. Maurice only snickered, shaking his head.

"You don't know your mother like I do." He ashes his cigarette with a grin. "She was a tramp, a *whore*." He stood from the kitchen table, folding his newspaper. His voice was nasty, making my head hurt. I missed my mom so fucking much, I couldn't do this without her.

"You were married." I argued. He seemed so much bigger then versus the end of his life. I may have been only a child, but he terrified me to the extent of wetting the bed until I was fourteen. His face was permanently pursed, every wrinkle telling a different story of anger and arrogance. I couldn't love him. Not then, and most certainly not today.

I held my ground, looking up at him with my fists balled. "What are you gonna do, you little shit? Cry? Hit me?" He laughed, his breath reeking of stale menthols. I'd love nothing more; my entire life I would have killed for the opportunity to beat the shit out of him. Denise shook her head, her back turned toward the sink. Denise was my last stepmom, lasting seven months with Maurice. She was only thirty-six, Maurice at a staggering sixty-eight. She could have done so much better, and I hope to God she did.

My eyes were wet, burning as I refused to blink. "I'm doing you a favor by not giving you to the state, do you understand me? Learn some fucking respect or I'll give you something your mom should've done a long-" I can't let him finish, my internal clock of instinct has run out. I swung my left hook, only to be stopped and caught by his grip around my throat. My back reaches the wall, the dishes in the antique hutch rattling. Denise shrieked, her hands over her ears from the commotion. I hate him, I hate him, I hate him. I couldn't think of any other words. "You'd better shape up, boy. I won't raise a disrespectful excuse for a son."

Jokes on the both of us, dad. You didn't raise shit.

Forty-Seven

TESSA

October 1ˢᵗ,

"Are you still there?" I asked loudly into the line, running into my apartment complex. The rain soaks my hair and clothes as my teeth chatter. I could barely hear his voice.

"Yeah, how's it going, kid?" Tim sighs as the sound of turning papers fills the speaker. "Fine, are you working?" I asked, stopping at my mailbox. It seemed like it'd been forever since I'd had a genuine phone call with someone that didn't include sex or crying. "Unfortunately, but I could use a break." He laughed, scratching the scruff on his face. We had decided to remain friends and avoid all romantic drama. He had listened to my troubles with Reese, avoiding any bias as Tim usually did. He was a great listener, which was what made us great friends. However, I was still holding onto my plane ticket for this weekend, never giving a direct yes or no.

I flip through the bills, pinching the phone between my jaw and shoulder. "Kinda shitty I'm forced to work on your birthday, everyone knows it's a national holiday." Tim sighs and I can't help but giggle.

"If I had to work, then so do you." I sighed, passing a birthday card from my mother. Probably the same old message. *'Happy birthday, my sweet girl.'* My brows crinkle at a black envelope with my name addressed as *Ms. Tessa Dawson* in big calligraphy. Tim's pleasant ramblings become background noise as I'm forced to shuffle all my belongings around in my hands. "Hold on a sec,"

"Is everything alright?" He asks more seriously as I tear the envelope. Maybe my dentist had stepped up his annual teeth cleaning postcard.

You are cordially invited to the funeral and reading of the will of
Maurice Lionel Finch
A beloved father, brother and friend
3P.M. October 4ᵗʰ, 2019

A beloved father was a shock. My brows remain lowered, I'm honored to attend the funeral, but the reading of the will was news to me. I exhale heavily, trying to wrap my brain around it.

"What's up, Tess?" Tim broke me from my trance, I blink rapidly, realizing I hadn't done so in a few minutes.

"I have a funeral on Friday."

"Kinda an odd day for a funeral, no?" His voice is of concern as I pitifully laugh. "It's an odd family." For once I don't feel like crying at the mention of the Finch family. "Do you want me to fly back? It's not a problem, really." He offered, making me sigh. Why couldn't all men have the compassion and sympathy that Tim held? He'd never changed. When I was fourteen and our dog passed, Timothy had stolen his dad's car to come console me. The moment he arrived, he embraced me tightly, rubbing my head as I cried in his arms. Men like this were rare these days.

I didn't have the heart to tell him Reese would be there; I didn't want him to worry. "No, I'll be fine. It was just a resident at Brindlewood." I walk up the stairs, tucking the mail under my arm. "Have you thought anymore about coming to Seattle?" Tim asks, breaking the few moments of silence. I run my tongue over my top teeth, considering the possible outcomes of this funeral. My thoughts drift to Reese, and my stomach does a somersault. I fantasize about him coming into my arms and us finally being reunited, or maybe me running into his. But what if we both turn away and pretend not to know each other after all this time?

"Honestly, I haven't. This funeral puts a wrench in things, if that makes sense." I sighed; Reese would be my deciding factor. Though we refused to reach out to one another, I couldn't help but feel the invisible string holding us together. "Right, I'll hold it as long as you need." A smile masked his defeat, always leaving me to guess what he was really thinking. Whenever he spoke to me, I could feel his smile. The sound of his voice was full of hidden amusement and warmth, even when he was serious.

"Thanks, Timothy." I sighed, entering my apartment. I toe my shoes off, kicking them by the door. "Always. I've gotta get back to work. I just wanted to call and tell you happy birthday, kid." His voice is soft, like there's more that he'd like to say. "I appreciate it. Talk later?"

Tim agrees, and I hang up the phone. I'm alone on my birthday, no family, no friends. It's a cold feeling. My phone vibrates a text from my sister, she'd be getting here on Friday.

3:12 P.M.
K- happy birthday sis! see you friday xoxo
T- thanks, kels. love you always

She doesn't reply, but I know the feeling is mutual. I almost dread seeing her, with her perfect life and perfect friends. Why did she wanna waste her time with me? I wasn't the cool older sister that did interesting things. I worked and came home to the same empty apartment. Every single day.

Kelseigh was the kind of girl who, based on what I witnessed on her socials, went to parties, tried new food, and met new people every day. I was always jealous of her charisma; she could talk to anyone about anything. While I stumbled over the same stereotypical conversations when forced around strangers. I think I was just always in my head, afraid of saying the wrong thing and embarrassing myself.

I don't remember thinking that way when I was with Reese. It's like the thought never crossed my mind. Everything I said was always met with understanding nods, or careful glances. He never made me feel embarrassed or uneducated.

I'm hurt that I haven't heard from him. I wasn't expecting flowers or a diamond necklace, but a text would have been sufficient. I mull over my cheek, ready to pull the trigger and text him. But I knew it would bite me in the ass. Hell, he was probably with someone right now. And I didn't want to find out the hard way.

"Knock, knock!" Kayla's sing-song voice could be heard from my bedroom where I was doing my makeup. I set the eye shadow brush down, turning my head to view her. Her ruby hair is pulled off her shoulders in a high ponytail, her makeup is dark and sultry like mine. I'm not sure where we thought we were going. It was a Tuesday, and though it may be New York, people still had jobs and priorities.

She's carrying a small white box with a bright smile on her face. "What's in there?" I blush, looking up at her with a playfully annoyed expression. I was in no position to be in the same room with an entire cake. One wrong look from someone and I'd be crying on the bathroom floor, eating with my hands. Kayla smirks, opening the box to four vanilla cupcakes, iced with a periwinkle frosting and pearl accents.

"You didn't have to do that, Kay." I smiled, wishing we were staying in like when we were kids. There was nothing I loved more than sitting in our jammies, watching movies and eating junk food. "Oh, but I did. Mainly for myself, but also for you." She teased, sitting on my bed.

"Tonight is about you. Not about Reese or work. It's your *birthday*, and I don't wanna worry about-"

"I got invited to the funeral."

Kayla softly shuts her eyes, assumably grateful I'm word vomiting now instead of over dinner. I figured there was no better time. "And the reading of the will." I've caught her attention, her ears perking and eyes growing wide. "The will? Are you saying you're in the will?" Her eyes are glowing, we've just become millionaires without any evidence. "I'm sure I'm just wanted for support. Or maybe he's honoring our deal."

She paces the room, nodding.

"I'll go with you." Kayla orders and I laugh, rising to my feet. "I'm afraid not. I'll be going alone." I pull my leather jacket over my burgundy dress. The first and only birthday gift I'd received today came from Kayla. She always stayed on top of trends, following whatever our friends were into. I wore the same scrubs and same sweatpants every day. The mere idea of buying clothes for myself was nauseating. I had other things to worry about. Still, I was grateful for Kayla and her excessive gift giving.

The wind blows against my thighs as the Manhattan nightlife ignites. I tug at the material of the dress, feeling more uncomfortable by the second. My curls are down over my shoulders and sticking to my lip gloss. God, I hated it. Kayla always bullied me into wearing it.

"Relax, you look hot." She swatted the fake leather that covered my arms. "I feel like an idiot." I groaned, trying not to pick the thong from my ass as we walked in. I'd never been to this side of Manhattan, it felt above my paygrade. Kayla grabbed my shoulders, looking deep in my eyes. Part of me thought she'd slap some sense into me. "Go get a drink, I'm gonna check on the table." She could tell I was uncomfortable. Hell, I was oozing insecurity. I only nodded as she turned me around, pushing me toward the bar.

The bartender hands me a laminated menu with four drinks, all of which sound confusing. I can feel my heart race, the familiar feeling of sounding stupid bubbling up.

"Get the Aviation." A man smirked beside me. He stood a foot taller than me with dark brown hair. His face is chiseled in the same way as Reese. God was it a turn on. I blink hard, trying to focus my eyes. "Aviation?" I asked, a brow raised as my mouth went dry. He chuckles under his breath, nodding. Everything about him exudes a masculine energy that demands attention. I can't help but admire his striking blue eyes and sharp, elegant features. He stands with effortless confidence, but not in a way that makes him seem arrogant. He's dripping in strength and stability.

I'm surprised when the purple drink is brought out, the maraschino garnish triggering a smile. "Thanks for the recommendation." I smiled, popping the cherry from the stem. He flashes me a pearly grin and nods with a sigh. "My name's Tyler by the way. I guess I should have led with that."

I wet my lips awkwardly, I'm unsure what to say back. He's cute, but I've had enough boy drama to tranquilize an elephant. "Nice to meet you, thanks again." I give a small wave, taking a sip as I walk backwards, stumbling over my feet toward Kayla. *Jesus, I was an idiot.*

"What the hell was that?" She asks in shock, her jaw nearly touching the ground. "What? Him?" My brows crinkled up in confusion, not seeing the same depth in the situation. "He was totally hot!" Kayla forces me to turn back around. My head is instinctively shaking no repeatedly. "No. No, I'm not interested!" I argue, digging my feet into the marble floors of the restaurant. She doesn't reply, shoving me harder.

I shoot her a glare, walking back in his direction. Every footstep feels like I have weights tied on my ankles. Tyler is still facing the bar, looking down at his phone. I stand on my tiptoes, tapping his shoulder. The way he looks around, pretending to not notice me, makes my cheeks flush. "Tessa."

I extend my hand with a sassy smile, maybe I'd sold him short. He deserved a conversation after giving me the most adult recommendation I've ever ordered. It beat the signature Malibu and pineapple juice that I regularly had. It was a classic, but maybe it was time for me to spread my wings. I will always have Timothy to thank for it.

Tyler chuckles, taking my hand. "Hi, Tessa." The way he looks down at me makes my stomach tighten, the way it once did with Reese.

"So, what brings you to this part of Manhattan?" I gave a lazy grin, relishing in my failure to make conversation. "Just visiting some family, you?" He leans against the bar with his elbow propped, his suit jacket tightening around his biceps. "It's my birthday, actually." My head tilts tightly to the side as I strike a playful pose. His laugh reminds me of summer nights, so warm and free. He's not ashamed, or uncomfortable. There aren't a hundred levels of trauma for me to break down. He's not the boy next door I devoted my teenage years to. He was just Tyler.

"Birthday? Well, in that case, I owe you another drink." He offered with a sly smirk. "Maybe another time, my friend is waiting for me."

"Is this friend a… Boyfriend by chance?" Tyler rubs the back of his neck, I can't help but laugh as I point back to Kayla, who is doing everything she can to be inconspicuous. When she feels our eyes on her, she gives a sheepish wave. "No boyfriend." I confirmed, tucking a curl behind my ear.

"Good." He holds his whisky close to his chest. The ice makes an angelic ringing. I can't focus on much else. My face is a thousand degrees, he was smoother than I thought. "Look, I'd like to take you to a movie or something. Y'know, for your birthday." He looked down at his glass, as if afraid of *my* rejection.

"Hmm, I dunno. I'm a busy girl." I teased, batting my lashes. "Busy?" He scoffs, running a hand over his jaw.

"Very."

"That's good to know, maybe I should take your number down. Just in case you have an opening?"

I chuckle under my breath, unable to hide the smile that creeps on my face as he pulls his phone out. It's sealed in a black case; I'm lost in the gold cufflinks on his jacket. My eyes trail until reaching his shoulders that are tightly kept in the linen. "Fine. But only because you made me laugh." I type in the number, saving it under *Tess*. I can still hear Reese's voice when I gave him my number. I was 'so serious.' It seemed like so long ago now, like a memory in the furthest part of my mind.

I'm left with a swarm of butterflies. My face is cemented into a smile as I sit at the table with Kayla.

She has a sassy 'I know I'm right' look on her face. "Don't say it." I roll my eyes playfully, taking a sip of my drink. "Who? Me? I'm not saying a word." She snickers, her lips pursed lightly.

I wasn't ready to fall in love again, but maybe this is my second chance at finding that real connection I thought I'd lost. Maybe this is fate, or a sign, something more. Whatever it is, I can't help but feel drawn to him and the possibility of starting over again with someone who seems so real and honest.

Forty-Eight

TESSA

October 4th

I tap my fingers against the steering wheel of the car. Traffic honks around me as everyone pushes through to their terminals. "C'mon, Kels…" I was beginning to feel anxious, ready to get the hell out of this place. I was a people pleaser, and I was holding up a line.

Finally, her blonde blowout could be seen bouncing with each step as she dragged her suitcase behind her. She waved excitedly, sprinting to the car. Kelseigh tosses her suitcase in the bed of the truck and climbs in the passenger seat. She looks radiant as always. She was the sun, and I was the moon, just as we were meant to be. "Hey, loser." I smile.

"Hey, weirdo." She giggled, pulling out her phone. "What a flight, I always forget how much I love NYC." She sighed, watching the rain patter from her window. I nod, feeling like slapping her. No one ever listens. "I told you; you can always move back with me." I reiterated as she laughed. "Nah," She pushes me slightly as I take a deep breath.

"Okay, so I packed a few options for the funeral." She turns her body towards me as I drive, and I nod. "Please don't feel like I'm making you go. I'm sure you have people to catch up with." My offer is more of a plea. I wasn't sure what was in store for me tonight, and I wasn't sure if I wanted a scene. "Are you kidding? Of course I'm gonna go. He was your old man friend; I don't want you there alone." She smiled, trying her best to be empathetic. It wasn't a trait that I didn't think she could possess. I nod, pulling my lips into a tight, uncomfortable smile.

My phone vibrates against the cupholder, I glance down, unable to read it. I assume it's my mom, making sure I got Kelseigh.

"Can you check that?" I sigh, not ready to talk to her at 8:30 in the morning. "Yeah…" Kels mumbles and reads over the text, a smirk growing on her face.

"Who's Tyler?" She giggles as I try to grab the phone from her. "Stop, just give it to me." I try to keep my eyes on the road while wanting to strangle her. "Let me know about Saturday." She reads his text out loud, and I feel my embarrassment rising. "He's a friend."

Kelseigh rolls her eyes. "I have to see you again?!" She reads his next text in shock, causing my heart to race. "He actually said that?"

Kels nods eagerly. Suddenly, we were sixteen and thirteen, reading Seventeen magazine and eating popcorn. "Okay, okay. Don't reply, not yet."

"Right, we don't want to seem *too* available." Kelseigh finishes my thought, just as she always did. I want to tell her that I love her, that I respect her and appreciate her. But I know she'll turn it into something stupid and I'll never hear the end of it.

We get back to my apartment, Kelseigh collapses into the couch.

"Don't get too comfortable, we have to leave by one." I sighed, grabbing a towel and a change of clothes. Kelseigh groans, stretching. "Just worry about yourself." She rolls on her side, eyes already glued shut.

I take a quick shower, freeing up the bathroom for a grouchy Kelseigh. I grab my black turtleneck, a flowy matching skirt that ends just above my knees and my stockings. I slide the skirt up over my hips, flattening the material as I look in the mirror, my lip twitching up at the way my thighs rub together. I envision being Kelseigh's size, she could be a supermodel. She was taller, thinner, everything I wasn't. Kayla always told me I was thick in the right places. My bust was bigger, but I had a small tummy and thighs that would be burning come tonight.

I didn't have much time to stress, this day wasn't about me. I finish my makeup, looking at the claw clip on the vanity. "Let me straighten your hair. Just once, please?" Kelseigh begged, pouting behind me in the mirror's reflection. It was so bad for my hair, but I strived for any bonding moment with her. "Fine." I smile, watching the excitement spew from her like lava. I don't think I've ever seen her run to her suitcase faster.

My hands are in my lap, watching in the mirror as Kels focuses on the task at hand. Her brows are scrunched, and I know she means business. I watch as she adds an extra three inches to my hair without the shrinkage. It's weird, I feel older with my straight hair.

I wet my lips as she pulled back the top layer, tying it into the same white ribbon from my trip with Reese. I feel bad for not telling her about him; it was just easier that way.

I notice Kelseigh's outfit, a black long-sleeved dress. No embellishments, no over-the-top design. It was like she was letting me have my moment after all these years. I smiled to myself, making a mental note to not pull out any awkwardness between us. "Ready?" I ask, slipping into my heels. Kelseigh nods, tucking her phone into her pocket.

The drive is rather easy to the cemetery. I found it strange for him to be buried somewhere so normal. Maurice wasn't an A-List celebrity by any means; but the media treated him as D-List at least. His hand in the stock market, his company, his drama, it was all a factor in his "fame."

When we arrive at Woodlawn, the entire cemetery is gated off by security. "What the hell? Whose funeral is this?" Kelseigh asks, sitting up in her seat. I'm glad I brought my invitation as this appears to be a V.I.P. event. "Maurice Finch." I mumble, turning into the gate. I roll my window down, handing it to the guard. He waves us on, and I give Kelseigh a weird look.

Inside are two black cars and a motorcycle. We don't fit in here. I take a deep breath, pulling my rusted Ranger behind a Mercedes. "Finch? As in *Playboy Finch*?" Kelseigh's jaw slacks, Reese's legacy lives on even in Florida.

"Don't think I don't keep up with the Stripe." She smirks as I put the car in park. I keep my side of Reese a secret. I don't need her looking at me any other way.

Kelseigh adjusts her dress, pulling down the mirror to check her makeup. "What are you doing?" I ask, feeling defensive. "Well, clearly, he'll be here. It was his dad."

"Kels, it's not a good idea." I shake my head with a sigh.

"Why not? I'm only here for the weekend." She shrugs, not picking up the tension in my voice. "He's just... Complicated." I try to explain as discreetly as I can. "Well, I'm not looking for a boyfriend, 'I.'" She giggles, opening the car door. I'm quick to try and follow.

My legs are shorter than hers, working ten times over to catch up. "I'm aware, but he's-"

Reese stands with his hands folded in front of him. An older man and a woman who looks like an attorney stand on either side of him.

He stares at the closed casket, his cheeks are sunken in, his skin especially ivory today. He looks so tired, like he hasn't slept. It's the first time I've seen him since crawling into my bed last week. He's defeated with the world, now an orphan at the ripe age of 29. His jaw flexes, his upper lip twitching with assumable rage.

"There he is." She whispered; I'm unable to reply. He looks up at us, his eyes briefly grazing over Kelseigh and resting on me. My feet are cemented to the ground, his gaze softening on me. I don't know what to say; I don't know what to do. He smiles weakly, taking a step forward. I shake my head, looking down. I didn't want to make a scene, not while my sister is here. Reese's bottom lip quivers and I feel like I've shot myself in the foot.

We take our place at the casket, my hands fold behind my back. I nervously pick at my fingers as the man speaks.

"Everyone knows Maurice was a tough son of a bitch. Our parents often put their bets on which one of us would be successful. I always knew it'd be him. I'm grateful to have worked alongside him as well as my son. He couldn't be here today, as he's preparing everything back at the house, but I know he sends his regards. Maurice was competitive, he was an asshole, but he was my older brother. He worked hard for everything he had, except that ten grand he snagged off me from our last poker game together."

Reese snickers, tucking away his anger and malice for the sake of family. The speech is sweet, subsequently leaving out any mentions of Maurice's troubling parenting or relationships. His brother paints him in a light that only made sense to me before Reese. The Tessa that came after Reese, knew this was all bullshit.

They lower the casket, no one cries. No one shows any emotion. It's cold and drizzly still, almost fitting to the death of Maurice.

"Thanks for coming." Reese crams his hands in his pockets, looking down at me. I can tell he wants to say more, but it's not the time or place. "Of course. This is Kelseigh, by the way. Kelseigh, Reese Finch." I introduce the two as she smiles brightly. "I'm so sorry for your loss. If there's anything I can do while I'm in town, please just let me know." She places a hand on his upper arm, but he seems not to notice.

"Yeah, thanks. Look, I need to talk to you. I'm sorry I-"

I cut him off, my eyes motioning to Kelseigh. "Soon. We'll talk soon." I smile, standing on my tiptoes to kiss his cheek.

I bask in the fragrance of his cologne, taking me back to August. When the weather was warm, the sun was shining, and I hated him. His arms wrap around my waist before I move away. "I'm sorry, Tessa." He whispers into my hair. All the blood rushes to my head, my knees buckling at the way he says my name. I have to pull away, if not for myself, then for the eyes burning in the back of my head.

"I know." I smile, unsuspectingly as Reese's tongue meets the corner of his mouth. He looks around in annoyance with both hands on his hips. I adjust my bag on my shoulder and turn around. It was time to head to Maurice's estate, and face what was waiting for me in this will.

"What are you not telling me?" Kelseigh asks as we close the doors to the truck. "Nothing?" My tone is defensive, as if I'm offended by her asking. "He clearly had something important to say to you."

I wave her off with my hand and a scoff. "He wanted to apologize for making my life hell while taking care of his dad."

Kelseigh nods slowly, she is weary to trust me but drops the interrogation. I couldn't take much more, I'd crack. I always do. I was a terrible liar and hated every second of it.

The drive to his estate is only about thirty minutes, long enough for us to get comfortable in the uncomfortable silence that comes with death. We waited at the top of the long driveway for everyone else to arrive; the motorcycle pulling in first. It's matted black, sporty and threatening. I was never a fan of motorcycles. I thought they were dangerous and stupid.

They put the kickstand down and step off. My mouth goes dry as Reese's identity is revealed under the helmet. "Oh, now that's hot."

Kelseigh giggles like a schoolgirl. I want to agree, I want to share the same level of excitement, but I can't. I only nod in agreement.

"When'd you become a motorcycle guy?" I ask as Kelseigh walks inside. Reese holds the helmet against his hip with a laugh. He wets his lips, rolling his eyes. "Thought it was time to change things up." He winks, motioning me to follow him. I don't move. "We will talk, I promise. I have something I wanna say to you too." I smile, feeling the weight of my anger with him melting. I want to work this out, I love him.

"Perfect." He looks at the ground briefly, flickering back up to meet my gaze. My heart skips a beat, feeling the love we once had.

Forty-Nine

TESSA

We walk in together once Reese's uncle and the attorney walk in. Kelseigh is in a chair in the corner of the room, holding a small plate of horderves. I smile at her, feeling uncomfortable as I straighten the material of my skirt. She gives me a reassuring look and I take a deep breath. I put on my most adult face, trying to hide my nervousness by exploring the estate.

"Maurice had taste, huh?" I smile, venturing down the hall. Reese nods, looking at all the abstract paintings and strange art pieces. It was like a museum. "Yeah, he was a pretentious old asshole, wasn't he?"

I look over my shoulder at him, a smile creeping on my face. He wasn't wrong. "Relax, he's dead. You can admit it." Reese smirks, taking my head and turning me to face him. He takes a step forward, my back now to the wall. I hate that I'm smiling, reminiscing about what we once had. "I guess he was a little snobby." I sighed; his body close to mine. My mouth salivated. God, I wanted to cave, but there were still so many things that needed to be said still. "Atta girl." His head falls back in soft laughter and I'm melting everywhere. Forget it, I'll gladly cave.

"I didn't know you had a cousin." I gave a snarky look, regarding his secrecy. In the two months I'd studied him, he never mentioned it. "Arthur's kid?" He winked. "He's alright. Worked for Maurice, yada yada." He rolls his eyes, turning his attention back to me, something I missed dearly. "Your sister seems nice." He smiled.

"Let me guess, you wanna sleep with her now." I folded my arms, sassily. I warned him that she'd have that effect on him. Reese scoffs and shakes his head.

"There's only room for one bratty Dawson in my life." He goes to put his thumb on my chin but is interrupted by the grace of God.

"Hey, Reese? We're all set in- Tessa?" Our heads dart to the right to see Tyler. His dark brown hair is pushed gently from his forehead, his brows furrowed with a goofy grin. Reese quickly looks back down at me. "You know Tyler?"

"We met the other night over dinner." He smiles, seeming unphased by my closeness with Reese. "Happy birthday again, by the way." Tyler smiles politely, his dress shoes clacking against the ground as he approaches us. I'm baffled that this didn't come up in conversation. Had I been so negligent by not asking him his last name? Anyone with half a brain would recognize the family resemblance.

"Is that so?" Reese's jaw flexes at Tyler's choice of words and I glare up at him, not willing to do this in public. I was so close to getting him back and now his walls were going back up. "We're ready when you are." Tyler looks at the two of us and turns quickly on his heels. It was clear, Reese was the hothead of the family, Tyler had the same views as I did on public outbursts.

As I go to follow, Reese grabs my arm. "You've got to be kidding me." He scoffs. "What?" I pull back as he tightens his grip. I don't acknowledge the pain that follows, it only fuels my frustration.

"My fucking cousin, Tessa?"

He's got it all wrong. "I was out with Kayla. He asked me for my number, and we went our separate ways." I pulled my arm from his grasp. "And by the way, you didn't even tell me happy birthday." It sounds so trivial, to be upset over something like that. And truly I wasn't, not until I had been told twice by Tyler and not *once* by the man who claimed to love me.

Reese parts his lips to speak but falls short. I preferred it that way. "Let's go." I ordered softly; he would never change. He was so quick to raise blame and argue, a match in a barrel of gasoline. I didn't have the strength or time. I wanted to collect my college tuition and get the hell out of there. "Okay." He sighed, running a hand over his face.

I sit beside Kelseigh, my legs bouncing in anxious anger. "He looks pissed." She whispers behind her hand, and I shrug. I try to be inconspicuous with my glance, peering over my shoulder. He stands with arms folded so tight he might bust out of his jacket. He leans against the doorframe as he stares into space. I can hear his heart rate from here. The idea of me talking to another man is taking over his mind. He's battling with killing Tyler, I just know it.

"Good afternoon, everyone. If you don't already know me, my name is Nicole Valdez. I was Maurice's attorney and the overseer of his benefits and estate. We're gonna keep this short and simple as I know you all have things to get to." Nicole flips through her paperwork as she sits at the table. She clears her throat, straightening her posture as she begins to read from Maurice's wishes.

"To my brother, Arthur Eugine Finch, I leave my estate, along with my vehicles. I leave him as sole proprietor of my stocks. And I leave him ten thousand dollars for the poker game of 2016." The mention of the same poker game makes the room erupt in laughter.

I cross my right leg over my left, my palms sweating. Tyler sips his whisky across the room.

His eyes occasionally land on me, giving me a soft smile. I'm terrified to look at Reese. I tried to keep my eyes on Nicole as she was the reason I was here. I take a shaky breath, becoming more tense by the second.

"Maurice also requested I play this video…" She pulls out a DVD, sliding it into the player on top of the television. I was surprised to see Maurice even owned one. I assumed him to be the type of person to only read for media consumption. Nicole presses play and my heart drops to see the background of Maurice's hospice bed. This was filmed recently, it had to be a new edition.

"Is it recording? Oh, okay. Hello, Tessa." He softly smiles, the oxygen tubes in his nose getting caught on his wrinkles. Kelseigh looks at me in disbelief. We're both in shock as we recognize Brindlewood's signature hospital blue walls. Everything about a personalized video screamed rekindling with your son. But here he was, calling me out directly.

"In two years, you have shown me so much kindness and compassion. It isn't easy taking care of someone like me and I realize that. I've been angry, malicious, and cruel to almost everyone I've been in contact with. When you get to be my age, you begin to lose sight of what's in front of you. I never want that to happen to you. You took on one of the hardest responsibilities in the world, helping my son. I can't imagine how that is going for you. He's stubborn like his old man, heh. I know I originally promised you tuition for nursing school, but I've been advised to appoint an heir to my company. And seeing as I will not make it to see your success in this, I've decided to leave you Finch & Company, along with one hundred thousand to get you on your feet close by. You'll work alongside Tyler, my assistant and nephew. He'll tell you everything you need to know."

My jaw is on the floor, I'm having a heart attack. A real-life heart attack. Kelseigh grips my thigh tightly, trying to keep herself from passing out. I peek at Reese who looks more confused than anything.

"And to my son, Reese Michael Finch. I leave you the gift of knowledge. Know that what I am doing is the right thing. I hope that in time, this will inspire you to work for what you want. Just as I have. When Ms. Dawson feels you've proven yourself, she may sign the company over to you. Or, if she chooses, she may keep it for herself. I know you'll understand that this was for the better of the company and is not a symbol of our relationship."

The screen goes black. No secret 'I love you' or anything left for Reese to relish in. It was no different than a corporate email. My heart aches for him, I want to hold him. But when I look back, he's gone.

"Congrats, boss." Tyler holds his glass up to me and I'm seeing spots. I need to find Reese; I need to tell him that I won't accept this. I hear the motorcycle start up out front as I stand to my feet, sprinting outside.

"Reese!" I called out. The wind whistles around me as I watch the dust and gravel swirl and ping off his bike. I watch him speed off, my hands on my head and tears streaming down my face. My body heaves at the pressure stacked against me.

A company I had no knowledge of, fame that I had no desire in, and a life without the love that I so craved.

www.ingramcontent.com/pod-product-compliance
Lightning Source LLC
Chambersburg PA
CBHW032033240626
47154CB00003B/897